Praise for

too beautiful for words

by Monique W. Morris

"Intoxicating and quietly devastating in its power."

—*Essence*

"Earnest."   —*Publishers Weekly*

"The voices leap off the page . . . this book is simply 'too beautiful for words.'"   —*Black Issues Book Review*

"An impressive episodic debut. . . . This is real fiction, related in prose that is always fresh, never mannered. . . . Refreshingly original, personal, and intimate."

—*Kirkus Reviews*

"Engaging . . . packs pain and power, heartache and hope . . . offers a compassionate bridge into a tragic area of black cultural experience."   —*Tampa Tribune*

"In the tradition of Sister Souljah, Sapphire, and Paul Beatty, Monique Morris's prose captures with exquisite honesty both the brutality of life on the streets and the humanity of the people who inhabit them. A stunning new voice in urban fiction, *Too Beautiful for Words* marks the debut of a wholly original talent."   —*Tennessee Tribune*

"*Too Beautiful for Words* is a cultural quilt that shows the textured patterns of collective memory. Through the voices of each character, Morris builds literary bridges so that people can navigate through the cultural meanings of blackness."

—Dr. Manning Marable,
author of *Speaking Truth to Power*

MONIQUE W. MORRIS is a former senior research associate with the National Council on Crime and Delinquency. For several years she has led national efforts to address racial disparities in the criminal and juvenile justice systems. She has made presentations on the subject to the NAACP, the American Society on Criminology's Division on People of Color and Crime, and the U.S. Congressional Black Caucus. She holds a B.A. and an M.S. from Columbia University. A writer, an accomplished artist, and a public speaker, Ms. Morris resides in Oakland, California, with her husband and daughters. This is her first novel.

Inspired by the Coup's "Me and Jesus the Pimp in a
'79 Granada Last Night"

monique w. morris

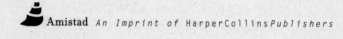Amistad *An Imprint of* HarperCollins*Publishers*

too

beautiful

for

words

Inspired by the Coup's "Me and Jesus the Pimp in a
'79 Granada Last Night"

A hardcover edition of this book was published in 2001 by Amistad, an imprint of
HarperCollins Publishers.

FIRST AMISTAD PAPERBACK EDITION PUBLISHED IN 2002; REISSUED IN 2004.

Designed by Chris Welch

Printed on acid-free paper

The Library of Congress has catalogued the hardcover edition as follows:
Morris, Monique W.
    Too beautiful for words / Monique W. Morris.—1st ed.
        p. cm.
    ISBN 0-06-621105-0
    1. African American criminals—Fiction. 2. African American families—Fic-
tion. 3. Oakland (Calif.)—Fiction. 4. Mothers and sons—Fiction. 5. Prostitutes—Fiction. 6. Young men—Fiction. I. Title.
    PS3613.O67 T66   2001
    813'.6—dc21   2001022328
    ISBN 0-06-093594-4 (pbk.)

04 05 06 07 08 WB/RRD 10 9 8 7 6 5 4 3 2

Misery is when you heard
On the radio that the neighborhood
You live in is a slum but
You always thought it was home.

—Langston Hughes

acknowledgments

I humbly appreciate the legacy of my ancestors, whose struggle informs every single day that I live and decision that I make. Without them, I could not be.

I acknowledge The Coup, especially Boots Riley, for supporting my vision for this work. "Me and Jesus the Pimp in a '79 Granada Last Night" is truly an inspiration.

I gratefully thank my mother, Katie A. Couvson, for her hard work and spirit of *kujichagulia* (self-determination) that has created a world where limitations can only exist if they are self-inflicted. I thank my brothers, Donte D. Couvson for opening my eyes to the fact that it is never "too late" and Xavier R. Couvson for receiving the guidance of those who wish to make him stronger. I thank my sisters, Dominique C. Couvson and Yvette C. Couvson, for their genuine love. I am indebted to my families, immediate and extended, for their support.

I thank my girl, JoHanna I. Thompson, for her sisterhood and friendship, and my manager, Nyanza Shaw, Esq., for her frank, constructive criticism and vision. I thank my editor, Manie Barron, for his ability to "feel me."

I thank the National Council on Crime and Delinquency and the Institute for Research in African American Studies at Columbia University for supporting my need to lobby for the voiceless.

I thank my friends across the globe and Sorors of Delta Sigma Theta Sorority, Inc., who have supported me throughout the years. I especially thank Lesleigh Irish-Underwood, whose years of love, coaching, and "spec-ing" I celebrate every day.

I would also like to send a special thank-you to Erika M. Irish for always pushing me to be an overachiever. One day I'll be as fly as you are!

Finally, I thank my husband, Gregory D. Morris. His foundation made it possible for *Too Beautiful for Words* to materialize. He is my love, my muse, and my rock.

part one

Jason

Dear Jesus:

In case you don't know, I don't live in a group home no more.

I got busted for runnin' heroin to this old house around the way. But I don't use it. I was just sellin' it to the fiends who come by the block all the time. None of the nuns where I was livin' came to court to get me, so they put me in here. First I was in juvenile hall. Now I live at the Youth Authority.

Anyway, I'm really only writin' you for one thing. Can you get me out of here?

Jason

Peaches

Lord, please forgive me for bein' late! Please have mercy . . .

It's already eleven-thirty in the mornin' and I ain't made it to church yet! I know it's only a block away from where I'm at now, but I can't help but keep checkin' on my watch 'cause I'm there at eleven-fifteen *every* mornin', baby. I always be checkin' to see what time it be 'cause I got a habit of bein' late for real important things. I guess you can say it's my own personal ritual. But it ain't no thing, 'cause I can't be doin' what everybody else be doin'. Can't help it—been this way ever since I was livin' with Grandma and Grandpa.

Livin' with them was like livin' in my very own convent—I mean, wasn't nothin' I could do without gettin' called some kinda name or gettin' some kinda punishment. I wasn't never no nun, so I was always fightin' Grandma and Grandpa when they tried to make me into somebody I wasn't. I mean, I ain't been a virgin since I was twelve years old, but they was tryin' to keep me up in the house all the time and wouldn't let no boys come over or nothin'. Even the ones that was just my friends couldn't even come over. It wasn't fair to me, but I just had to do my best to try to live by them rules.

To them it was all 'bout a whole lot of prayin'. Every mornin' before I went to school, we would get up and pray. We ain't always had breakfast, but we always had our prayers. Since Grandpa was a deacon, sometimes we even got caught up spendin' half the night in the church house— just singin' and dancin'. You know how we be when the Holy Ghost jump inside us and we can't shake that feelin' that just make us start talkin' all crazy and feelin' filled with the Lord!

Yeah, them was the days. On some Sundays we even had hotcakes cookin' on the stove to keep our stomachs from rumblin' up in that church. At first we would have to stomp the roaches out the kitchen, 'cause you know there was always a whole family full of them things runnin' around tryin' to feed theyselves off of our crumbs. Then we had to make for sure there was some flour in the kitchen, and if there was, then we would eat our hearts out! We wouldn't never have no syrup, so we would warm up some butter and brown sugar, and pour that over the top. Sometimes I could whip up some molasses and put that on top. Mmmm! Mahalia used to be singin' in her usual deep and soulful voice—just fillin' our old house with the joyful sound He likes. That would be right before Grandma would step in and start hollerin' for me to come help her get ready. I can hear her now.

"An-gie!" She always broke up my name like it was two words instead of one.

"Yes, Grandma!"

"Come on in here and help Grandma put on this here brassiere so I can get this dress on."

I remember stumblin' up them steps and draggin' my feet into that musty old room to help her pull those lugs she called her "bosom" up into that huge bra that would help keep her chest from slappin' her knees all day. Together we'd be gruntin' and pullin' to a beat like some of them prisoners on the chain gang. On a good one-two rhythm, we could get them big-ole breasts in that bra in less than a minute, but on a bad day, baby, it could take up to ten whole minutes! Yeah, sometimes I miss them days . . . especially just bein' able to be around Grandma and Grandpa. But ain't no use in cryin' over things you can't change. So I just as soon let them days be in the past where they belong.

I mean, it's 1979, baby! Things way different now than they was back when I was livin' with Grandma and Grandpa, anyway. Some years ago, folks took to callin' me Peaches— it was part of a whole new life I took up—but I'll always just be little Angie on the inside, waitin' on Grandma to call me in to help her get ready for Sunday's sermon. I mean, I don't be wearin' no pigtails and saddle shoes no more, but I'm always gonna be Deacon and Mrs. Johnson's little grand-baby. They ain't around no more, and I guess that's all right—especially for me right now. They would kill me if they knew I was late gettin' to church.

The church is just ahead now. It's so beautiful, with that gray stone and that big-ole cross on top of it. It ain't as tall as the big white Mormon church that you can spot from just 'bout any freeway drivin' through Oakland, but it be holdin' its own on this side of town. It got some big stone steps leadin' up to the door that's made of wood. That big-ole door was painted black when some of the kids around here started postin' all kinds of signs on it. It left some marks that damaged the wood, and I sure hated the way it looked. But then one day, I saw some painters out there workin' on it. And they really cleaned it up, you hear me? Now the church looks better than it ever did. It's a real simple thing, but it's the most beautiful buildin' in the West.

I'm walkin' up the church steps now—but I'm still late. I can't stand it when I'm late, you hear me? I be missin' too much. You'd be surprised how much you could pick up from bein' at the right place at the right time every day. Only problem with gettin' in the church is that big-ole front door up there. It don't matter how many times I pull on it, it be too heavy to get with just one hand. I mean, it's real heavy, baby.

Our Father, Who art in Heaven,
Hallowed be Thy Name,
Thy Kingdom come,
Thy Will be done,
On Earth as it is in Heaven . . .

I love it in here. There ain't no church—and I mean *no* church—like the First Baptist Church of the Almighty Jesus Christ! The inside got pews set up on both sides of the church. There's two sections, too. So many people be comin' to this church that they had to add another level a little while back. It looks good, too—got more room in here to just sit around and look at the paintings and stained glass windows. There's a bunch of pictures of Jesus and Mary along the walls up in here, but you'll see my favorite one behind the altar.

I love them stained glass windows up there. Right behind the altar you can see one big painted window with two smaller ones on each side. The one in the middle got a picture of the sun, the sky, and some mountains. It looks real pretty on some mornings when the sun shines through. It comes right on through and can blind you if you stare at it long enough. It's almost like lookin' right at the sun. That ain't my favorite one, though. My favorite one is the one that's the furthest to the right. It's the small one that's almost in the corner. But, even though it's all the way over there, you can see it from wherever you is in this church.

It's showin' Jesus ministerin' to a crowd of people. He risin' higher than everybody else. He got His arms stretched out, and everybody around Him is kneelin' at His feet. He got men, women, and children acceptin' His lesson. I like it 'cause it show how even though everybody ain't love Jesus, there was always the ones who could see how special He was. I'm talkin' 'bout the people with *real* sight, not just the kind that come from your eyes. Naw . . . uh uh. I'm talkin' the kinda sight that gets in your bones and makes you *feel*— makes you *know*—you doin' the right thing. That's the kinda love for Jesus I'm talkin' 'bout, baby.

I look at that stained glass over there every day. Sometimes I just go over and take it in. Most of the time, I don't say nothin', though. I just be sittin' in the back pew in here for a whole hour from eleven-fifteen to twelve-fifteen. That's when the reverend take his lunch break. I like to come in here when he gone, 'cause this way, he don't be botherin' me.

Oh, I guess you thought I was worryin' 'bout bein' late for one of *his* sermons? Hell naw, I can't *stand* his sermons. His sermons don't be nothin' but a whole bunch of whoopin' and hollerin'. I mean, he just be jumpin' around like a fool on dope. Anyway, ain't nobody got no time to be sittin' in here watchin' folks get the Holy Ghost over somethin' they don't even really understand. And I hate the way he always got somethin' to say 'bout me—'bout my work, my life, and everything else he don't get 'bout me. I came to one of his sermons a few years ago after Grandma and Grandpa died. That was in 1972, right after the first time Jesus had went to see what was happenin' on the Chicago scene. He always go there now. He been runnin' back and forth between here and Chicago for the last two years, but I don't mind it. Um . . . excuse me . . .

Jesus, Lord, please forgive me for sayin' your name in vain, but you know I ain't always talkin' 'bout you, Lord. I know you understand . . . and I know you forgive me. Amen.

So, yeah, as I was sayin', I came to one of the reverend's sermons one day and in the middle of his speech he started pointin' the finger at me, you hear me? Out of nowhere! First he was talkin' 'bout Job and his sores, right? But then he saw me 'cause I was sittin' close to the front, and started in on Jesus and Mary Magdalene! It ain't make no sense at all. He started talkin' 'bout how turnin' her life to Jesus saved her, and how if somebody in the church got a lost soul, they need to turn to God to save them. First I got mad and was ready to take my bag and get out of there fast! But then I thought 'bout it, right? And the Lord showed me that the reverend was just sendin' me a message that I can't never leave *my* Jesus. See, the message said that I can't never really

too beautiful for words

leave 'cause then my soul would be lost. I would be runnin' around them streets with nobody to watch over my back. It was a message from the Lord, you hear? Anyway, that's how I saw it. Yeah, that reverend—he was pointin' the finger for sure, but what he couldn't see was that I was already saved. It ain't matter to me, though. I got the message.

Jesus saved me ten years ago, baby. Sometimes I can't believe it's been that long since he rescued me from that nothin' life I was headin' into when I was in high school. He showed me how to feel and be fine all the time and how to stay committed to one man and one thing. I mean, before Jesus, I was just givin' myself to people who ain't deserve me—and I wasn't even gettin' nothin' out of it. But you know, Jesus taught me the right way. He taught me how to get money for my love. See, I *been* saved, and that reverend just don't get it. Yeah, I know it sounds crazy, but I sure do got me a pimp that is named after the Lord.

So now I just come in here when the reverend gone on his lunch break. The little stories in each of them windows remind me of all the lessons I done already learned in Sunday school. I mean, I done spent many a Sunday mornin' in this church with "Mrs. Johnson," readin' from the Scripture and tellin' stories with the other kids in the class.

But you know, we all be doin' stuff that we ain't real happy 'bout—even the holy do some sinnin'. I ain't 'bout all that showin' for others, though. I know when I do dirt, the Lord know it. And I know that every once in a while I just gotta be reminded of how to do good. That's why I like to watch them stained windows, 'cause they show me the good things I be forgettin' sometimes. It's funny, too, 'cause even though the faces in them pictures is all white, I can see in them all the people I done known in my life. See, to me, it ain't never been 'bout who the people in them Bible stories was, it's 'bout what they be sayin' to me 'bout how to live my life.

Anyway, I usually be in here just prayin' everything away. I mean, I be askin' for all kinds of forgiveness up in here, baby. It's kinda funny if you think 'bout it—the way people be doin' what we do out there on them streets without givin' the Lord a second thought, then be comin' in here and actin' like we gotta tell the Lord that we sorry for sinnin' and grinnin' on the outside. Like God can't see outside of these here walls. It's kinda funny, but I guess it just be makin' people feel better to do it that way. I know it do that for me.

That's why I be up in here for an hour every day. Well, usually. Today is a little different 'cause I gotta do some things. It ain't like I ain't got time for the Lord today, it's just that I gotta get back home before I get caught out. Jesus is comin' home from his latest trip to Chicago, and I gotta make sure I look good for my Daddy. He comin' back to check on his business—and to see me and Jason, our baby boy. Jason is me and Jesus' son . . . and the best thing to ever happen to me. Ain't a thing I do that ain't for him—I mean nothin'. That's my baby, and you should see him. He soooo beautiful! He look just like his daddy—got his hair, his eyes, and everything.

Dang! My watch say it's twelve already! I gotta go get ready, 'cause if there's one thing I do know, it's that Jesus ain't catchin' me out here lookin' like this, do you hear me? He ain't catchin' me!

Lord, I know you understand that I gotta go. You the only thing that really understand me and everything I do. Please bless me, Lord, and all the men in my life so we'll be all right down here on this Earth. And thank you for not trippin' off what I do with my life. Amen.

God ain't trippin' off me. I mean, I done thought 'bout this a lot. If the Lord was real mad at what I do, He would have let me know it by now. I mean, wouldn't I be struck down or somethin'? Jesus don't take no mess. But the way I figure, so long as I keep on prayin', me and my folks should be all right. I ain't perfect or nothin', but I sure ain't the one to be fightin' with the ways of the Lord. Anyway, Grandma always said to keep on with the Lord's Prayer and I would be all right no matter what. She said ain't nobody strong enough to be a real challenge to God. Not on this Earth anyway.

So I don't be challengin' Him—not the Jesus up in Heaven or the one down here in my life. I just share myself between the two. All I do is take the love I feel for the Jesus I can't see and show it to the one I do see. It was real easy to do, especially when my man told me his name was "Jesus." That was just the Lord sendin' me another message. I just took to askin' for forgiveness for havin' to say His name in vain, and started my new life from there. And I know God understand . . . I know He do.

Dang! It's twelve-fifteen already? I gotta go . . .

Ooo-wee! The wind is blowin' out here for real! And I just got my hair did. I had it pressed and slicked back so I could put my wigs on real easy. I'm glad I be doin' that, too. 'Cause if I didn't, I would be lookin' like somethin' else right 'bout now. The wind sure ain't botherin' them little girls over there though. Look at them. They ain't worried at all—they still jumpin' around and singin' them nursery rhymes with each other.

"Ring, ring, ring to the rhythm machine, right on! He rocked in the treetop all day long . . . Huffin' and a-puffin' and a-singin' his song . . ."

Listen to how they just keep on singin' even though they ponytails flyin' like bats out of hell. They can barely hold on to them hips long enough to finish singin' the rhyme.

"Momma's in the kitchen burnin' rice, Daddy's outside shootin' dice . . . Brother's in jail raisin' hell, Sister's on the corner sellin' *fruit cocktail!*"

Dang! Them nursery rhymes done changed since I was a little girl. These girls out here singin' 'bout they daddies shootin' craps and gamblin' on the corner and they mommas burnin' up some food. I guess it's safe to say that them girls probably do got a brother in jail and a sister on the corner . . . but sometimes things call for certain ways of life. I mean, I ain't trippin' off of what they singin' 'bout. What trouble me is that them little girls the ones singin' 'bout it. They too young for all that.

This weather is kinda strange, 'cause it don't usually be this windy in Oakland—maybe in some parts of Frisco—but not here in Oakland. Maybe the city's just gettin' clean and ready for Jesus. I know I'm 'bout to get real clean and ready . . . Wait . . . Who that callin' me?

"Hey, Peaches!"

Oh, it's just Maurice. He across the street, but I don't feel like walkin' over there right now. He been around for years, even hired me for a couple of dates. I know he married and everything, but he be trickin' too. He think he got it goin' on 'cause he be out here talkin' fast and showin' off that little bit of money he got in his pocket, but he ain't got nothin' on Jesus. That's why Maurice ain't runnin' my show and Jesus is.

"Heey, Mauriiice," I sing back. He likes it when I sing his name. He say I sound like Gladys Knight, but I don't think I can sing as good as her. I sing to him anyway, though, and keep on walkin'. Maybe he'll come see me later . . . ooh! You hear that? Somebody playin' my song real loud from a car radio! It's a song by Michael Jackson.

That boy done quit his brothers and now he got his own record out. Believe me, it's out of sight! I say it's the best thing out right now. The name of it is "I wanna rock with you . . ."—haa-aay!

I always start dancin' like this when I hear a good song. I can't help it. It's in my blood. Anyway, I can't wait to hear what that boy gonna come up with next. Maybe if I work real hard tonight, I can get Jesus to buy that record for me.

I'm glad Jesus comin' home for a while, 'cause I be missin' him when he gone. A few years back, Hollywood started makin' movies full of colored folks, showin' a lot of folks how to have some fake Hollywood game. Since then, everybody been wantin' to be a pimp. I got cats comin' up to me left and right tryin' to get me to choose them. They be talkin' all this trash 'bout how Jesus done left me and how there ain't really no protection out here for me. I mean, I be havin' to explain to them that I ain't no renegade. I got a pimp, and his name is Jesus!

They leave me alone after a while, but the police sure don't leave me alone. They be botherin' me all the time. But I learned what to say to them to get them so that they leave me alone. I just be sayin' the same thing I say to them other pimps. I be talkin' 'bout Jesus, and most of the time that work all right. The police don't be messin' with the white hos that much, but they sure love messin' with us colored girls.

Sometimes the police be puttin' a hurtin' on colored girls out there with nobody to pay them to leave them alone. Them movies done made pimpin' the scene, but it be hard to keep up sometimes. We gotta keep sharp, stay on our toes, and make sure they ain't got no setups pretendin' to be lookin' for tricks.

\ I did like one movie, though. It came out 'bout . . . um . . . six years ago. Yeah, they filmed it right here in Oakland, right around the time that I had Jason. I know you done seen *The Mack*, right? We was in the audience in that one scene with the Players' Ball. The camera got a shot of Jesus, and he in that movie lookin' fine, you hear me? If you look real hard, you might could see me, too, 'cause I was sittin' right behind him. That actor Max Julien looked so much like Jesus in that movie, I thought I was gonna jump through the screen and start givin' *him* my money! I'm just messin' with you . . . but for real, Max is fine. *Fine!* Just like Jesus—except for that Afro. Jesus got good hair 'cause his momma is a Mexican and his daddy is a colored Creole from Louisiana. So, you know, when Jesus be tryin' to fluff up his hair to be like the rest of us, he be lookin' kinda funny. I like it better when he just slick it back and look fine like Smokey Robinson.

Jesus got a bad arm, but I ain't never minded that plastic thing. When he be takin' it off he's fine, and when he be puttin' it on he's fine. Jesus' fine be all in his face . . . and in another, private place.

Ain't too many folks out here on the streets today. Usually, there be young boys lined up on the corners or leanin' on somebody's car playin' they music. Today, though, ain't nobody really around. It seem like everybody who is out now is on they way somewhere. I guess ain't nobody got time to be hangin' out right now. The West—you know, West Oakland—be like that sometimes, with nothin' on the streets but a few folks here and there, old Victorian houses, classic cars, and liquor stores. The streets ain't that clean 'cause the garbage man only come every two weeks, but it's still all right. We still find our way to have a good time.

See the liquor store on that corner over there? Buddy be runnin' that store like it's a street mall. They sell everything up in there. You can get heroin, weed, dust, uppers, downers—whatever they pushin' on the street, they pushin' in that store. You can go in there and get bread, milk, candy, *and* dope. It's a dope fiend's paradise. The police come around sometimes, but most of them is gettin' a cut from it all, so they be in there just long enough to collect they cash, and then be out. They just leave it alone as long as they share be waitin' for them at the end of the week.

One time, though, they ain't get they *real* cut, 'cause—you know Buddy—he always tryin' to get over on somebody and keep a little somethin' extra for hisself. Well, that time, he kept a little too much and pissed off the beat cops. They rolled up on that store with a raid so thick the city almost shut the store down. Yeah, Buddy was actin' all scared, but it only lasted a week. I heard the police started gettin' paid twice what they was gettin' before. Everything was all right then— right and smooth again. Good thing, too, 'cause ain't nowhere else to get somethin' to eat within ten blocks of here. All the real grocery stores be in the white folks' neighborhood.

"Hey girl. How you doin'?" some man is askin' me as I walk by, and his eyes is tellin' all his dope fiend secrets, baby.

"Hi," I say. I always be polite to strangers, even when they be fiendin' for somethin' I ain't got.

"Hey . . . Saw Jesus down the street. He was talkin' 'bout how he gonna be wit' you later on."

Lord, have mercy! He talkin' 'bout me? He gonna be so mad if he catch me out here lookin' like this. I gotta make it home before he gets there and see me walk in lookin' like a catastrophe instead of some caviar. I ain't never had no caviar, but ain't it fish droppin's or somethin' like that? Anyway, that's what Jesus be sayin'. I gotta be beautiful when he see me, so he don't get mad and turn me out to work the nasty trick stroll. Right now he got me on the good one— the one where the tricks be too scary to act up or get loud. They usually got families theyselves, so everything they do be quiet style. That's how I like it. It's much better than workin' with tricks who ain't got nothin' to lose. The tricks I turn dates with be clean, you know, most of the time.

Anyway, besides that, I like to stay fine for Jesus. He can't never leave me—you know, *leave* me—as long as I do. As long I stay his dream girl, I'm always gonna be the Top Ho, his number one. Right now, that spot is mine, but I know them other girls would cut my face in a heartbeat if they knew he would drop me 'cause of it.

"Where he at?" I ask. "He down the street right now?"

I gotta scratch my nose 'cause it itches, but I know this fool gonna think I'm a fiend.

"Hey, you lookin' for some coke?" he asks.

I knew it.

"Naw . . . I don't do that stuff, baby. Anyway, like I said, where Jesus at?"

"Slow down, momma! He went for a ride. I told you he said he was gonna see you later on."

Oh, yeah. Well, then, that still leaves me some time. Anyway, I ain't too comfortable with this fiend all up in my business like I know him real good, 'cause I don't. But like I told you before, I'm always gonna be nice. Anyway, I don't know him, but he gotta know me, the way he carryin' on. Maybe he know me from a party at Jesus' house or somethin'. I don't remember all the tricks we see at parties. That ain't my job. That's for Jesus to do—and he real good at it. He be rememberin' everybody.

I'm gonna leave this fiend while he still feelin' around his pockets. Anyway, he got too much goin' on to be worried 'bout me. I'll probably see him later on, but only if he got money and Jesus think he good enough for me. I ain't got time to waste on no second-level tricks. I gotta go get ready for my Daddy—so come on, let's keep walkin'.

Around here, every house got a tree planted outside. They ain't like the palm trees that be around Lake Merritt, but they be sproutin' from the concrete like they gifts from the Lord. And I love when the trees be shiftin' back and forth like they is now. Like I said, it don't usually be this windy in Oakland, but when it is, I like to watch the trees. Look at that big old oak tree over there . . . over *there* . . . in front of that pink and blue house. That tree been there for as long as I can remember. One time it was in the middle of winter, and the rain was comin' down real heavy—like a storm. But them branches and leaves was so thick, they was protectin' the street and anybody who was standin' under them. There was this old lady standin' underneath one of them with her grocery bags, and I mean, she was all dry! I tried it the next day when I got caught out in the rain. It worked then, too. It was warm up under there and everything. Tell you this, if I don't say nothin' else, Oakland got the best trees in the whole Bay Area. That's how the city got its name, anyway. We known for bein' the land of oak—at least that's what my schoolteachers used to say.

See that old, boarded-up green house over there? I'm talkin' 'bout the one that's three houses down from the pink one. Right there on them steps is where I first met Jesus, you hear me? I ain't kiddin'. See, Grandma and Grandpa lived in that house before the city came through and boarded it up. Every day, I used to sit on the front steps and wait for my girls, Gayle and Wanda, to come home from school.

We had been friends for a few years by then, but we never really hung together outside of the neighborhood. We was always walkin' around the West, but they ain't take me nowhere else with them. That used to be enough for me, though. Gayle and Wanda was real smart, so they went to Skyline. They got on a bus and went way across town for they schoolin', so that didn't leave too much time in the evenin' for them to be hangin' around with me.

I went to McClymonds, right here in West Oakland, so I could walk. And you know, I always got home way before they did. Most of the time I wouldn't even go inside first. I'd just wait on them steps till they came by. When we finally did get together we would have a good time. We used to laugh and talk a lot on them steps, but I always knew they was better friends with each other than they was with me. It ain't matter, though, 'cause they was all the friends I had. Besides them, there wasn't no other girls who would pay attention to me. I can't figure out why, that's just the way things was.

Gayle told me it was probably 'cause I liked to show off my body to the boys. If that was the truth, then there wasn't nothin' I was gonna do to fix that one. I loved showin' a little leg to boys whenever I could—just a little, though. Just enough to get their attention. Grandma sure hated it when she caught me flirtin' with the boys in church. She was mad at me since she caught me in the house one day makin' it with this boy from school. She was always talkin' 'bout how no boy would ever want to marry me if he knew I had already gave away my "goods"—that's what she called it. But I wasn't worryin' 'bout bein' married, so it didn't matter no how. Anyway, I loved the way them boys would feel next to my skin. When they touched me, I felt like I could make them do whatever I wanted, especially if I did a little actin' along the way to make them think they stuff was the best I ever had.

She only caught me once, but that was enough for her. She started callin' me a "Jezebel," a "hussy," or anything else she could think of to make me think I was bad. But it only bothered me a little when she got so mad, 'cause I knew what I was doin'. I was givin' them boys what they wanted—somethin' to talk 'bout, somethin' to brag 'bout. The way I seen it, dark girls like me had to have a little extra goin' on if we was gonna get the fine boys. If I ain't know nothin' else, I always knew how to use my body—how to shake what my momma gave me.

Yeah, she gave it to me all right. Passed it right on down, so I hear. I don't really remember her or my daddy. They died right after I was born. Grandma and Grandpa never really told me much more than that. Of course, I wonder sometimes 'bout what happened to them—what kinda child wouldn't? Once, I even got up enough nerve to ask Grandpa 'bout it, but I ain't get no real answer. He just said somethin' 'bout an accident, some white folks, and me stayin' out of grown folks' business. So I just left it alone from there. I don't really like to keep askin' questions when somebody done already told me what they know 'bout somethin'. I ain't never been pushy like Gayle and Wanda—that's why I got to choose Jesus and they didn't.

One day, I was waitin' on the steps for Gayle and Wanda to come home when I spotted the finest man I had ever seen around this neighborhood. He was walkin' real slow-like, and I remember I saw that only one arm was swingin'. But back then all the boys was walkin' with a sway, so, you know, I ain't even notice that the other arm wasn't real. And when he got close enough for me to see, I was so blown away by his face and them clothes, I ain't even care 'bout that arm. Whew! That man was fine. I felt like God had reached down and slapped me silly with the sight of his fineness!

He got to where I was sittin' and then stopped. He was kinda light-skinded, and he was wearin' a long, black leather coat draped over his shoulders and a green and yellow pin-striped suit. His hat was cocked to the side and his alligator shoes was like nothin' I had ever seen before. He was just standin' there lookin' at me, leanin' back and to the side. I mean, he was sharp and his gangsta-lean was workin'! He was leanin' so far back I thought he was gonna fall over, but he was real good with it. He sprung up real fast and pulled his shades down, showin' off them brown eyes like they was a secret weapon. The other weapon that I could see was all covered up by his hat, and that was his hair. Man! That long, wavy hair on his head!

I was tryin' not to stare at him too hard, even though he was workin' overtime to get me to fall on my knees and start worshippin' him right then. I was fightin' it though. I just kept lookin' at my saddle shoes and playin' around a little with the front part of my skirt, right where it rubbed against my knees. He stopped to look at my legs, just like I wanted him to, then he finally spoke to me.

I remember him sayin', "Hey, baby . . . You *gots* to be right! Lookin' fine like wine . . . ripe, sweet, and better with time. What you doin' on them steps?"

I laughed, 'cause I had heard that one before, but never like he said it. When he said it, it sounded real, like he really did think I would get better with time. And I believed him as soon as he said it. I could dig it, man.

His voice was real deep, but he kept on changin' it—makin' it go high when he wanted to. And even though he was doin' all that with his voice, it ain't even crack a little bit, do you hear me? He was as cool as they come. He might have looked young in the face, but I knew he was a man.

"Aw, I'm just waitin' here for somebody," I said, tryin' not to smile too hard.

"Well, you sure is fine. What's your name, baby?"

"Angie."

"Aaangie?" He let my name roll out like that: Aaangie.

"Yeah."

"Who you waitin' on, Aaangie?"

"My friends to come home from school."

"School? You still wastin' your time in school when you gots all that talent?"

"What you talkin' 'bout, man. You ain't got no sense. How you know I got talent?"

"'Cause I can see special gifts, baby. I gots special powers that come with bein' me."

I thought he was high . . . talkin' 'bout "special powers." I was not tryin' to hear that, but then he kept on and got my attention for real.

"So," he said, "what you finna do when you graduate? What kind of job you think you finna get?"

I had been thinkin' 'bout tryin' to be a beautician. I always liked doin' hair, but I wasn't for sure, so I ain't tell him that.

"Well I ain't really gave it much thought. I'll probably go on and get me a job in Frisco . . . yeah, that's what's probably gonna happen."

"Well, if you decide to give it some more thought, why don't you come by my crib and see if you might be interested in a stylish gig more suitable for a special talent like you."

"What, you runnin' a business or somethin'?" I was actin' like I ain't know what was goin' on, but I had been figured it out. I might not be that bright, but with the leather coat, the pimped-out suit, and all that sweet talkin', I would have been a stone fool not to recognize it.

"I gots the best business, baby."

When he said that, my heart skipped a beat. I thought it was gonna jump through my body. The best business! I had stumbled into a gold mine. He kept rappin' 'bout how pretty I was, and how he thought I could do more than just scrape by on three dollars an hour sellin' stuff that people could live without. He said he could tell I had a lot to offer—that I had somethin' people would die to get a piece of—and I liked that.

"So let's cut to the chase then. You classy or do you turn out hos like them nasty ladies on MacArthur?" I asked.

He walked up all close to me, and I remember he smelled

so sweet—like love without sex. From his soft, clean, honey-colored face to the milky white of his teeth, this man caught ahold of my heart and yanked it straight through my body. It was a wonderful feelin'—natural and dark. And it only got sweeter when he told me that I could come to one of his parties and see his "family" for myself. He asked me for a piece of paper, so I dug into my backpack and gave him one—with a pencil and all.

I hadn't ever thought 'bout bein' a ho before, but I did want to do whatever could keep me close to that man standin' in front of me. I remember wantin' to look at him forever! I knew Grandma and Grandpa would kill me if they even saw me talkin' to him, but none of that made a lick of difference. I wanted to know how I could be with that man, and I had to find a way out anyway. Grandma and Grandpa was threatenin' to kick me out the house when I turned eighteen—and I was seventeen then. They wasn't thinkin' 'bout me, so I wasn't thinkin' 'bout them.

When he gave me the paper back, it had an address on it that wasn't too far from Grandma and Grandpa's house. I could have walked there if I ain't had no ride to the party. He started to walk away, but I knew I couldn't let him leave 'cause somethin' was missin'. I read what was on that sheet of paper three times before it hit me—he forgot to put his name on it. I had told him all my information, and I still knew next to nothin' 'bout him.

"Hey!" I yelled. I had to stand up for this one—put my hand on my hip and everything. "You forgot to write your name down!"

"I didn't forget, baby. Greatness can't write his name on paper. My name rolls off the tongue, baby, not the pen."

I remember how he said it—with that cocky attitude that had me all caught up from the get-go. I mean, he flashed a smile and had me needin' to change my panties!

"Well then, *tell* me your name and I'll write it down myself," I said.

"My name is Jesus, baby."

"No, I'm serious. Tell me your name!"

He looked at me and smiled again, and I just knew he was lyin'. But I went to his party anyway.

When me, Gayle, and Wanda first rolled up to the house, I noticed that the people standin' on the front porch had on some serious threads! The porch was decorated with some flowers and some outdoor heaters. The house was a Victorian, but the paint on the outside was new, not like the chipped paint on the other houses on his block. It had some steps leadin' up to the door, then more steps before you actually got up into his house. I saw lights on in every room that could be seen from the street, and behind each shade in them windows was shadows of bodies rockin' back and forth. I couldn't wait to get inside.

When we stepped foot in that house, everybody was walkin' around hollerin' "Jesus." As soon as I heard them, I knew he had to be tellin' me the truth 'bout his name, 'cause wasn't none of us in no church or Bible study. So I felt kinda silly not believin' him from before. But I just played it off.

Honey, his pad wasn't nothin' like I had ever seen, and I was sure Gayle and Wanda hadn't seen nothin' like that before. It was laid out! I mean, Jesus had fur and leather all over the inside of his pad! And when I saw that new-smellin' lambskin rug on the floor, I couldn't wait to take off my platforms and get my toes into it! He had them strobe lights workin' like his house was the disco spot. He even had a full bar—with a bartender and everything! It was lavish, man. And the women, they was gorgeous.

I heard somebody say that night that Jesus had only been a pimp for three years, but I didn't believe it. I remember thinkin' that if he had all that after only three years, then bein' with him in the long run could change my life forever! I ain't said nothin' to Gayle or Wanda, but I was sold then and there. There was a lot of women there at first, but then some men started comin' in, and I thought I was gonna die from the sight of all that money in one room. I loved it, but Gayle and Wanda ain't like it too much.

I remember Gayle turnin' to me and talkin' 'bout she think they a bunch of hookers and pimps. So what, right? But she was always actin' all stuck up like that. That's why we not friends no more. She always thought she was better than me.

"Look at these girls . . . I bet they're all high and I *know* they're all whores," she said.

"Wanda, just hang on a minute. These people look nice to me," I said, tryin' not to get too mad.

"That's because you're stupid."

I can laugh now, 'cause I know she just ain't understand. She just ain't see what I saw. I saw a life of glamour that would be so easy for me to fit in. I saw a way for me to get out of that life of bein' cooped up all the time and never havin' nothin'. I saw a way for me to use my body to get what I needed. And I needed somethin' better than a roach-infested, foodless kitchen, you hear me?

When Jesus came through that crowd of people, I'll never forget it. He was wearin' a black silk shirt and some blue and pink patched suede pants. His hair was all slicked back and his shirt was tucked in, but unbuttoned to his stomach. I was turned on—way on. So it was only a matter of time before Gayle and Wanda was left to fend for theyselves. After watchin' the way they was actin', I knew they was gettin' too stuck up for me. I mean, it was time for me to get some new friends anyway.

Jesus walked right up to me and started sayin' a whole bunch of real nice things 'bout my clothes and my body. I had gone out of my way to look good that night, even put on my pink hot pants that Grandma never knew I had. He walked around me real slow-like, with his eyes watchin' *all* my curves, baby. I was hot and I knew it. Everything was goin' perfect till Gayle started actin' like she was my momma instead of my girlfriend.

"Damn, baby. You sure is workin' them pants," Jesus said. He touched my booty just a little with his hand. I liked it, but Gayle ain't like it too tough.

"Don't touch her booty," she said kinda loud. Her face was all frowned up like somethin' stank.

I remember turnin' to look at her so she would shut up, but her mouth kept on goin'.

"Look," she said, "I don't know what kind of whores you're used to dealing with, but we are not about to get turned out, so if that's what you're up to, then you can hang it up right now."

"Gayle, what you doin'?" I asked. I was tryin' to whisper, but it was comin' out kinda loud. I couldn't believe she was embarrassin' me like that. There I was, invited to Jesus' party, and Gayle wanted to show her ass like she ain't had no sense. Our friendship wasn't doin' too good right 'bout then.

Jesus' face turned that funny color—like all the blood in

his body done went right up to his cheeks. Then he broke into that laugh he got when he mad and don't want nobody to know it. He grabbed a cigarette from this girl who was standin' next to him, and put it in his mouth for a drag. Then he just let it dangle off his lips and just kept on talkin'.

"Aaangie," he said, "this bitch come with you?"

I remember my hands started shakin' 'cause I really ain't know what to expect. I mean, we had walked up in this man's house and was makin' a scene out of nothin'. Before then, I ain't never really been around no pimps, but I'd heard 'bout pimps whippin' some ass if a girl made a scene out of nothin'. That night, Gayle and Wanda sure enough ain't know they place.

Gayle said somethin' like, "What did you call me, nigga?"

Then Wanda jumped in it, talkin' 'bout "ain't nobody just gonna call my girl a bitch."

That's when it really hit the fan. All I remember is two of them girls in the party walked up and started slappin' on Wanda and Gayle like they was little kids. Then Jesus started cussin' and threw them both out the house. He asked me again if they was with me.

"Aaangie, you brought them bitches to my house?" he asked.

"No, Jesus. I know them from around the block, but they ain't come with me. We just walked in at the same time," I said. And I said it with a straight face, too. I ain't that bright, but I ain't no fool.

After that night, I never talked to Wanda or Gayle again. I know they see me sometimes. Wanda and her baby still live around here, but I heard Gayle got some big-time job and moved to San Leandro. They both still think they better than me, but I know what I'm doin' now—just like I knew what I was doin' then.

After things calmed down, Jesus showed me around his crib and introduced me to all kinds of folks. He walked me over to a man in politics and then to another who was a famous basketball player. They was all real low-key, but they was covered in girls dancin' around them and feedin' them grapes and other kinds of fruit. Jesus had the place jumpin' with scenes that reminded me of some pictures I used to see in history class. Some of them girls was dressed in white toga sheets and others was dressed in African clothes. He had some Chinese-lookin' girl doin' a dance that had a crowd of men droolin' over her somethin' fierce! I mean, the girl couldn't even get through dancin' before them men was tryin' to put a bid in to Jesus on who could go first in gettin' some of her.

I was just standin' next to Jesus, followin' behind him like a stranded puppy—except that for the first time in my life, I felt like I was at home. He stopped to talk to one of the bidders for the Chinese girl, so I turned away. Bein' so new, I wasn't tryin' to get all up in his business like that. So I just turned my back and tried to stay calm while takin' in the scene. I wasn't alone for long, though. A tall, thin, real *black* girl came up to me and grabbed my hand. She ain't say nothin' at first. She just smiled at me and rubbed on my hand real soft like she was strokin' mink. I ain't know what to say since she wasn't sayin' nothin', so I just stood there till she finally decided to start talkin'.

"Hi, my name is Alexandra," she whispered in my ear.

"Hi."

"Baby, why don't you come with me?" she said.

Her eyes was callin' me, and there wasn't nothin' I could do to fight it. She took hold of my hand and pulled me into this empty bedroom in the back of house—real far from all the noise from the party. She walked ahead of me and held the door open. I should have been wonderin' where she was takin' me, but all I could do was concentrate on them diamonds around her neck. At first I wondered if them things was for real—I ain't never seen nothin' more than cubic zirconia—but then she pulled up her dress and dug deep into her stockin's. At first I was tryin' to figure out what she was doin', but then she pulled out a thick wad of ice-cold cash, and I thought I was gonna lose my mind! And it wasn't full of no ones, neither. It was full of tens, twenties, and hundreds. It was the most bread I had ever seen in my life!

My eyes was 'bout to bug right out of my head, and I think she knew it, too. She just looked at me and smiled—still not sayin' much of nothin'. But that time I couldn't hold my tongue. I had to let her know she had showed me the magic potion.

"Where you get all that bread?" I asked her.

"I earned it," she said, winkin' at me.

"Dang, you must have been savin' since you was ten years old!"

"Aw, baby, that's just what I made this week."

With all she was holdin', I was scared somebody might have seen all that bread and was plannin' to rob her. I looked around the room we was in and ain't seen nobody else around, so I went back to admirin' all them goods she had pulled out. She saw me look around the room, so she went over to the door and shut it. Still smilin' at me, she rubbed her hand over the part of her thighs where the wad of cash was and said, "Sometimes it gets a little too big for me to handle all by myself."

I looked back at that wad of cash and had to clear my mind, 'cause it was startin' to get too cloudy up in there. I looked back at her diamonds, then back at that cash, and sat on the edge of the bed. She was still smilin' at me, and I was still tryin' to figure out what was goin' on. Then Jesus walked in, and I knew right then what was 'bout to go down. He was through with his other business, so I guess he came back to check on how we was doin'.

"You findin' everything all right?" he asked.

He walked over to the bed where I was sittin' and pulled me up from it. I stood up without too much help, but my stomach was jumpin' all over the place from the nerves that was eatin' right through me.

"Yeah," I said. "I mean, everything is so . . ."

"It ain't nothin' compared to what we could make together."

"What? What you talkin' 'bout?"

"Oh, come on, honey," Alexandra said. "You ain't that dense, is you?"

I knew what everything was 'bout. I mean, I had seen some of it from the street, but I didn't think it would happen like that—not so soon. I thought I was gonna have to do more to be a part of it, or wait awhile before somebody would see me as bein' worthy enough. But I just kept lookin' at the floor, not sayin' a thing till Jesus stepped in and made me know that he was serious.

"It's all right, baby. Take your time," he said.

"Oh, I ain't rushin' you," she said. "Just take your time . . . What's your name, baby?" It turned out she was only two years older than me, but I ain't mind that she was callin' me "baby."

"Angie," I told her.

"That's it? Just Angie? We gonna have to fix that, baby girl."

She put her hand on Jesus' shoulder, then he turned his head and started kissin' on her. He was rubbin' his hand into her hair and holdin' on to her body real tight. My stomach was actin' up real good by then, but I was tryin' my hardest to look like it wasn't nothin' I ain't never seen before. I just kept concentratin' on keepin' my knees real tight and my mouth stiff. The shakes in my stomach was startin' to spread to my whole body, but I was hangin' on—till Jesus turned his eyes to me.

Yeah, he was kissin' Alexandra, but his eyes was fixed right on me. It was like he was talkin' to me without sayin' a thing. You probably ain't never heard of such a thing, but it was real to me. That was really the first and last time I ever looked Jesus directly in the eyes, but they showed me that night that there wasn't nothin' to be scared of. His lips wasn't fixin' no words at all, but them eyes was tellin' me everything I needed to know. They made me feel scared, but they also made me feel calm. It was like he was makin' me real sure that he would always be the only one I need. He was always gonna be there for me. From that point on, I really couldn't go back to the way I was livin' before, 'cause everything that had been fixed in my life up to that point had just been unfastened.

"We 'bout to embark upon a whole new decade—a whole

new way of life, baby. The sixties 'bout to be over," Alexandra said. "The question you gotta ask yourself is how you gonna live the seventies and the eighties, baby?"

Her long eyelashes was battin' at me when she asked the question, and before I could answer her, she reached out and started strokin' my lips. I ain't sure how long I would have been standin' there watchin' them make out if she hadn't brought me into it. My body was froze before, but when she touched me, it was like everything just thawed right out. She was makin' a pass for sure, but for some reason, I just knew in my bones that they was doin' somethin' special for me. That kiss was for me, and the burnin' in my chest told me that I wanted some of it, too.

I don't remember thinkin' too hard 'bout her question, but I did know I wanted to be beautiful—beautiful like her, beautiful like the girls in the party. Most of all, I knew that I wanted Jesus. And that night I had him. I had her, too. Before that night I had only made it a few times before with that boy from school and a boy from church, but somethin' was makin' me want to give everything to Jesus. I tell you, I wanted Jesus to love me. I was a machine, and I wanted it all. It was a funny kinda high, the whole thing. I felt like I was floatin' on cloud nine without all that dope folks be puttin' in they bodies. I mean, I couldn't stop myself. Me, Jesus, and Alexandra made it so many times I can't even count, but I had it all together—and I wanted it to stay that way.

I felt so happy that night, like I had been filled with a new holy ghost—with a love greater than anything I had ever felt in my whole life. It wasn't just 'cause of all the sexy positions we was doin' and stories we was tellin' to each other, neither.

I wasn't bein' put down by nobody in that room. They thought I was pretty. They wanted to be with me. I was bein' made into a new woman and was 'bout to have a new way of livin'. That night with Alexandra and Jesus was my first step into a life where I could be beautiful and where I didn't have to feel like I was lesser 'cause of my family situation. Bein' with them was like comin' into a new family that loved me for all the things that I was good at, without yellin' at me or criticizin' me all the time. When they touched me, they touched my roots. My life changed, and there wasn't no goin' back. There was somethin' real strong and powerful in Jesus' touch. I was filled with a sensation that left me tinglin' all over. I loved it, and I was fallin' in love with him, too.

He put it to me that I was gonna be his latest investment—but that it was gonna have to be my choice.

"Ask yourself where you want to be in the next ten years and then figure out who can get you there."

I ain't had to figure that one out. Like I said, if he had it goin' on like that after only three years . . .

"I want to be with you in the next ten years," I said. "I want to be pullin' hundred-dollar bills from my drawers the way Alexandra do."

"Then get on your knees and crawl to me. Let me know you understand that bein' with me means you gots to let go of most of what you know now and come anew. We gonna redo everything, baby. You finna be new and improved."

I wanted him to know right then that I was down for him and the family. So I did what he said. I dropped to my knees and crawled right on over to him.

Alexandra was still watchin', but she wasn't sayin' nothin'.

She was lookin' on with a straight face, lookin' like she wanted to slap me down. I couldn't really figure that one out, though, 'cause she had gone from makin' it with me to lookin' like she wanted to whip my ass. I just ignored her, though. The most important person in my life that night was Jesus. And he was gonna get anything he asked for.

"You ready to do this?" he asked.

"Yeah . . . I am, Jesus. I'm ready." I remember sayin' it with all the feelin' I had up inside me. I wanted him to know I was sure.

"Well, I ain't callin' you 'Aaangie' no more, momma, so erase that name from your head, 'cause it ain't you."

"What you gonna call me then?"

He was quiet for a minute, then he grabbed ahold of my titties and started rubbin' them in slow circles. He was holdin' them when he finally said, "I'm finna call you 'Peaches,' 'cause you fine and ripe!"

Like they say in the choir—ride on, sweet Jesus! I was ready to go. It was funny when he said it, 'cause my titties is 'bout the same size as some peaches. They still stand up pretty good, but back then they was real perky, so it was perfect. I liked the name "Peaches" from the first time I saw him fix his mouth to say it. And now I don't go by nothin' else.

Oh, look at me, tellin' you all these stories. You gonna make me late. And there ain't no time to waste. Now that I'm his number one, I gotta look good all the time—especially when he come off a long trip and first see me. I know people around here been talkin' 'bout him, sayin' he losin' his game 'cause he done gained a little weight. But, baby, that ain't no thing. That just mean that I'm doin' my job so he can eat.

Anyhow, wait till you see me later. You might even want some Peaches. Naw, I'm just messin' with you . . . unless you got fifty dollars and a few more minutes. I mean, this is business. How 'bout it, baby?

Jesus

"What you doin' right now?" Jason says.

"I'm finna get on up and see what's happenin' on the corner," I say.

"Oh . . . what time you leavin'? 'Cause I was finna head to your house. I thought I could swoop you and we could hit that spot I was tellin' you about. Come on, nigga. I ain't seen you since you been out."

"Hmmm. You think you ready, nigga?"

"I'm for real about this."

"Serious?" I ask the question, but of course the muthafucka is serious. He been writin' me for years now, hollerin' about how he wants to be a pimp. And he been callin' me for the past two days, tryin' to hook up.

"There finna be hella hos out where I'ma take you, blood. Come on, you know . . ."

"What does that mean?"

"What?"

"Hella."

"It means 'a lot,' man . . . I got *hella* bitches, *hella* hos . . ."

"Aw . . . you young cats . . ."

"Anyway, so what's up for right now? Come on, you know I ain't trippin' off all that shit that happened before. That's all in the past. I ain't no player hater."

"Well, I'm glad to hear that, 'cause I ain't gots no time to waste."

"Jesus."

"What, nigga?!"

"I'll be there in a half."

"Yeah, all right, Jason. I'll be sittin' on my steps. Hurry up, nigga."

He's laughin', but I'm serious.

Like I said, Jason been callin' me ever since I gots out of jail a few days ago. Every time he calls, he says he serious, but tonight we'll see if he really gots the balls for this business. I know he ain't strayed too far from his old man, but a nigga still gots to be careful who he let into his circle. Muthafuckas be jealous, man. And that's dangerous 'cause then they be walkin' around stakin' out your territory, plottin' and schemin' on how to make you weak.

See, that's what they been tryin' to do with me. You think I don't know what people out there be sayin' about me? Talkin' all that shit about how I'm losin' my bitch magnetism. They just jealous, baby, but I ain't trippin'. They just tryin' to search theyselves for even one of the balls I got danglin' from these drawers.

Everybody want to be a pimp these days—all those fake-ass, wannabe players and Macks want a piece of this shit.

Shit, they all dyin' for a piece of this game, but those of us already in it know they ain't really gots what it takes to be a pimp. All these young fellas gots is personality, and that's all right—if you already gots your shit sewn up. But if you serious, then that ain't what it's *all* about. You gots to be cold-blooded. You gots to be about your bread, man. You gots to be prepared to take care of your main money-makin' source. See, you gots to be a businessman with all the trimmins' of a superstar—'cause that's what you is on the streets.

Once some bitch chooses you, you gots to be prepared to defend that investment—protect your property—'cause there will be other Macks out there waitin' on you to start slippin'. And if one of them do happen to catch you in a moment of carelessness, that's when you gots to exercise your options—you gots to make your presence felt. You gots to be anywhere and everywhere—not always in person, but always in their minds. Hos gots to think—no, they need to *know*—you gots the power to be their *real* salvation.

When I look in the mirror, of course, I see a man. But when other niggas see me, they see somebody who can deliver them from this hell we livin' in. Me bein' who I am ain't never been about performin' no miracles, but it's always been about givin' people what they need. These hos know what it's all about, and if they don't, I teach them. I control this muthafucka, man—just me.

This is *Jesus* you talkin' to, baby! And all them hos know I'm a vengeful pimp. I'm a jealous pimp that's true to form and true to salvation, baby. Like when I first saw Peaches sittin' on them steps starin' at me like she was, I wanted her soul. And I knew I could get it. It came with a load of bullshit, but when she chose me, she made the decision to follow my rules and live by my word. She was lookin' to be saved. My work was done before I even gots started.

That's what I'm tryin' to teach that boy now. He gots to learn the rules of the game from somebody. And with me bein' a legend around here, I want him learnin' them from me. These other sucka-ass players don't know shit, man. Shit, they can't even tell a real Mack from an international player, man. They can't see that a Mack gots game that can't always be seen by the average person, 'cause the shit goes too deep. An international player might get pussy around the world. He might even get some shit out of it, like in that movie with Richard Gere playin' a gigolo. But he wasn't no Mack. He wasn't workin' them bitches the way a Mack would. He ain't have no hos, so he wasn't no pimp. But fake-ass muthafuckas be content to be players and gigolos—callin' theyselves Macks—but they ain't nothin', man. They ain't smart. They ain't gots no business sense—all they gots is personality. And again, that's all right for some folks, but Jason finna get more than that. Like I said, personality all by itself don't get you to the top of your pimpin' game, especially with everything else that's goin' on around here.

The dope game been givin' our business a run for its money lately, but I'm finna give this boy a Mackin' lesson that'll make the dope competition look like it ain't shit. When we through here tonight, he might even be ready to get started on acquirin' some real hos. He been messin' around with some of them neighborhood girls—gettin' them to buy him shit—but until lately, I ain't really thought he was ready to enter the game for real. Looks like he might be, though.

I'm finna show him how girls come around every ten minutes, lookin' for a pimp to control they shit. Maybe tonight he'll show me that he do gots what it takes. It shouldn't be too hard—the muthafucka *is* my son.

It shouldn't be too hard for him to see how bitches be lookin' to be saved, man. I'm tellin' you, they always lookin' for somebody to choose. They need somebody to handle them—and they're always willin' participants. I ain't never twisted a bitch's arm to choose me. Wouldn't be choosin' if I had to do that. They come beggin' for me, man, hollerin' *"Please, Jesus"* and *"Just help me, Jesus."* Some of them hos even be comin' up to me like they in church, talkin' about *"I need Jesus in my life!"* Those be the easy ones to turn out.

See, I don't care if my hos go to church. Matter fact, I like it when they go and read the Bible, 'cause it ain't doin' nothin but reinforcin' what I already been tellin' them. The Bible say love Jesus. I say love Jesus. The Bible say Jesus will save you. I say Jesus will save you. The Bible say spread love. I say spread love. See, it's all the same thing.

All this just came to me when I was creatin' my own rules of the game. Before me, wasn't nobody pimpin' hos without keepin' them on drugs and shit. Everybody else's hos be strung out on dope. That's how they numb their minds to what they be doin'. But me? I gots my hos believin' what they do for me be biblical. Man, them bitches do anything for me—for Jesus.

Before I was Jason's age, I birthed the philosophy that my momma named me "Jesus" for a reason. It only took me a little time to figure it out. Back in the day, I used to get teased for bein' named after Jesus. Niggas around these parts wasn't used to a nigga with a Mexican side to his family—so you know, they couldn't get down with the culture and shit. I

tried to tell them about me, tried to show them that I was as
black as them, but they couldn't get with it. Some of the old
black ladies tried to call me anything but my name, talkin'
about sayin' my name was a sin in the Bible. Listenin' to them
had a muthafucka like me startin' to second-guess the value
of the only *good* thing my momma ever gave me! But when I
saw how girls used to be all over me, talkin' about they liked
bein' around somebody who looked like me and how much
they loved hollerin' my name, I realized that I couldn't just
waste this gift. That would be blasphemy.

Once I realized pimpin' was my callin', it was only natural
that I keep my name. My momma pronounced it the Spanish
way—you know, like "Hay-soos," but my pimpin' name has
always been "Jesus." My daddy bein' from the South, he was
all about the crucifixes and other religious shit. And he was
down with havin' me bein' named after the son of God—
now tell me who gots the complex! With genes like that,
there wasn't no way I was finna cave in to other people's
problems with me. My shit was together, man. Fuck what
people said about me and my family. I was finna win.

That's why I'm out here waitin' on my son now. There
ain't no guarantees in this life, but where other men fail, we
win. You know how they say "Pimpin' Ain't Easy"? I ain't
never said that, 'cause it came to me natural—it *was* easy.
See, I was born a pimp. I make hos.

Yeah, so I'm out here waitin' on Jason. I ain't trippin',
though. I been out here every night since I gots out the
joint—just sittin' on my front steps and enjoyin' the fresh air.
See, it don't matter where I be, I can still monitor what's
goin' on. And I ain't gots no reason to put on a show. These
bitches know who they gonna come to when work is over

and the sun come up. See, Jesus was a man who walked among the common folks. He was the son of God, and *all* He did was hang with the hos and the gamblers. Them was His people, man.

So that's what I do. I can walk, or sit, among the folks that don't nobody want to see, man. See, right here is where I earned my M.B.A.P.H.D. degree—my Mackin' Bitches And Pimpin' Hos Degree. That's what these cats don't understand about me, I'm a complicated man with simple ways. I gots to be, 'cause life out here can make a muthafucka go crazy if he let it.

Back in the day—all the way up until I went to the joint— I was the Truth. Cats even called me that instead of "Jesus" sometimes. "The Truth," "Jesus"—I answer to them both. See, I ain't never been about what these new cats call "space-age" pimpin', or none of that nonviolent pimpin' shit. The Truth is all about layin' a Mack hand down when hos get out of line and think they ain't gots to follow simple rules and directions. Don't cringe, baby. I told you I was a vengeful pimp. I let them know when they done crossed the line and finna answer to me. And oh, yeah, they jump back in line real quick.

Look, we smoke, drink, sleep—all of it—together. And if a bitch get out of line, sometimes I ain't even gots to be the one to check her. My other bitches do it for me, see, 'cause they recognize the value of our family. They know we all gots to fight to protect the family. This is all a part of the life.

All these years out here, and I can't tell you how many hos I done had. I had so many hos turnin' tricks for me that them other pimps quit tryin' to lure my girls away and started tryin' to talk to me about bein' interested in a merger! Ain't no tax deductibles in this game, though, so I let them know that I had *one* religion goin' on here—and there wasn't no room for more than one god. Once hos start worshippin' another god, it's time to turn them loose like they got bad breath, man.

Bad enough I had to put money aside for the police, but that shit was worth not havin' to bail my bitches out of jail 'cause they done accidentally offered to turn a trick on a cop. A nice weekly allowance—that's what I'll call it—kept the police away from all my girls. Cops around here be a trip, too. Them muthafuckas be just as easy to pimp as my hos.

I remember when, about twenty-five, damn near thirty years ago, some of them cops gots all impressed with my power. It don't even seem that long ago, but it was. It was when I was in a Hollywood movie about the local pimpin' game.

The police was out there watchin' hard when them cameras started rollin' into the Paramount Theatre. Yeah, I was up in there looking *bad*, man, and I had all my girls lookin' fine too! They was filmin' a fake Players' Ball for the movie, but it turned into a real one, 'cause all the real pimps and players from around the Bay Area turned out. They was all tellin' me the main actor in the movie looked like me. If you ask me, I'm much prettier, man, but it ain't no thing. His actin' did me a lot of good. Right after that movie came out, I had all kinds of pussy thrown my way—and I tell you, man, the Truth set it free!

It's cold out here tonight, so I'm finna turn on this heater. I had it put in long before other muthafuckas around here had enough bread to do this kind of shit. I had it put out here on the porch for all them parties I was throwin'. It was good for business, too. Muthafuckas loved takin' pictures in front of my shit—like they was hangin' with a bona fide superstar. Oh, yeah, baby.

And best believe that nobody around here touched my shit. Some of them dope fiends messed with other people's shit around here, but for the most part, they don't come near my house 'cause they want to live for another high. For all fifteen years I was in the joint, nobody touched my shit, but now that some of them been trippin' off that rock, they tryin' to test a nigga.

Man, I had to kill one of them crackheads a few nights ago—the same night I gots released from the joint—for tryin' to lift my portable TV out the backyard. The nigga actually jumped over my back fence and was fumblin' around with my shit, man. I guess he thought that I couldn't catch his skinny ass on the late night, but I did. I spotted him from my kitchen and I came flyin' out the house with a mission to make an example out of him. And I had that muthafucka hemmed up tight on the grass in my yard. He was hollerin' for me to let him loose, but that just made me hold on tighter. Then he pissed me off, offerin' to do some faggot shit I had heard over and over in the joint. He fucked up though, 'cause what he said triggered some jail shit, and I just flashed. I saw some scissors on the dominos table I gots back there, so I knocked the muthafucka across his head with my prosthetic, grabbed them scissors with my real hand, and cut straight through his skin.

I was feelin' it, man, and the more he hollered, the deeper I dug them scissors. When I was done, I tripped on how I was finna get rid of that muthafucka. But not too hard, though. I just threw his little ass in the Dumpster down the block. I'm sure cats around here know I did it. I ain't do nothin' to hide that it was me. The police ain't busted me for it, though. And it ain't finna be on no ten o'clock news, neither. All I did was kill a crackhead—them news reporters don't give a shit about that.

But seriously, bein' in the joint for so long gots me trippin' on how much things done changed out here. That crack cocaine shit came out while I was locked up, so a lot of this is new to me. Yeah, some of the cats comin' in the joint was strung out on that shit, but I never imagined the kind of zombies that be walkin' around these streets high off that little rock. I came back here and saw how that shit was threatenin' to kill the game. Even some of my hos was on that shit! I had to cut them crack bitches loose, though. Bad for business. My Top Ho been tellin' me how some of them bitches was spendin' my money on them rocks faster than she could walk two steps to get my bread; and I told you, man, once hos start worshippin' another god, it's time to let them go. So that's what I did. Crackheads sacrifice everything for that dope, man—it ain't like the stuff I use. My shit is basic.

See, I don't need no shit that's finna make me hyper. I just stick to my little "soother." That's what I call it, my "soother." It ain't nothin' but a little weed and a little heroin. And I don't care what muthafuckas might say about my crutch. I live life to enjoy it, and my stash ain't like crack. It don't get in the way of business, so fuck it. Matter of fact, I could use some now, but I'm finna wait to light up until Jason get here. I gots some in my pockets somewhere. One of them dope dealers gave me some free shit to celebrate my bein' out the joint, and for lettin' one of my hos turn a trick on him and his friends. I was happy to oblige. Rita, the ho I sent over, is a freaky bitch. They're gonna ask for her again, but the next time, her trick won't be for free. Damn, where is my stash? I know I put it in one of these pockets.

"Hey, old man . . . lookin' for some more hop?" says some young dope dealer from across the street. I ain't gonna say nothin' back to nonsense. He thinks he knows what game is 'cause him and his friend gots some new shoes and some fancy sweat pants. I'm just gonna pretend to ignore the shit like it don't even deserve my attention. He been standin' out there with his friend for the last hour, sellin' dope to some crazy-lookin' white folks drivin' up in fancy cars. Ain't nobody rollin' up to them now, so I guess they bored or somethin'.

But these young bucks be goin' wrong, man, 'cause they rest on what they see. They don't hear me say nothin', so I guess they think I ain't trippin'. What they don't get is that life ain't about what you see, it's about the way you make people *feel*. I ain't what I used to be—I know that—but my shit still ain't as fucked up muthafuckas want it to be. Anyway, that kid probably don't know me from his own daddy, dumb muthafucka.

That's the only problem with livin' here now. Things are fallin' apart. All them houses that was owned by muthafuckas who halfway cared about this neighborhood done fell apart. Paint been chipped on these houses for years, but there ain't never been no boarded-up buildings and broke-down homes like there is now. I guess over the years, folks around here just let everything go. Like the house on the opposite corner from this one—it's huge, and gots a front door that's set back off the street. Shit, my house gots a nice-sized porch, but the one on that house is major. But the muthafucka don't gots nobody in it! It's all boarded up and shit.

Maybe when I get back in my groove out here, I'll sell this one and buy that one. It would be a big fix-up project, but my bitches would take care of that for me. Or maybe I'll buy that muthafucka and rent out the rooms to bitches who need a place to stay. I could do a whole lot with that big-ass house.

"Ain't that fiend some kind of broke-down old pimp or somethin' like that?" the other young dope dealer just said. These boys bein' real stupid to confuse my quiet for not carin'. They finna learn, though. I don't care if they do look like they only about fourteen or fifteen, they treadin' in deep water now.

"I know you better act like you gots some sense before these first few years you been livin' be your last," I say. I just gave them a warnin' shot.

"Aw . . . we just playin', pops."

They're laughin', but I'm serious.

"Yeah, don't get sensitive, man. We just playin' wit' your old ass."

They're too young to know what they're toyin' with—not seasoned enough to be out here on these streets. And I'm not the kind to just sit back and be disrespected, so they're real lucky I'm in a good mood right about now. Yeah, they're lucky I'm waitin' on my son, and feelin' fatherly, or this little exchange we havin' might be endin' differently. All I'm about to do now is reach into the little openin' I gots tucked away in these steps and flash my gun so they know what's comin' if they keep it up. There won't be no quiet next time. Of course, this means I'm gonna have to move the gun, but that don't matter right now. I gots to show them that this "old pimp" ain't "broke down" at all.

Yeah, you see how fast they scatterin' and tryin' to go inside the house? Now they want to apologize and go back to being boys. A few seconds ago, they was dyin' to be men. Funny how the sight of a gun can shake the wrinkles from a man's drawers. And believe me, intimidation be necessary, especially when you settin' boundaries. It's all a part of the game, baby just a little intimidation be showin' these mutha-fuckas how far they can go. And it suits me to scare the shit out of a muthafucka.

Suits me like all the hos I had workin' for me before I had to cut some of them crack bitches loose. I still gots my good ones though. Man, I gots the black ones, white ones, Hawai-ians, Mexicans, Filipinos, Chinese . . . you name it, I gots it. I'm runnin' the international house of pleasure, man. I gots them all. I mean, don't everybody love Jesus?

Ain't nobody been gifted like Peaches, though. She was special. That's why I made her my number one. She was my Top Ho. Don't get confused, though. I wasn't trustin' the bitch. She was still turnin' tricks like the rest of them—for fifty dollars a pop, too—but she was always a little special to me. And fine! That girl could get a rise out of a fag. That's why she brought in so much business. But I always knew she would. I had been a pimp for only a few years when I met her, but I could tell her potential from the first time I laid eyes on them big legs and juicy lips. And she always had my back, no matter what.

She would fight another ho down in a heartbeat for me—but that wasn't always a good thing. I mean, when bitches fight they leave scars and other shit that's bad for business. Other times, though, bitch fights was funny, especially when Peaches was in them. She had this way of bein' real sexy after she threw a punch. She would touch her tits—like they gave her super powers or somethin'—and hold on to them until I came over. It was like her signal that the fight was finna be over soon. It was almost like a call for me to jump in it.

Oh, yeah, my other hos was jealous, especially Alexandra, who was my Top Ho before Peaches came into the picture. But fuck it, you know? Alexandra was startin' to get old-lookin' and she just wasn't pullin' them the way she used to. Anyway, I ain't like them other pimps—I love all my hos.

But Peaches was a little more. She put a soft spot on my heart. That's why I let her keep the baby when she got knocked up. She tried to put on her sweet voice, but I could see right through that shit before she could even get started.

"Jesus, baby . . . I ain't had a period in three months," she said one day right after we finished fuckin'. And, man, as soon as the words left her mouth, I was pissed.

"Goddammit! I told you to take care of that shit!"

And I lost my temper. I was cussin', then I slapped the shit out of her—but I only used my real hand, not the plastic one. I was so mad 'cause she was supposed to be the leader of the team. I couldn't have my role model for the other girls gettin' pregnant. Before I'd know it, all my hos would be comin' up pregnant and shit.

"Please, Jesus . . . please. It . . . it's yours."

"How am I supposed to know that shit? You gettin' rid of it."

"Please . . . Jesus, it's yours. I know it is 'cause I only been doin' blow jobs with everybody else, remember? You told me three months ago to only do blow jobs. Please . . . remember?"

When I thought about it, she was right. I had her servin'
up head for those months, 'cause I was startin' to fuck her on
the regular. She wasn't bringin' as much money then, 'cause
it didn't cost that much for head. But that didn't matter. I was
usin' her to bring other bitches into the family. But with that
whole baby shit, Peaches fucked up. She violated the rules.
She was pregnant, and usually that shit would *not* be toler-
ated. Anyway, I never had regular relationships with girls, so
her tellin' me she was havin' a baby caught me off guard.
Already I must have been lettin' her get away with too much.
She was gettin' too comfortable, and that had to be stopped.

"Look," I said to her once I calmed down. "You ain't like
the rest of them bitches. You know this already, so I'm finna
make an exception. If this is my child—and I will know if
he's mine—I ain't gonna kill my son, so we just gonna have
to wait it out and see." Shit, I wasn't finna kill a Baby Jesus!

She tried that "what if it's a girl" shit, but I knew if it was
mine, it was finna be a boy. Her face lit up, like I had saved
her life—again. And I had. But she had to know that in the
same breath, I could take it away.

"If it ain't mine, I'm killin' you," I said.

Hell yeah I was serious, and she was scared—just like she
should have been. She was so scared she started stutterin'
and shit about how she loved me and how this kid was our
"love child." But I had to let her know that if she was finna
stay pregnant, she had to move out of my house. I couldn't
have no pregnant ho livin' with me. What would I look like?
As it was, she was the only one I was givin' the honor of carryin' my son . . . at least the only one I know about.

I'm a pimp, baby. I can't be concerned with keepin' track
of all the places I might have planted my seed. It ain't my

business to do that no way. These bitches supposed to be on top of their craft, just like I'm on top of mine. Like the Temptations say—this papa's a "rollin' stone." I can't be bothered with shit like birth control.

Damn, I hate bein' outside on nights like these. It's startin' to rain now. Even though I gots the heat comin' down on the porch, it don't always work out so good 'cause of my arm. I had a new one waitin' for me when I gots out a few nights ago, and I'm still gettin' used to it. This arm is all a part of my new beginnings, but it gets ice cold when it's fifty degrees and damn near one hundred degrees when it's lukewarm outside. I gots to adjust to this shit again after fifteen years without one.

I've had a prosthesis since I turned my life around and gots me the pimp status you see today. But I was born with one good arm and one bad one. I could always use my left hand, but my right one would just hang there to the side not doin' shit. The shit was useless, but it was also a lifesaver.

I was eighteen and workin' at a pet store downtown when I gots the notice sayin' to report for army duty. I had just graduated from high school, so they thought they could jump on a nigga's young ass and get him over to Vietnam. You know, they was recruitin' niggas left and right in 1966 to go get shot up over there. But my arm kept me out of that shit.

It was all a part of the master plan, though. I know this 'cause it was durin' my time at the pet store that the vision came to me. I was cleanin' up some bird and cat shit one day when it came to me that doin' that kind of work was not where it was at.

One day this rich old cracker came in there talkin' to me

like I was supposed to be his very own ass-licker. He came in there makin' me run through all kinds of hoops, talkin' about "Get this, boy" and "Boy, get that down." He might as well have followed everything he was sayin' with "nigger." Shit, the muthafucka's voice was sayin' it all.

But then I realized he wasn't doin' nothin' that I couldn't do. I could walk through life demandin' respect and makin' other people work for me, too. He wasn't no smarter than me. He was just white and born into a world that told him he had a right to some shit. Well, that's when I started thinkin' that I gots a right to some shit, too.

I remember he was walkin' down the aisle—not *askin'* me to get some cat that was in the back of its cage, but *screamin'* at me to get it. His mouth was open so wide I could damn near see his tonsils. I never did get the cat, but I gave him a cussin' like he ain't never had before. He didn't say much after that except somethin' about how my "people" would always be treated like we "deserved." You know what I wanted to do to that muthafucka, but I didn't have my "degree" yet. I didn't know how to get away with handlin' muthafuckas like him.

I swore then that it didn't matter how I did it, but I would build an empire that would make simple muthafuckas like him be my hos. I knew he was born into the world's biggest pimpin' school. I could tell that by the way he was talkin' to me. But you know what? It didn't even matter. I know that if I saw him today, he would probably still talk to me like he did before, but see, this time I would know how to handle it. I gots my equalizers now—the bread in my pocket and the lead in my gun.

Of course, the muthafucka that ran the store fired my ass,

talkin' some shit about how I couldn't ever step foot in that place again. What he didn't know is that I didn't *want* to go back to that muthafucka. Shit, that day I walked a few blocks over to the strip, and ran into my main man from high school, Slim. He was standin' on the porch of this other muthafucka's house when he spotted me. He had about three or four bitches hangin' on him who was lookin' at me like I was finna be they next trick. But I wasn't no bitch's trick, and Slim knew that shit. Turns out he was callin' me over there just to shoot the breeze, but while he was rappin', I was soakin' in the scene and the stares from Slim's bitches.

I realized that I had a choice. I could rebuild my life and get with the program, or I could end up just like my broke-ass daddy. He ain't never had shit from his job as a janitor, and my momma, well, she had a mental condition and ain't never done nothin' for me. I was her only child, and all she could do was follow behind what my daddy told her to do. She didn't even learn English so she could talk to a nigga. All she did was pray, stare at the radio, and fuck my daddy. It ain't no big deal, though. Like I said, she was doin' what my daddy told her to do. Just like she was supposed to. Slim was the one who really put me on to the way to survive. He laid it down in high school, when he first started talkin' seriously about the life. He said his uncle was a major pimp in the Fillmore over in Frisco, and that he was finna make a run for it in Oakland. I laughed back then, 'cause I didn't think that muthafucka could do it. But when I ran into him that day I left the pet store, I saw that his way was workin'. He was black and ugly, but he could talk a good game, and he was pullin' hos left and right. Shit, I *knew* I could do it if he could.

I was a pretty muthafucka, and I knew I had it in me. All

through high school, girls was always tryin' to get with me 'cause I looked so good. I could always get them to do anything I told them to do. It was never a problem for me, and I must have been trippin' not to see it sooner. So, after I cashed my last paycheck from the pet store, I left Oakland for a while. I went to Frisco, where I could start over—you know, and develop my own game.

The Tenderloin is the funky underarm of Frisco, man. Don't nothin' be lurkin' behind them buildings but dirt—the kind that walk and the kind that breed. This ain't the neighborhood tourists be tryin' to see; it ain't even nothin' the city government wants to see. I was livin' in the Tenderloin, and let me tell you, them was some tough times. I was over there livin' in one of them hotels for a few months, with only a few girls workin' for me. They was enough to scrape by, but nothin' to make a muthafucka stop workin' the streets. I was workin' day and night tryin' to find somebody that didn't look like shit. Then I found her. Her name was Alexandra, and from the look in her eyes, I could tell she wasn't no stranger to sellin' her body. Turned out she only did it when she needed food or the rent paid, but all that changed when she chose me, and I made it happen—for her and for me.

She was a renegade ho until I charmed, romanced, and turned her out to the streets a changed woman. I just remembered what Slim said when we was in high school about makin' bitches bow to a bigger game. I always had a way with them bitches out there, so I just rolled over that play for somethin' that could put food in my mouth and a serious roof over my head. Before long, Alexandra was comin' back with wads of money the likes of which neither one of us had seen up to that point. Man, I learned that bein' paid was a high all by itself—and it left us with a tasty hangover.

We was a good team, 'cause Alexandra believed in what we was makin'. She would get busted at ten o'clock, bailed out by twelve, and back at it fifteen minutes later. That was dedication, man. But we was developin' a reputation with them judges,so before everything could get shut down, we moved back to Oakland and started up new. The infection in my arm caused me to have to cut it off, but I gots a brand new one that was better than the old one ever was.

The way I saw it, my fake arm was just a symbol for my new life. I had the old useless weight replaced by a pimped-out version of the flesh and blood original, baby. It makes my shit superhuman. Just ask any of them hos. They know me. Just ask anyone who be around here. They all know me. They recognize Jesus the Pimp. And I'm always finna win— I'm the Mack with the game that lasts forever. And the name to match.

Peaches

I know it ain't much to look at, but it's my home. Jesus
helped me find this apartment 'bout six and half years ago. It
was when I got knocked up. I stay here now 'cause it's easier
on Jason. It ain't nothin' fancy, but it's on the fourth floor of
the buildin' so I got a little view of what's goin' on outside
when I look out the window. My furniture ain't nothin' fancy
neither, but at least it's mine.

Here he come now . . . that's my baby.

Oh, he be playin' like that all the time—just quiet and to
hisself. Watch, he just gonna sit there on that old tricycle
that he always be ridin' between the livin' room and the
kitchen and play with that toy gun. I let him put water in it
sometimes, but only when we be outside.

Look at him. Ain't he sweet? He got those beautiful
brown eyes that look like the eyes on a panther. Don't he
got panther eyes? See how they slant upward on the outside

and curve down by his nose? I love his eyes—look at them lashes. They look just like Jesus' eyes, I think. I can't really remember what they look like in real life—I can only look at them in pictures. I can't study them like I study Jason's, 'cause you know, I ain't allowed to look in his eyes no more. They my favorite part of the face, though, so sometimes I be takin' a little peek. I gotta be fast, you know, 'cause if Jesus catch me I could be in serious trouble, you hear me? Anyway, I be tryin' to be the best ho I can be, and part of that is makin' sure I don't never look into my pimp's eyes.

But I can look at Jason's eyes any time I want to. I stare into them beautiful eyes whenever it please me to do it. I just wish they ain't have to see everything that goes on in this world—or even up in this apartment. But there ain't nothin' I can do 'bout that, can I? I just do what I can.

Since he was born, his daddy been trainin' him to be a "Baby Jesus"—that's what he be callin' him. He be walkin' around here talkin' 'bout my baby's genes already make him one of the best pimps around. You know I love Jesus, but Jason ain't gonna be another one of him. There ain't no guarantees that Jason gonna be as good at the game as Jesus—and, anyway, I want more for my baby. This is all right for me and for his daddy, but it ain't all right for that precious baby over there. I know, I know—he's six—but he always gonna be my baby, you hear me? Anyway, can't nobody be Jesus but Jesus. There's only one.

He sure do look like him, though. I be lookin' at Jason sometimes, wonderin' what parts of me he got at all. Look at him, playin' with that water gun like he Officer Friday chasin' a criminal. Yeah, I be playin' with him sometimes—when I ain't too tired—but tonight ain't one of them nights.

I only got 'bout another hour before I go out on the stroll, and that ain't hardly enough time to get my head on right. I mean, just lookin' at Jason be makin' me feel a hundred times better, but it's always hard to go from playin' "Mommy" to playin' "Hot Momma," you know? Anyway, I like sittin' here lookin' at him do what he do best—be my sweet baby.

"Jason, baby . . . Come on over here and give Momma a kiss," I say to him. I ain't even had to say it, really. You saw how as soon as I opened my mouth and said his name, he was breakin' his neck to get off that bike and come to me. He loves his momma.

See how he just kisses me like I'm goin' out of style? But I ain't never gonna be out of style to him. That's what make this so perfect. When this booty starts to saggin' and these titties get tired and want to lay down, he still gonna love me. He always gonna love me. I tell you what—this child here done made me rethink everything I thought I knew 'bout life and love.

"Mommy, you gotta leave tonight?" he says. This ain't the first time he done asked me that question.

"Baby, you know Momma gotta go to work," I say. I keep on smilin' like this 'cause I ain't real happy 'bout him knowin' how hard it be for me to leave him every night. Like I said, he know too much already.

"Why you always workin' all the time when it be in the nighttime?"

Poor baby. He see this world, but he ain't got no understandin' 'bout how things work in it.

"'Cause that's when you be sleep. I go to work when you can't miss me. Now, I need my rest, so you go on in the corner over there and play . . . Momma loves you, okay?"

"Okay."

"Love me?"

"Yes."

Jason on his way to go play in the corner between the couch and the window. He like bein' right there, so he can play. I don't let him get too close to the window, especially not this late at night. But over there, he can just play to hisself.

I don't never let him go without givin' him a little slap on the butt. I ain't really knowin' why—I guess it's just somethin' I picked up from Jesus. The first time he did it, he said he just wanted to cop a feel. The second time he did it, he said he was just bein' friendly—and then he just kept on doin' it. Started doin' it to all the girls. I guess it's just somethin' that rubbed off.

Funny how little things rub off on you, and you catch yourself doin' somethin' you ain't never thought you was even payin' attention to. Like with me. I think I just got a little of my grandpa in me, but I got a whole bunch of Grandma. Especially when it come to the church. Good thing Jesus ain't never got mad 'bout that. I heard some of them other pimps ain't as open as Jesus when it come to they hos goin' to church. I say they ain't got enough goin' on if they feel like they gotta be threatened by God. They should love Him, not be scared of Him. I mean, how you gonna feel threatened by God? That don't even make no sense. I mean, no sense at all.

I see you lookin' at my picture of Jesus over there next to the window. I got it framed two months after me and him first met. I wasn't rushin' into nothin'—I already told you how I knew he was the man for me. I love that picture, too, 'cause see the way he smilin'? He smilin' like that 'cause he had just won "Mack of the Year" for the second year in a row. I ain't had much to do with his winnin' that year, but I sure did my thing at the picnic, you hear me? Jesus told us we couldn't work. He said we was there to have our fun. But you know, everything is work.

We all went out of our way to be fine that day. It was all 'bout sex, baby, and I had the best. You hear me? The best. I keep that picture hangin' up 'cause it remind me of why I gotta work so hard. He gotta keep on winnin' and keep on makin' me the star attraction. I gotta show them other hos out there that they ain't got a clue 'bout what's goin' on right here.

I also like that picture 'cause the sun aimin' at his teeth and put a little shine on his lips like he just been kissed. Well, I guess he had been kissed. Winnin' the Mack trophy be a big deal around here. All the pimps want to be a winner, and all the hos want to be with the man who be winnin'. That day was so much fun—but times ain't been like that in a little while. On some bad days, I even be thinkin' that I gotta find me somethin' else to do. But them thoughts—like the bad days—just be comin' and goin'.

That one next to it is Grandma's old picture of Jesus Christ. I hung that one up a few years after I hung up the other picture. Kinda strange how it happened that I hung up the picture of the Jesus I knew all my life *after* I hung up the one of the Jesus I knew for only two months. But you know, I had a hard time dealin' with the memories that came with the old one. Maybe it's 'cause it used to be Grandma's and Grandpa's—I ain't really knowin'. But I do know that whenever I look at it, I think 'bout how Grandma and Grandpa just cut me off when I told them what I wanted to do with my life. They was from Mississippi, and I know they was old-fashioned and ain't really understand me when I told them I was droppin' out of high school to work for Jesus, but I ain't expect them to drop me altogether.

First, they thought I was gonna be a nun. Then they thought I was sick. Kinda funny if you think 'bout it. They thought I was losin' my mind—said they was gonna call the doctor 'cause I was havin' these dreams 'bout runnin' away with Jesus. I think they thought I was playin', till that day I packed my bags and said I was movin' in with him. Grandpa had a fit, you hear me? He started yellin' at me, sayin' I was leavin' the church for a life of sin. And Grandma, well, she dropped to her knees and started callin' out to my dead momma. I just walked out the door, 'cause that was all too much for me. I tried to explain that I wasn't leavin' the church—I was just switchin' focus, but she couldn't get with it. She just kept pointin' to that there picture of Jesus and kept on askin' where she went wrong. Nothin' but hollerin' was goin' on in that house. I mean, I even got told I was full of the devil. I couldn't get a word in at all to defend myself, so I just walked away.

I tried to go back to the house a few times after that, but when Grandma started hearin' from the folks at church that they had seen me in places they ain't thought was a good place for me to be, Grandma shut the door and never opened it again. The last time I set foot in that old house was when I was comin' in to say good-bye when they died. They had already started boardin' up the house 'cause Grandma and Grandpa said they ain't had no kin left. So once I got in there, I just grabbed the picture and got out. It kinda hurt, but it wasn't the first time I ain't had no parents.

Now when I look at the picture, it ain't so hard, especially 'cause I hung it up next to the one of my Jesus. I put them together so I could just look up in that one spot and remember that when things just seem like they goin' real bad, I can rest on my two Jesuses to make everything all right.

They look so different to me in them pictures, too—one white, one not. One a man, one not. But them blue eyes and that blond hair ain't never said nothin' bad to me. Now that everybody around here hollerin' 'bout they "free," they be walkin' up and down the street passin' out flyers sayin' colored folks is brainwashed. There be people standin' on Broadway yellin' into bullhorns, takin' 'bout Jesus was a colored man, and that the man who painted the picture I got hangin' up was really drawin' his brother or his cousin or somebody. I don't know what they talkin' 'bout. Anyway, I can't see why it even matter to them folks. I love both my Jesuses, and I couldn't wait to hang my two pictures together so I could bring all my problems and my good news to them at the same time. I don't care what they look like.

I be talkin' to them pictures, too. No, I ain't crazy. I just got this little habit of talkin' to things that can't talk back. I started doin' that years ago when Grandma would lock me in my room and tell me that I couldn't come out till I fixed myself and stopped doin' whatever I was doin' bad. Well, I can't just not talk, so I started talkin' to all the things that was around me—my baby doll, my little wood cross, the pictures in the schoolbooks. Don't matter, though. I'm really the only one who know I be doin' it.

Anyway, it feels good to look into them eyes and pray for everything to be all right. One day, when I have my two Jesuses to myself forever, I'm gonna feel real peace for the first time in my life . . . I mean *real* peace. The kinda peace where you forget where you is 'cause you so comfortable. The kinda peace where you ain't gotta worry 'bout how good you look or how good you turn a trick.

Oh, I'm sorry. I try not to cry over things like this. I'm gonna go in the bathroom so Jason can't see me. I ain't never liked it when he see me cry. It ain't fair that he gotta see so much sadness so early on in his life. It don't matter how much I try to explain it, he can't understand yet. I mean, no matter what they see, I ain't run into a kid yet who ain't a little boy or girl on the inside. Oh, look at me. Here I am cryin' for myself when I ain't got no time for this. I gotta get ready for tonight.

I know I seem sad now, but I be tryin' not to trip that hard off the way things done changed. Jesus used to have me in his house with the other girls, and when I got knocked up, he was right to put me out. I couldn't be havin' a baby all up in a house where serious pimpin' was goin' on. It ain't a good match. I wasn't too worried 'bout it anyway. I was pregnant and that's all that mattered. I just did blow jobs to make a little money to keep some food comin' in. And that kept me busy. I had lockjaw so bad that I could barely keep it open to scream from the birthin' pains. But Jesus took good care of me. I ain't had to go to Highland Hospital. He took me to Kaiser, and I got real good service. The other girls was soundin' like they was happy for me, but I know they was tryin' hard to take my spot as the number one. They was doin' everything they could to get in the master bedroom— you know, Jesus' room. But what they ain't realize was that they ain't no competition for me, 'cause I had his baby. And it was a boy.

I mean, things did change once I had Jason, but it ain't no

thing for me. I still make more money for Jesus than most of the other girls. And I'm always gonna be Jesus' number one in his heart even when I ain't the number one moneymaker. He always gonna be comin' over here and spendin' time with me and Jason. Sometimes I be gettin' lucky, and he'll leave a little money on the counter for me to spend on some extras—like some nice shoes or somethin'.

Well, I feel a little better now. I feel like I gotta throw up, but at least I ain't cryin' no more. And washin' some of them tears out of my eyes done helped. Don't think I ain't happy with the way things is . . . I just be trippin' sometimes. No big deal. A good face washin' always makes me feel better, but it sure don't do nothin' for the red in these eyes. They just stay red and keep on soakin' in everything—even things they don't want to see no more—like that eviction threat over there. I know you can see it over there on the hamper. Who could miss it?

The landlady stuck it under the door before I came in today. She been sayin' she gonna throw me and Jason out on the street if I don't pay her what I owe. I do be givin' her what I can, but when I ain't got no money, how I'm gonna pay the rent? I gotta pay for my own clothes, and for Jason's clothes, and all the rest of my money be goin' to pay for enough food to feed me, Jason, and Jesus sometimes. Sometimes Jesus take money back to go buy the things he need, and when he ask for it, it ain't like I can't give it to him when I got it. She know times been hard, but she ain't worried 'bout me. She got her own business to run, and I understand, even though it still don't do nothin' for me.

I understand what it's like to be in a business. I mean, even though lately I been feelin' more like a worker bee than the queen, I gotta keep my spirits up so I can make others' spirits stay up. Ain't nobody gonna pay for a sad, angry date. That's why I been thinkin' it might be time to make a change. I mean, it ain't like I *can't* pull them like I used to—I do keep my steadies and I got new ones comin' around every night, so I be doin' all right. It's just gettin' too hard to stay happy for them. The only reason why I still do it is 'cause of Jesus. I promised him a long time ago that I would be a part of his team till I wasn't bringin' in no more bread. But I been hoin' for over ten years now, and you know, I just think it might be time for a change. My body can only take so much.

I'm hopin' things gonna get better. I know Jesus will take care of everything. See his picture watchin' me? He be tellin' me that he gonna take care of everything and keep me from havin' to do this much longer. Jesus will make everything all right. He'll fix everything so that I ain't gotta see too many more mad letters from the landlady or too many more nights without my baby boy. Jesus always take care of Peaches. Just look over there in that corner and see for yourself. He'll tell you things gonna be all right. He gonna let me keep my promise—and he gonna help me make it come true.

Five years ago I promised myself that I was gonna quit trickin' in 1980, and now I only got one year left. I promised myself that I was gonna get another job before Jason got old enough to know what I really be doin' when I ain't with him. I can't tell my baby what's right and what's wrong when he forever seein' me doin' wrong. I'm thinkin' 'bout tryin' my hand at bein' a waitress or a baby-sitter or somethin'. I just know one thing—I ain't doin' this till I look run down like them old hags who be workin' the corners as renegade hos 'cause ain't no pimp desperate enough to handle they wrinkled behinds. Anyway, I already talked my plans over with Jesus and he said he understood. He said it was okay if I ain't want to turn tricks no more. He said I could just help recruit new girls into the family, but I'm thinkin' I don't even want to do none of that. Anyway, Jesus said he been savin' money for me and that there is a whole bunch that me and Jason could live off of if I need to do somethin' else for a while. I wish he could give me some of that money now, 'cause it sure would help with the rent.

"Mommy?"

It's Jason. He done come into the bathroom to be with me. Maybe it's 'cause he heard me in here cryin'. His little voice sounds so big when we standin' in here. It just echoes all over the place. What's that in his hand? He tryin' to hide somethin', but it's pokin' out through them tiny fingers.

"What you got in your hand, baby?"

He always shrug his shoulders like that when I ask him a question. Then, just like he doin' now, he show me what he got. Look, he got some change in his hand.

"What's this for, baby?"

"For you, Mommy. You can keep it."

"Oh . . . it's for me? Thank you."

He so sweet—to be so young, and so givin'. That ain't somethin' a lot of kids around here got at his age.

We walkin' out of the bathroom, 'cause it echoes too much in there. I swear sometimes that the people who live upstairs be puttin' they heads to the vent so they can listen to what I got goin' on down here. I can hear them talkin' sometimes, and they sure enough be repeatin' stuff I done just said. We should be all right to talk in my bedroom, though. It ain't like this apartment is so big, but our voices don't carry that much in here. Anyway, ain't no vents to listen through.

I'm puttin' him on my bed so he can lay down. Once he lay there for fifteen minutes or so, he'll just go to sleep and I can get ready to do what I gotta do.

"So now you ain't gotta go," he sayin' to me, still sittin' up and wigglin' his little toes back and forth. "Mommy, now you can stay home."

I wasn't expectin' that. How am I gonna tell him I *want* to stay home, but I *can't*? You can't tell no six-year-old nothin' without gettin' a whole bunch of questions back. And I just ain't got the heart to explain what really be goin' on when I leave him at night.

"Sweetheart, I gotta go to work. Momma gotta keep makin' money so we can eat and live here . . ."

"I already give you money."

"I know, baby, but Momma gotta get some more. I gotta have enough so Daddy be happy. You want Daddy happy, right?"

"I give you money like Jesus."

Jason took to callin' Jesus by his name after he got the worst whippin' of his tiny life for callin' him "Daddy." I ain't never understood why Jesus ain't want Jason to call him "Daddy." I guess he only want his girls to do that. Kinda funny how the only person who supposed to be callin' him "Daddy" is the only one not allowed to call him that. Jason ain't trippin' though. He learned real fast and, like I said, just took to callin' Jesus by his name. I make sure he know that's his daddy, though—even if he can't call him so.

"I give you money . . ." he startin' again.

He did give me money, and I wish it was enough to matter. I mean, I can't turn eighty-five cents back over to Jesus and expect to keep myself all right. Imagine me handin' eighty-five cents over to Jesus—he would slap me to pieces!

"I can't stay, baby. Not tonight. But I'll stay with you all day tomorrow, okay?"

"Nooo . . . stay now."

"I gotta work, baby. I gotta get some money for Daddy."

"He don't need no more money."

"Yes he do, baby."

I hate it when he looks like that. His eyes get big and that bottom lip hang down so far it almost be touchin' his chin. It's that look in his eyes that be makin' me nervous. It ain't like I think he gonna do somethin' stupid. He too little for all that drama. But I do think he gonna start hatin' Jesus over me. I think he gonna be all right tonight, but that's why I gotta get out of this life, 'cause I ain't ready to raise no child who hate his daddy. I ain't never had my parents. And he gonna have—and love—both of his.

Jason real smart, though. Every five minutes, he gotta know what's goin' on. I can't keep answerin' his questions the way I do. He gonna start catchin' on to things he really ain't got no business knowin' if he keep up this pace of learnin'. I know it's my business to make sure he don't catch no bad feelings toward Jesus, but it's gettin' harder and harder to tell the truth and make it seem like I'm a Cinderella with her Prince Charmin'.

"Baby, you love Momma, right?"

"Yes."

"You love Daddy?"

He still poutin' and lookin' at his toes wiggle around. I don't know why he ain't sayin' nothin'. I'm gonna say it again. Maybe he ain't understood me the first time.

"You love your daddy? Jason, you love your daddy, right?"

Okay. He noddin' now. Good.

"You think Daddy's nice? Daddy treats us real nice, you hear me? He loves us. He gonna always take care of us."

"Mommy . . ."

Jason done pulled his feet in closer, and now he pickin' at his toes with his fingers. He look like he ain't sure he want to say what's on his mind. It seems like he havin' trouble lookin' at me in my eyes.

"Yeah, baby."

"I don't like Jesus."

"What? Why, baby?"

"'Cause he missin' a arm . . . and he seem like a pee-pee head."

Oh, no. This is my fault. I must be doin' a bad job of makin' him understand what's goin' on here between me and Jesus.

Jason done crossed the line and said somethin' I ain't never wanted to hear. I can't never let Jesus hear him say nothin' like that. No, he can't talk bad 'bout his daddy.

"That's enough. Listen here, you don't cuss, you hear? You better learn to like your daddy, 'cause he all we got, you hear me? He all we got. Now, get up and go to the bathroom, clean yourself up, then you can come back in here and get in the bed."

I know sometimes he see Jesus hit me or talk real bad to me, but what Jason don't get is that them times be my fault. I drive him to do that stuff. He can't help that he only wants the best from me. I gotta learn. I gotta learn to always give my best so I'm always showin' things like they supposed to be, especially when it comes to the business and the family. When I act crazy, like when I try to talk back or when I be late for somethin', he ain't got no choice but to break me. I know all this must be causin' Jason to think bad 'bout Jesus, and I gotta fix this fast before he say somethin' to Jesus and all hell breaks loose up in this place.

I don't know what to say right now, though, so I ain't gonna say nothin'. I'm just gonna wait for him to come back in here and make sure he goes to sleep before I leave. I hate leavin' when he still awake.

"Don't forget to brush your teeth and flush the toilet!"

He ain't answerin', but I know he heard me. I hear the water runnin' in the bathroom now. Good, he in there gettin' ready for bed like I told him to. Sometimes he just let it run while he playin' in the corner with some dust—or somethin' else he really ain't got no business touchin'. Sometimes it be real nasty, too. But I don't think he doin' that now.

I know, I'm tryin' to change the subject, but only 'cause I can't believe he really thinks that way 'bout his daddy. I do everything I can to make him understand what me and his daddy all 'bout. Dang, I ain't even all that sure what I'm fightin' so hard for anymore—but don't tell Jesus. He don't need to know, and I really don't want him to know. Thinkin' 'bout all this is startin' to make me sick.

All I can do, for real, is just get ready for another night. I can't stay here with Jason like I want to, so it don't even make no sense in bringin' it up again. It really don't matter how I feel no how, 'cause I still gotta work. And if I gotta work for money this way, at least it's all for my baby and my man. They all that matter, anyway. Even when I'm turnin' a trick, I'm thinkin' 'bout them. I have to keep thinkin' 'bout them or I might start trippin' and lose everything I done worked so hard for—even Jesus. Look, I know how I am, and what works for me. It almost happened before, and I don't want it to happen again.

It almost happened the first time I ever brought up leavin' the life. I came home one day and just told him that I was thinkin' 'bout quittin'. First he got mad and slapped me. Then he put it to me like this.

He said, "You the only one that's finna lose out if you give all this up, Peaches. You only gots one thing goin' for you now . . . and that's me." I hated to hear it, but he was right. He always be right.

But then he thought 'bout it some and came back to me sayin' that if I wanted to leave, I could—and I could use the money he been holdin' for me. I ain't sure why he changed his mind or how much money he plannin' on givin' me, but I work hard now to keep his pockets full of cash so that when I do go, he'll remember all the tricks I turned in his name—and the promise I get to keep.

I know you don't understand. Don't nobody really understand. Sometimes I can't even understand it. Like tonight, I feel like I gotta throw up, but I'm gonna stick with it anyway. Almost every night I go out now, it seems like I be throwin' up. It's just that I start thinkin' of things, and my body just do it on its own—like my stomach just be decidin' that it gotta get clean before goin' out. Deep down inside maybe it's 'cause of the nasty smells and the dirty cars that I be in. Maybe it's the smell of piss and old, funky corn chips that be all over some of the tricks that be makin' my stomach turn—

or the thought of what my lips do when they ain't kissin' on my son . . . oh, excuse me. I gotta throw up.

I gotta run into the bathroom and move Jason on out the way. I hate it when he see me have to throw up like this, but there ain't no way to hide it from him. It's just another one of them things I wish his eyes ain't had to see.

"Move, baby," I say. That's all I can say before it comes out. Oh, Lord, here it comes.

I know Jason lookin' at me, but I'm just gonna ignore him. I'm just gonna flush the toilet and let him keep gettin' ready for bed. Now I gotta wash my face again and brush my teeth. I'm just gonna hurry up and finish, so I can get to the other room. I . . . I gotta get it together.

My stomach is still turnin' even though I done emptied everything there was up in there. I'm startin' to get a headache, too. Dang, I gotta get it together! My head be feelin' better when I put it between these two pillows. They do somethin' for my head that can't nothin' else do. Jesus gave them to me, and this one right here even smell like the cologne he be wearin'.

I can't wait till next year when I can leave the street. I mean, I still be tryin' to believe that what I do is real special—and Jesus still tellin' me I got a gift from God—but I can't help but think that maybe God done gave me some other gifts, too. I gotta be able to do somethin' else other than turn tricks. I got a girlfriend who been tryin' to turn me into a political kind like her, but I know that ain't never gonna happen. She always show up with that high yellow skin and nappy hair tryin' to tell me to run away with her. She can do all them crazy things, 'cause she light-skinded, so people forgive her. Not me. It's too late for me.

Maybe if I put my head to it, I can land a steady gig that will finally let me tell my son what I do for a livin'. I saw a sign up at the bus stop the other day that said there was a whole bunch of jobs open at the University Hospital in Frisco. It said they was hirin' in the laundry department. Maybe I could do that. I could at least give it a try.

Anyway, enough dreamin' 'bout what could be. I gotta live for today—right now. I gotta rest my head right here in these pillows for a few minutes, 'cause there's only a half-hour left before I gotta meet Jesus at our regular spot. Don't worry, I'll be on time—or close to it. But right now I just gotta rest for a minute.

What is that breeze on my leg? Oh, Lord. It's my baby's breath. I guess he finally done cleanin' hisself up for bed. He right up under me, too, ready for me to tuck him in. Oh, he got that face of an angel. Look at him. You see what I'm talkin' 'bout?

"Mommy, why you cryin'?"

"Momma's not cryin'."

"Why you throw up again?"

"My head just hurts, baby. I'm gonna be okay, though."

"I'll make you feel better, Mommy. When I get bigger, I'm gonna buy you the biggest castle in the whole wide world, and it's gonna take up the whole block, and you gonna be the king, Mommy."

So sweet . . .

"Sugar, only men can be kings. Daddy's a king. Momma can be . . . can be the queen."

"Then you be the queen."

"Hmmm . . . Baby, you're just too beautiful for words."

"And I'ma be the prince!"

He's already a prince. Only my precious little man would want to rescue me when I'm havin' a bad night. I'm pullin' him up here in the bed with me so he can go to sleep. All it takes to put him to sleep is just to keep rubbin' his cheeks like this—real soft-like. And I sing to him, too, almost like I'm whisperin'. I always sing the same words 'cause I want him to know how much he means to me, and that I mean every word I say to him.

"You're much too beautiful for words," I sing. "You're much too beautiful for words. You're much too beautiful for words. You're much too beautiful for words . . ."

Jesus

Baby Jesus:

I just gots your letter. The guards like to take their time to get us our mail, but I finally gots it. I heard what you was asking, but I can't do nothing to get you out from behind bars. But I can help keep you from being poor and always needin' somebody else to do something for your ass. Nigga, I can teach you the best way to have your own shit. You won't never be broke again if you play it right.

Just handle the time you gots to spend in that detention, then come out a stronger man. Part of being a man is knowing that you can handle whatever life deals you. If you been sentenced to some jail time, do it. Then come out better than you was before you went in.

And about Peaches. I don't want to talk about her. It's grown folks' business what happened between me and your momma. I ain't gonna lie to you. I didn't mean for everything to go down the way it did, but I had to teach her a lesson. Being a pimp is serious business, and I keep my hos in line. It ain't nothin' personal to you and it wasn't nothin' personal to her. You'll understand someday. You a young Mack, so I know one day you'll understand. How old are you now? You about ready to start learnin about life and how to live in it as a man. I'm gonna teach you how to be a man. You gonna be just like me.

It don't matter how old you get, just remember that shit with your momma was a accident. What I write here, I mean. We blood. I ain't gonna lie to you. You about to need me like everybody else.

    —J

Jason

Dear Jesus:

I just turned eleven years old and I just moved into a new group home. It's okay. The people seem nice, but I don't know how long that's gonna last. There is this one boy who got a flat head on one side because he said his foster family didn't turn him over when he was a baby. So now he got a big bruise and a flat head. The other kids seem cool, but I think I'm the coolest one here. I'm the only one who been to juvi hall, and I'm the only one who got family that's runnin' the street. I don't got no bruises and shit, neither. I guess y'all turned me over cool when I was a little baby.

Anyway, I got everybody in here doin' what I tell them to do 'cause they don't want me to tell you they did me dirty. Everybody in here done heard about you, Jesus. Even Mr. Maurice from the block where we used to be at be givin' me free stuff at the liquor store. I be gettin' Now and Laters and Twinkies from him for nothin'! He say he wanted me to tell you how he was takin' care of me while you was away.

One of your girls came up to me today and said I look like you. Then she asked me if I wanted to go hump her. I said no, 'cause I wanted some money. She laughed at me. Why was she laughin' at me? She said that someday people would listen to me when I grow up. She said maybe even the mayor would listen to me, but I don't know why she said that. Don't no mayor want to listen to a poor nigga like me who live in the 'hood. I don't have nothin' to say to them anyway, except to ask them how come they don't never clean the beer bottles up off the street so I can stop scuffin' my shoes on the glass.

I want to make money so I can get me a car. I saw these other pimps who had nice cars and nice clothes. My group home leader cool, but he don't be buyin' me clothes. I want to make my own money so can't nobody tell me what to do. I want to be like you and have my own stuff. Jesus, can you teach me to be a pimp?

Jason

Chinaka

It's amazing how selective amnesia can wash over the pride that it took years of Revolution to build and replace it with a gut-wrenching apathy so severe that it gouges the soul of those who labored in its name. Even more piercing than having to watch brothers and sisters just stop fighting is having the power to do nothing—in the larger scheme of things—while they destroy themselves with the tools handed to them in malice.

Of course, now I've found a way to deal with it, but I still suffer from the labor of love. I am ill with an unquenchable thirst to prevent the failure of my people by demanding more respect, more access, and more opportunity. I've been expecting more from this country for years now, ever since an elder offered the prophecy that I would die for the liberation of my people. And I probably will, considering the fact that I will continue to fight until this whole system is blown up, and we are saved from the economic chains of the oppressor and the anger that lingers within ourselves. I have to expect more—*for* people, *from* people—if dying for the Revolution will ultimately be worth it.

But it wasn't always that way.

This story begins for me in 1968—when I left San Jose State with ten dollars in my pocket, three boxes of books, and a huge chip on my shoulder. The Olympic events in Mexico City had just returned Tommy Smith, John Carlos, and Lee Evans to our college campus with nothing but this fascist, racist government riding their backs. By raising their fists in a moment of triumph, those brothers put a spotlight on the racism and oppression their people suffered every day. These brothers had to endure the most insulting of occurrences—being called "boys" before the world as their grown bodies were treated as spectacles to be marveled at, while being denied the titles they won as the fastest human beings in the world. But we cheered them on anyway and eagerly awaited their return home.

Yes, they were our Black ambassadors, and we couldn't wait for them to come back so that we could tell them just how proud the rest of us Afro-wearing, gun-toting, black-fist-in-the-air-waving revolutionaries were to see them make our statement in that arena. They had a platform, and they used it. Bobby used to say, "Seize the time!"—and that's exactly what they did. Those brothers paid dearly for it, but they were also loved for it. Contrary to popular belief, the Revolution—for one suspended moment in time—was displayed in the mass media for all to see. And my eyes made love to it.

Those days were something else! I hadn't always been so

revolutionary in my thinking, but it started when I was twenty-one years old, ten years before I found the woman who would ultimately help me realize my purpose in life. They were at the end of what seemed to be an eternal extension of brick and urine, and at the beginning of the end of my cocoon.

My education and awareness were gradual—like any period of significant growth, but they came nonetheless. As a student, I spent every free moment I had in the college library, sifting through old newspapers and magazines, looking for any and every fabrication I could find on Black Nationalism. Most of it was appalling and, I might say, a gross simplification of how we lived our lives. But at least it was available.

I was always a scholar. I thrived on information. I could read any piece of literature and spot a lie in a heartbeat. But it wasn't until I'd gone to college that I was ever really capable of *finding* the information to counter the lies I'd been spoon-fed since birth. I read everything, focusing on all of the major African, Latin, Asian, and European scholars who questioned authority. I read all who questioned the way things were and offered concrete suggestions on how things could change. I cracked open the *Communist Manifesto* by Marx and Engels and realized I had found the philosophy that would liberate Black people in America and all over the world. I devoured readings on the Cuban revolution, and celebrated brothers Che and Fidel. I discovered the brilliance of the red book—I thought Chairman Mao was a genius—and knew there was only one way for me to live my life.

I was a Communist. I was for the liberation of the oppressed people on this Earth. And when I read the Black Panther Party's ten-point program and platform, I found my calling.

"We want freedom to determine the destiny of our Black Community"—yes!

"We want education for our people that exposes the true nature of this decadent American society. We want education that teaches us our true history and our role in the present-day society"—exceptional!

"We want an immediate end to POLICE BRUTALITY and MURDER of Black people—we practice self-defense and the right to bear arms"—right on!

"We want land, bread, housing, education, clothing, justice and peace"—this was it!

When I was not in the library, I spent time—time I probably should have spent studying—with the Professor. He taught me all I could process about how to classify the racism I had experienced my whole life, and the language that I could use to educate others about that system of oppression I had come to understand as "capitalism." I probably spent too much time with the Professor, but he was instrumental in educating brothers and sisters on the campus on the core elements of Black Power and the Revolution. Again, considering the fact that I was the only sister recruited to San Jose through an academic scholarship, I probably should have done more course-related studying than I actually did.

But the taste for Revolution overpowered the desire to graduate with a degree in brainwashing. I had enough of that. It was time to learn—and to share—a new philoso-

too beautiful for words

phy. Nothing was, or is, more important. So, after that summer of '68, I left school and went home. I packed my bags, came back to Oakland, and looked up the Black Panther Party.

The stories had trickled down to San Jose about all the heat they had been getting from the pigs up here who were more concerned with preserving the oppressive power structure than with protecting the innocent, so I knew what to expect. The world was afraid of us. Brothers and sisters struggled to educate *as well as* protect our own, but our guns always got more attention on TV than the educational programs. Even so, education was always my informal contribution. I hooked up with Eldridge and we took to the streets, passing out flyers and trying our best to erase the ignorance that was sedating the activism of our people.

It wasn't until the early seventies, when a sister was running the Party, that I finally became a legitimate member. I was never into the official titles—and I really was not into compromising my person in order to succumb to the sexual advances of Party leadership—but I was always about the message.

When that sister finally took over the leadership of the Party, I became charged, and finally accepted official membership into the organization. It was the best decision of my life.

Throughout the years, I was always frustrated by the fact that most folks didn't understand us—thanks mostly to the propagandizing of Governor Reagan. We were more than just a bunch of "thugs with guns." We were revolutionaries. We were educated, and many of us went on to contribute to the developing "Black Intelligentsia." Others went on to be community leaders and organizers. We were the vanguard and the new direction of Black Power. And yes, we stood strong by the belief that capitalism was the oppressor—then and now. It's the *real* poison.

And so—ten years after my return to Oakland, after most folks had grown tired of fighting the government's conspiracy to destroy us—I got a call from Mustafa, one of our front linemen. He said that the neighborhood pigs had discovered where we were hiding one of the Party founders upon his return from being exiled in Cuba.

I knew what we had to do.

Never one to shy away from excitement, I accepted the challenge. I was to be the decoy for the operation, even though I was risking death or going to jail for a long time. These pigs were already after me for a murder conspiracy, inciting a riot, and vandalism. But I would do them all again if I had to, because all of these were crimes of war. Never mind what this country was doing to my people every day or what it had done to generations of African, Asian, and Native people on this land. These pigs felt the need to make *me* one of the Bay Area's Most Wanted.

Technically, I should have been granted immunity given the conditions I was being forced to live in—but that would never happen for a sister in this country. I could have fled like many brothers and sisters did, but I preferred to just live as I live. When it's time for me to die, I'll die. Until then, I wasn't—and I'm still not—going anywhere. Born and raised in Oakland, I was not going to let them run me away from my people.

After I accumulated approximately ten arrests and warrants, you could see how being the distraction for the police was a heavy risk. But I was down for it anyway. And the plan was simple enough. I was to throw a Molotov cocktail at the squad car, run until my legs couldn't carry me anymore, and pray I didn't happen upon one of those trigger-happy badge toters. So there I was, in the shadow of Black Power fists and the brothers and sisters who died so that I may live, about to lay it all on the line once again for what I believed was right.

But Black Power fists in the air are hardly the aphrodisiac for those who preferred pimping and prostitution to Revolution. So you can imagine my surprise when it was a hooker who saved my ass on a cold night in 1978, when I was running from the police. If they'd caught me, I'm sure I would have been killed for throwing the Molotov cocktail at them and resisting arrest—because I certainly did not stop when they yelled "freeze."

When I met her, I was breathing as softly as possible in order to avoid the pigs who were chasing me, knowing that if they did catch me, I'd probably be found dead somewhere on the streets. I knew that the morgue would probably see me before any paperwork had been processed or telephone calls granted. Pigs like the ones chasing me that night never filed any official reports—they lived for the moments where they were free to make every revolutionary act punishable by death. On several occasions throughout the years, comrades surrendered to the pigs, thinking that they would not end up with a bullet in their backs. But they were wrong. Little Bobby Sutton was shot while trying to surrender. Back on the East Coast, sister Assata was shot up, then chained to a hospital bed while delivering her child, and none of these acts was ever declared in the official reports. At least, they were not visible on any of the reports that I have seen. But I was still alive, so I was already beating the odds.

Only weeks before, I'd read an article in the newspaper that the FBI had officially declared that the Party was dead. I remember reading the words of J. Edgar Hoover's protégés, who proudly boasted that their administration's efforts had effectively neutralized one of America's worst enemies. They did not know about those of us who never "treated" our brains with dope and, instead, opted to fine-tune every tool of war we ever learned.

After I'd thrown the Molotov cocktail, the police began to chase me. They were on my trail, and almost caught me, until I ran into an abandoned building in an effort to lose them among several flights of stairs and a small colony of transient heroin addicts. Mustafa told me about the apartment and had drawn out a floor plan that mapped the escape route. I was not sure whether I would make it through the route, but everything was just as he'd described. On the fourth floor of the apartment complex, there was a room at the end of the corridor that held a few stacked mattresses soiled with sweat and urine, a few cases of empty beer bottles, and a tiny compartment that led straight down to the street. It was a trap door and resembled something that could be seen in a comic book caper, but it was real enough to get me away from the pigs who chased me. After a free fall that nearly scared me to death, I landed on the ground and hit my tailbone. I knew I had a bad bruise, and the fall hurt like hell, but I had to keep quiet or they would have caught me for sure.

In front of me was a long, narrow passage that led directly

into an alleyway. As I crawled through the passage, following the cracks in the ground to make sure I did not plant my hand smack into something that would completely disgust me, I heard voices coming from the open end. When I reached the part of the path that allowed me to see out, I spotted a small-framed sister bending over to adjust the straps of her stiletto heals. She glanced at me and flashed a smile. I motioned for her to stay quiet just as a male voice called out to her by name, indirectly ordering her to stand from the crouched position that greeted me.

The voice was that of a pig I assumed must have been called as backup to other ones that I hoped were still in the building preoccupied by the sight of rampant drug usage. I stayed quiet, listening intently to each word that echoed through the alley and seeped into my temporary shelter. I figured the last thing she would do is rat me out to those pigs, but I did not expect for her to be so calm around them. I lay motionless next to the cold ground inside of what seemed to be a shrinking hole, holding my breath and praying that those pigs did not see the passageway or me lying inside of it. Even though I was willing to die for what I believed in, I was not ready to die that night.

I was surprised when I heard her speak, because her voice was deep. I guess because of her relatively small frame, I figured she would have a small voice, too. But hers was husky, almost hoarse. I was sure she had gotten a lot of play from that voice. Brothers in the Party used to gravitate toward sisters with deep voices, saying a deep voice was more like the voice of a revolutionary. This one was the voice of a prostitute.

I also remember being amazed by her poise. Her voice was still laced with a lack of confidence that I had come to recognize in brothers and sisters who came face to face with pigs, but she still had the kind of poise I would have expected from a seasoned revolutionary. This sister was a prostitute—a ho—but there she was, communicating with those pigs like a veteran diplomat. It did not surprise me that she knew them. Everybody knew that the reigning pimps in the area were paying off most of the pigs in the precinct. But what did surprise me was how friendly their relationship actually was. The pigs chasing me that night *must* have been on that sister's pimp's payroll.

They talked to her for about five minutes, asking her about some brother named "Jesus" and some other sisters with less recognizable names. I figured out that whoever that brother was, he was the reason it was so easy for her to slip away from these pigs without getting busted. After I heard no more voices, I was ready to get out of that hole in the wall and stand in thanks and camaraderie. I pulled myself forward and reached my hand out to the edge of the opening, only to be stopped by a stiletto point supporting five-inch heels that almost stabbed right through my hand. She was actually pretty smooth and gentle with it, sliding it closer and closer to the inside of hole, pushing my hand back out of sight. It was a strange, cold, tickling feeling between my fingers that I sometimes get today when I scratch away an itch on that part of my hand.

I stopped trying to move when I heard more voices. She had moved my hand back because it wasn't safe yet. Those damn pigs were still on the corner. In my eagerness to leave,

89

too beautiful for words

I almost missed her signal—but I caught it in time to stay put and soak in the sight of her thin, strong ankles.

"Okay, Peaches, I'm only going to ask you this question one more time. I'm going to make it simple for you so you understand everything coming out of my mouth. If we find out that you're lying to us, and that you've seen that nigger bitch, we'll bust your ass so fast you'll be turning tricks for a pimp named Bertha in Cell Block 205. Got it?"

They were using their usual intimidation tactics. At least she didn't get roughed up in the process.

"And—also, you should know," one of them said—it was a different voice from the first one—"if you're hiding her any-where around here, that's aiding and abetting. You can go to jail for that, too."

"I done already told you. I ain't seen nobody. I'm just waitin' for somebody to pick me up, and that's it. Anyway, ain't nobody been around this way for at least a half-hour," she said.

When the pigs finally left and she moved so that I could pull myself out of the wall, I was shocked by her scantly clad body. A long, straight wig with bangs covered her own hair and set off the oval shape of her face. Her eyes were large, anxious, dark brown eyes that almost matched the hue of her skin. She had a full nose and thick, round lips that were covered in lipstick two shades too light for her complexion. There was never a question about her natural beauty, but it was almost hard to find it through all of the makeup she caked on. Her body was barely covered by a pink bra and hot pants that crawled up her private areas. She wore a fake fur bolero that stopped at her breasts, leaving the rest of her exposed to the cold night air.

She was not shy about showing her body. She was obviously proud, and even stood in a way that accented her perky breasts and shapely legs. She smiled a wide, genuine smile that exposed a set of teeth that probably could have benefited from regular visits to a dentist. But for some reason—maybe it was the novelty of it all—I couldn't get enough of her. It was not sexual, but it was very curious. She must have known this, too, because she just stood there watching me take it all in. Then she started laughing.

Her laugh was the most amazing sound I'd ever heard. It started out soft, then grew louder the more amused she became. It was a gut-wrenching, almost wickedly infectious laugh. At its peak, the laugh was piercing and reverberated throughout the alley. I remember thinking that her loud noises would prompt the pigs who were just there to turn the squad car around and come rushing back to check out the scene. But they never did.

"What you doin' down there?" she asked.

"Running from the pigs."

"Pigs?"

"Yeah . . . the police."

"Oh, baby, that's just Cuffs and Junior. Anyway, that's what we call them around here. They ain't no real harm."

"Hmmm." Maybe not to that sister, but definitely to me.

"So . . . why they chasin' you?"

"I'm Black. They are after all Black people."

She wasn't buying it, but I was telling the truth.

"You gotta had did somethin' other than just be Black, baby."

"Well . . . Have you ever heard of the Black Panther Party?"

"Um . . . yeah. They the ones that used to be always passin' out them flyers."

"Right. Well, I'm a member of the Party, and we had some real important business tonight. You could say I was the decoy for the business."

"Decoy? What's that?"

"It's . . . well . . . let's just say I was the distraction."

"Oh, yeah, I be the distraction all the time. So, that's what y'all do in that Black Panther group? Spend all your nights rollin' all on the ground hidin' from the police?" She was chuckling again at my expense.

"No. Of course we don't spend *every* night out here like this. I'm actually a teacher's assistant over at McClymonds High, but I'd crawl on the ground every night if it would bring on the Revolution."

"You say you teach at McClymonds? I went there!" She completely ignored my comment about Revolution—how typical.

"Yeah?"

"Yeah! I ain't know they had colored teachers over there."

My heart skipped. Colored? I couldn't believe my ears. She actually referred to Black people as "colored"—and she was serious! I thought I was talking to my grandmother. Until running into this sister, I thought the term "colored" had died with the sentiment of Negroes. But I was wrong.

Before that night, I had been completely submerged in a world of conscious, intelligent brothers and sisters who had dedicated their lives to the reeducation of Black people. I had become so consumed by the thought of addressing the underdevelopment of our communities that I had forgotten what it was like to spend time with folks who thrived there. The consciousness was something I took for granted considering the academic environment that I had buried myself in, but this sister was a reality check.

I had spent years doing all I thought I could to spread the word about the new consciousness that we were building in Oakland. After talking to this sister, it was clear that we missed a spot.

"What's your name?" I asked.

"You can call me Peaches."

"Well, thanks for your help, Peaches."

"What's your name?" she asked.

"Chinaka."

Her face frowned and washed over with confusion. Clearly she was not familiar with African names. My birth name was Jessica, but with my revolutionary lifestyle came a new name. I told her my revolutionary name, Chinaka, instead of the one that I was born with, because I only used "Jessica" when I was over at the school. "Jessica" had become the alias that allowed me to operate in a semifunctional way in White society. In any event, I could immediately tell that it was Chinaka whom she was destined to meet, not Jessica.

"Chink . . . what?"

"Chinaka. It means 'God decides.'"

That seemed to get her attention. After I slowed down the pronunciation so that she could catch on, she was eager to talk about my name and make some relation to a pimp—the brother she and those pigs called "Jesus."

"Wait. That's his real name or some name he made up for the streets?"

"That's his *real* name, honey. You should meet him, too. He's incredible . . ."

Um . . . how about *hell no?!*

"I don't think that's ever going to happen, Peaches. Look, I really appreciate what you just did for me, but there is no way I'm turning to a pimp for *anything*. This whole lifestyle is just a smaller version of the oppression I fight every day. Why would I run right into the arms of the Beast?"

I had lost her, but it did not matter. She'd saved me that night from the pigs, so I was indebted to her. Despite her ignorance, Peaches helped the Revolution, but for the life of her, she could not understand why I would crawl on my knees for something that seemed so unattainable. She even laughed at me—the nerve!

I always found it amazing that she just could not grasp the ideology behind my struggle, all while working the corner every night for some illusory "business" that was supposed to liberate her from an obvious emotional and financial strain. I kept asking her if life was so good, then why was she as broke as me? "Jesus" was her answer for everything, but none of it made sense. The conversation and questions began that first night, but there were many nights after that one when we would just meet and talk.

At first I showed up around there because I knew that she would hide me from the police during one of their decisions to pursue so-called vigilantes, then I started to come back because I recognized in her a kindred spirit. I trusted her. I noticed that while she could not articulate it, she loved Black people as much as I did. Why else would she have helped me, a perfect stranger? Through all of her rambling outbursts about how nothing mattered but Jesus, she had to care. I knew she did.

There were nights I could see her face light up when she saw me coming. Of course, she always talked of the trouble she could get in for hiding me, but I could see it in her face that she relished the thought of being a part of something progressive, something militant—even if she knew nothing about it. It did not take me long to realize that in a different world and, maybe, if our paths had crossed sooner, Peaches might have been a revolutionary. One night I even told her that.

"Girl, I ain't never been that kind . . . I ain't all political like you," she said.

"That's why you get used every day."

"I don't be gettin' used. If anybody gettin' used, it's them. I use them just to get what I need done for me and my baby."

She was in denial, of course, but so was I. On many nights, to keep her from getting beat by that pimp of hers, I actually paid her my last money for the time that I spent trying to convince her she could leave the life. I would drive up like a john in my Granada and we would go for a long ride so that I could talk to her about the ills of capitalism and the many ways pimping is destroying our people.

Of course, people thought she was tricking with me during the time we were together—and that was the idea. We always kept our meetings private so that she would never be put out by that pimp who walked away with all of her money every night. She would just jump in the car like she did with everyone else, and we would go to some private street and rap about making change.

I tried to convince her that this pimp she claimed to love so much was actually part of the exploitation that made her situation inevitable. I tried to share with her the alternatives. She didn't catch everything I said—in many ways most of what was coming out of my mouth was over her head. But there was something in her that made her want to hear everything about my experiences anyway. She always wanted to know about the Revolution, but she was never really interested in how she could be a part of it.

In a way, I looked forward to talking to this sister. Talking to her was like teaching in that high school. She didn't have much education, but she was full of questions, and the teacher in me just could not let that quality die. The way I saw it, Peaches was dying for a doctrine that would save her life. She seemed comfortable with the idea that she had found it in that Jesus she believed in, but I always felt there was a reason I ran into her that night in the alley.

The elder who changed my name suggested that I needed divine protection given how prone I was to volunteering for near-fatal missions. He was also the one who, out of nowhere, offered a prophecy that I would die for the Revolution. But in the same breath, he called me "God decides" to protect me and to give me some perspective. After a meeting one day, he escorted me to a side room where he initiated a short ceremony that officially changed my name from "Jessica" to "Chinaka." My new name felt as natural as joining the struggle for freedom.

To tell the truth, I've often thought that God was navigating every move that I made and every turn that I took so that I could get closer to the person who needed me most.

I never knew who that person would be, but I always believed—and still do—that God does. It was always for my people, for the Revolution, and for an end to this capitalist exploitation that made the lives of precious sisters like Peaches seem minuscule in the greater context of things.

We would see each other at least one night a week. In the time that we spent together, it became apparent that she needed me. She needed me for her sanity as well as for her physical health. But I needed her, too. I realized that I needed her so that I could learn how someone so "dirty" on the outside could be so pure on the inside. I had never come across anyone who loved like her, and I was obsessed with understanding how she could love so hard and not be loved back. I needed to know how she did it. It was an amazing conquest, and over time, she taught me well.

No one ever knew Peaches as more than a hooker. They especially did not ever envision her to be a private aider and abettor to a diehard revolutionary like me. But together we were willing to sacrifice everything for those few moments to rap about change and what constituted loyalty and love. She once told me that she spent so much time with me because of her desperate passion to live another life, even if only vicariously. And I did it for love—my love for her and my love for my people.

Being with her made it easier for me to confirm that I would throw away every earthly possession I had if it would bring on the Revolution. Our people were in desperate need of something else, something more. And I think Peaches would have given it all up, too—in a different place and a different time.

"You can either be a part of it or fight it," I would say.

"I'll just be a part of it—and be the best at it," she would respond.

Man, she was brainwashed by Jesus. That brother—if I could have called him that—must have been thorough.

Jesus

Baby Jesus:

Why you asking me if I could teach you to be a pimp? Why you think I call you "Baby Jesus"? You was born to pimp!

One thing I know is that I better not ever hear about you tryin' to force a bitch to be your ho. Bitches choose to ho, it ain't a pimp's job to turn them out. Ain't no bitch going to ho without some reason of her own. It's your job to fine-tune that reason, and make it work for you. Pimpin' is easy, baby, if you gots what it takes, and if you think you can handle bread, respect, and power.

You gonna have to get over your momma, though. I can't waste my time on you if you a momma's boy.

Momma's boys don't make good pimps. So make sure you in the right mind before you come to me. Learn the streets and get a name going for yourself. This is serious business, man. You gots to be ready.

   ¬J

Peaches

Things done changed since the last time y'all heard from me.

Sometimes settin' out a plan for your life ain't nothin' but a huge waste of time. I mean, things ain't always gonna be the way you want them to be. I know I said I was leavin' the life two years ago, but the game out there just be too thick. I can't do nothin' but this, especially with me bein' almost thirty years old now. Hoin' is what I do best. And I sure can't go back to that high school. I couldn't stand them classes when I was in them before. Everyone was callin' me stupid and sayin' that I couldn't hardly mix words or make figures add up. If I wasn't makin' the grades back then, I sure can't go back now. I'm too old, and it's too late.

I left Jesus for 'bout two months in 1980 like I said I was gonna do to get me a job in Frisco. I know it don't seem like a long time, but bein' out there alone with Jason felt like a whole lifetime to me. But I ain't gotta tell you how hard it be for a colored girl to get paid around these parts, especially since I ain't never had no real job before. I couldn't find no job anywhere I looked without havin' some references, and I couldn't get around to keep lookin'—not on that little money I had in my pocket.

Chinaka offered to help me out, but I couldn't take her up on it. If I was gonna leave and do it on my own, I had to leave everybody. Anyway, I can't do what she do. I can only do what I do. So when it didn't work out, I had to come back to Jesus, beggin' for him to help me get it together. I had to come back to Jesus. I needed him to save me, 'cause I just couldn't live like that. I told him I would do anything for him if he let me and Jason back in, you hear me? Anything. He been puttin' me to the test, too. He said he wasn't gonna give me no money like he was before 'cause I had to prove I wasn't ever gonna leave him again.

Remember how he said, at first, that it was gonna be okay? Well, right before I left, we was havin' some hard times, and when I went to get a job in Frisco, all my dates took to some of the girls workin' for other pimps. Well, I ain't gotta tell you that Jesus got mad at me! I understand, though, 'cause I did leave when he really needed me. But I just couldn't take it no more. Anyway, I only got 'bout six months left out here on the dope fiend stroll before Jesus say he gonna move me back to the better one that I was workin' before I left. Things ain't been the same since I left and came back. I mean, you know how I used to throw up before I went out on the stroll? Well, it's even worser now. It be all I can do some nights to keep from throwin' up while I'm out here on the streets. I hate sex, but I do it 'cause I gotta pass Jesus' test. I gotta make up for leavin'. I gotta show him I'm thankful that he let me back in.

The way I been workin' these past years, he gotta know I'm sorry. I mean, I be out here workin' till 'bout five or six o'clock in the mornin' sometimes. But it don't matter. I would work for him twenty-four hours a day if I could. I mean, if my body could take it. I need him in my corner out here in this world. He all I ever had goin' for me. He the only way I can stay right, the only way I can stay in this formula. He the only way my baby gonna survive right now. Leavin' for them two months showed me that I really do need Jesus in my life.

He left me a little money yesterday. It was okay, but the landlady been on me, 'cause I'm behind on the rent again. She still don't cut me no slack, but I'm tryin' not to make it no big thing. I still look pretty good, but I need to get things back to the way they was so I can pay the rent. I know he still like me better than everybody else, 'cause I'm still the only one with his baby. Jesus know I believe in what we doin', though. He know I ain't never gonna go against him for real. I mean, three weeks ago, just to prove I could still out-turn some of them younger, new girls, I brung home one thousand dollars to Jesus all by myself! I still got my talent, and I ain't gonna try foolin' myself into thinkin' there's more to me. There ain't nothin' more.

That's what I be tryin' to explain to Chinaka. That's my girl and all, but she don't get it. She got other things goin' on for her. She real pretty and bein' light-skinded done gave her a good life around here—nothin' like mine. She come from a good home, so she learned a long time ago how to do right by herself. She 'bout four or five years older than me and got her life crawlin' through alleys and teachin' over there at the high school. I ain't got no brain like she got, so I can't do what she do. I just be listenin' to her. I ain't never gonna do none of that stuff, but I *love* to hear 'bout it. It keeps me thinkin' 'bout how things might be better for Jason in the long run. Yeah, I be thinkin' that maybe if Chinaka get her Revolution, my baby won't have to hustle like me and his daddy. Maybe.

Tonight I did good, though—made close to nine hundred dollars. So I just went on ahead and dropped the rent off in the landlady's mailbox before headin' back to my buildin'. No, it ain't a far walk. See that white house across the street with the Volkswagen parked in front? Yeah, she live right there.

I gotta be careful when I go over there, though. Especially when I be wearin' these kinda clothes. I ain't real comfortable bein' around her house no way, but especially when I'm dressed in full gear. She already been sayin' she know what I do, and that she gonna throw me out on the street 'cause she don't want no hos in her buildin'. That's why I just gave her the rent money. Now she can't throw me and Jason out on the streets. I was lucky when Grandma and Grandpa put me out, 'cause I had Jesus. He took me in when they threw me out. But I don't ever want to put my baby through all that. See, the streets is fine for me, but it ain't no place for a nine-year-old, you know? Not these streets. Not these corners out here. I'll be dead before that happen.

So I just be creepin' on through them streets before anybody see me or she catch me out here lookin' like this. She'd probably throw me out right away if she seen me like this. I ain't wearin' nothin' real glamorous, but it sure is good for what it do. This outfit here—with these bikini panties and this fur—just keep the tricks linin' up for me. The little fur jacket is fake, but it sure do look good against my skin, baby. I had it on that night I met Chinaka, and even she couldn't take her eyes off me with this on. And my Tina Turner heels always cap it off just right! No . . . they ain't really her heels. It's just a sayin'. It mean my shoes is real high and real sexy. Some tricks want me to pretend I'm the real one—dancin' and singin' on stage with my long wig flyin' all over the place while they be pretendin' to be Ike standin' in the back. They be crackin' me up when they want crazy stuff like that—but them be the ones that pay big, so I do what they say. They like it when I put on a show.

But now all them shows is over. I done raised my money for the night, and I got three hundred dollars left in my pocket to give to Jesus. I really done worked as much as I can for now. Ain't nobody up this hour no way, exceptin' the fiends comin' down off somethin' or some young kids ridin' through the West after comin' from a party downtown. They be good for business though, especially them square ones. We be the only way they gettin' some of anything at all, so they be payin' real good. I always raise the price for them—and the price get real high when I see one of them Berkeley College stickers on they car. But now it's just time for everybody to go on home.

I ain't sure if Jesus is home right now, but if he is, I'll give him this bread I got left. Part of me don't want him to be up there. Sometimes he don't come to collect till he wake up in the mornin'. So in some ways, I'm hopin' tonight gonna be one of them nights. If he don't come till later, it'll give me some more time to get my story right.

What was that sound? You hear them footsteps? Sound like they in the buildin' somewhere. Oh, it's just a man comin' down from upstairs. I hope he ain't gonna try nothin' funny. I got a blade stuck in my garter belt in case he do.

"Mornin'," he says.

"Hey," I say back. Good, he ain't tryin' nothin' funny. Anyway, he don't know I was ready to cut him if he was. I told you before I always be nice to people—and especially when they comin' in and out of my buildin'.

Anyway, we here now. Be real quiet. I really ain't wantin' to wake up Jesus and Jason if they in there sleepin'. I can't handle Jesus tonight. I broke rule, you know. I paid somebody else before I gave Jesus his due. It ain't right, and Jesus could really put me under pimp arrest for doin' it. But I told you, I *had* to pay the rent, even though that don't change what Jesus could get away with doin' to me for it.

Somethin' like this happened to one of the girls on the stroll last week. She claimed some other pimp from around town who she used to work for stole her money. That's what she said, but everybody knew she was usin' it for dope. I ain't passin' judgment on the girl. I mean, life can get real hard out there. Ain't everybody ready for this kinda life—or good at it.

So anyway, it happened right on San Pablo, right in front of all of us. Her pimp, Slim, beat her like she was a dog, and then he shot the dope dealer she paid his money to. He got his money back, and I bet ain't none of his hos ever gonna break rule again. That's why I'm a little nervous 'bout what I done did tonight.

I know pimps gotta be 'bout they business, and a ho is supposed to be all 'bout supportin' her pimp with the same energy he protect her with. I know we all gotta be 'bout business, and we all supposed to take care of ours. I mean, I get the skit—I know the way things supposed to be—but tonight I really ain't had no choice but to do what I did.

The way I see it, my choices was to be laid out on the street with my baby boy or take a little whippin' 'cause of breakin' the rules—that is, if he find out. Jesus do be gettin' mad over stuff like this, but I can't deal with that right now. So the trick is to be quiet when goin' in the apartment, just in case Jesus already in there. Matter of fact, I'm gonna take off these here shoes so I don't make no noise at all when I go through the front door. That way, there won't be no clickin' sound and no reason for Jesus or Jason to wake up.

I'm just gonna put my keys down over here on this table and sleep on the couch tonight. If I hold my keys real tight, they stay real quiet—can't wake nobody up like this.

It ain't that I'm scared Jesus gonna drop me or somethin'. I mean, life been better since he let me back, you hear? Jesus made me what I am, but I know he need me to help keep him on top. He gotta understand why I did what I did tonight. I hope he do anyway. He gotta know that some nights don't be so easy.

This is really the first time I ever broke rule this bad. I'm hopin' he just cut me some slack if he do find out, 'cause this is gonna be my last time for doin' anything like this. I promise. I'm gonna learn to handle my money better so I don't gotta lie to Jesus. Anyway, ain't no thing, 'cause I don't see nobody. He ain't even in here.

"Peaches, why are you prancin' around here like you tryin' to hide from somebody?"

Oh, God . . . that was Jesus. He's already in here, and he's still awake. His voice don't sound happy, neither. Okay, I need to stay calm. I gotta stay calm, or he gonna know somethin' is goin' on.

"Oh . . . Daddy . . . Baby, I ain't hidin'. I was just, you know, keepin' quiet so I don't wake Jason up. He wake up real easy, you know that." That's all I can think of right now.

"I know you up to somethin' if I don't know nothin' else . . . Where's my money?"

He ain't even playin' tonight. He must know somethin' is up. It must have been a bad night with them other girls. I can't let him down. I'm gonna have to tell him the truth. I know he ain't gonna like what I gotta say, but I can't let him think I ain't pullin' them no more. I will always be one of the best so that someday I can be his number one again—even if he did turn me out to the nasty street corner.

"Well, here go three hundred dollars," I say.

"That's all you made for all them hours? Did you charge seventy-five dollars tonight like I told you to?"

"I . . . Daddy, I had to go pay the landlady 'cause she was gonna throw me and Jason out on the street . . ."

"What, bitch?! You lost your mind or somethin'? Is that what you're tryin' to tell me?"

"No . . . yeah . . . I mean, wait a minute . . ."

"I ain't waitin' for shit. You gave somebody else my money?!"

Lord, please help me!

He ain't waitin' to hear nothin' I gotta say . . . Aahh! He just slapped me, and the sting is still there. I better talk fast before he really get riled up.

"Daddy, please hear me out . . ."

"Bitch, there ain't nothin' for you to say! You gave some-body else *my* money!"

He's right . . . and he got every right to be mad at me. I know he mad now, but I hope he can just stop to understand what I'm goin' through. I . . . I hope my tears show him the sorry I can't fix my mouth to say.

Our Father, Who art in Heaven,
Hallowed be Thy name . . .

"You can cry all you want to, bitch, but them tears ain't finna get my money back! I ain't takin' this bullshit!"

He throwin' the money I just gave him back in my face a few bills at a time. Part of me wish I could keep these bills that's fallin' in my face, but it ain't gonna do me no good no way. I'm tryin' to give him back the money, but he not takin' it. If he would take the money, maybe he would stop tuggin' at his plastic arm like he tryin' to pull it off. Oh, God, he look like he tryin' to take it off. I hope he ain't tryin' to take it off so he can hit me with it.

Please, Lord . . . don't let him be takin' his arm off. Please stop him *from gettin' so mad.*

One time he slapped me with that arm and I got a concus-sion. I went to work anyway—even made a few dates, but when I got dizzy and fell out, Jesus told me to go home and get some rest. Gettin' hit with that arm is like gettin' hit with a baseball bat. It ain't no joke on the brain and it hurts like hell.

"Please don't . . . Daddy, please don't hit me with the arm. I'll go back out right now."

I'm tryin' to grab for my stuff, but he knocked my keys off

the table and now he kickin' them across the floor so I can't get them. He done already moved my shoes on out the way. I'm thinkin' that maybe I should run for it on barefoot—but if I do, he might hurt Jason, and I can't let that happen. Dang. I never should have gave the landlady his money.

Thy Kingdom come,
Thy Will be done,
On Earth as it is in Heaven . . .

"I'll go back and get the money," I'm sayin'. "I'll stay out there till I bring home more than what I had before, Daddy. I. . ."

He ain't listenin' to me. I'm tryin' to get up from my knees now, 'cause I know he ain't gonna never give me the stuff I need to go out and find some more dates. He mad and . . . Oh Lord, he hit me . . . with that arm. He beatin' it into me like he playin' hockey or somethin' with my head. It hurts so bad. I'm tryin' to cover. I done rolled onto my stomach and everything, but it ain't workin'. He done hit the blade I had in my garter belt, and sent it straight through my thigh. I can't take this pain. I promise to do everything right from now on. I won't never do this again.

He keep hittin' me in the same place with that arm and it's rippin' through my skin. Oh, it hurts so bad. I need to get away, but I can't. I can't talk, and even if I could, I don't know what to say.

I can't get up. I can't do nothin'. All I can do is cry.

"Bitch, shut the fuck up, before I really give you somethin' to cry 'bout . . . givin' my shit away like *you* runnin' this show . . ."

I want to shut up all this cryin', but I just can't. My heart is beatin' so fast and my mouth is tryin' to stay closed, but it can't when that arm just keep comin' down and hurtin' so much. I can't say nothin'. All I got is these tears.

I'm tryin' to crawl way from him. I think if I can reach the table, I can hide and he'll stop hittin' me with that thing. I can only make it halfway, though, 'cause the energy it's takin' to scream the pain away and keep my head from bustin' open is takin' away what I need to keep movin' away from him. I hear my mouth callin' out for Jesus, but I think this time, I'm callin' out for the Lord. I just can't . . . take this pain no more.

Oh, Jesus . . . please help me, Lord. I promise to do better if he just stop beatin' me . . .

I got blood comin' from my mouth 'cause my teeth is broke from the last swing of the arm. It hit me in the mouth, and my lips is puffin' out. I feel like my teeth is fallin' out one by one. And I know my hands gotta be broke, at least they feel that way. This is the worst whippin' I done ever had. It's worser than any of the beatin's I got from Grandpa or Grandma. It's worser than the feelin' in my gut when they closed the door that last time. I just pray he don't close the door on me, too.

Jesus really mad tonight, even though I did it all for . . .

"Momma!"

The lights in here just got turned on, and I know the sight of me layin' on this floor right now must be a little scary. I hope Jason ain't lookin' too hard. He don't need to see this. I really wish he wasn't woke so he wouldn't have to look at me like this at all. But with all this noise, I ain't surprised. I'm gonna have to fix all this when Jesus finish whippin' on me.

When this is over, I'm gonna fix the whole thing to what it was before. Well, I hope I can.

I can hear my baby cryin'. He's callin' out for me over and over again. I just want him to stay away so Jesus don't get mad at him and start beatin' him the way he beatin' on me. I don't want him to see me like this. He can't think that his daddy doin' this 'cause of somethin' that's wrong with him. This beatin' is my fault. Oh, I just wish Jason would just turn his back. I wish he would just turn and walk away.

"Stay . . . back . . . Jason . . ."

That's all I can fix my mouth to say 'cause my gums is on fire. Anyway, I think Jason got the point. My talkin' sounds a little crazy right now, but it's 'cause of this blood and spit comin' out of my face. I know I'm scarin' my baby like this, 'cause I can hear him cryin'. I hope he still think I'm beautiful enough to be a queen in his castle.

"Fuck you, bitch. I'll teach you to take my money, and to steal from me . . . This is what happens to bitches who get out of line!"

And Forgive us our Trespasses,
As we Forgive those who Trespass against us . . .

I'm gettin' real tired now. I can't hear everything that Jesus and Jason is sayin' to me. My eyes can't see straight and what I do hear be comin' in bits and pieces, like the music used to come through on Grandpa's radio in our old car that ain't had no antenna. I just keep hearin' cryin', hollerin', and the word "money" all blurred in my mind. But I can't do nothin' 'bout it now. I . . . I just can't.

I can't feel nothin' nowhere but in my head. Somethin' is

real heavy on my brain, and it just . . . hurts . . . so bad. Oh, Jesus! Please stop. Jesus, please make it stop.

And Lead us Not into Temptation . . .

Jesus . . . he walkin' away from me now, but that ain't stoppin' the pain. He leavin' with his arm, so maybe he done. I'm gonna clean up this apartment real good when I feel better. I just gotta go to sleep right now. But when I wake up, I'm gonna clean this up real good. He'll forgive me then.

I wish he would have listened to me, though. He need to know 'bout why I did it, and I need to tell him I ain't never gonna do it again. I just hope he don't drop me for this, 'cause then my life will be over. I can't make it in this world without Jesus.

My eyes gettin' real heavy now, like I done just been up all night with the worst headache I done ever had.

"My momma . . . real sick . . . dyin' . . . help!"

I can't really make out what Jason sayin' for real, but when I open my eyes, I can see him talkin' on the phone.

"We live at . . ."

I always thought death would be different. My head feels heavy, and I can't move it no matter what I do. But, inside me, I ain't feelin' nothin' like death. Ain't no feelin' at all, really—just like life. I always thought death would bring me the big feelin' I was supposed to have while bein' alive. Huh, I must have been lookin' for the wrong thing.

Jesus . . .

I know Jason next to me now. He done hung up the phone and now he just sittin' next to me cryin'. I really want to tell him everything gonna be all right, but I can't. I don't think nothin' or nobody done ever loved me as much as him. Knowin' my baby, he probably touchin' me . . . but I . . . ain't . . . knowin'. Can't . . . feel . . . nothin'.

". . . ambulance comin', Momma . . . love you . . ."

Lord, please make my baby be all right. Somebody around here gonna have to take care of him. I sure wish I could reach Chinaka right now. Lord, please take Chinaka to him. I want her to raise him on up. Maybe she could get him to be all political like her. He too young to handle every-thing on his own. Lord, please make him be all right.

I can hear them sirens outside, but it sound real low, almost quiet. Usually they be ringin' so loud I gotta cover my ears to keep them under control, but now I gotta struggle just to hear them a little bit. Maybe the police gonna help my baby out this time. Maybe.

"I love you, Momma. I love you . . ."

I love you, too, Jason.

I love him so much, and I wish I could tell him so. I hope he know how much he mean to me and how beautiful I will always think he is. If I could get myself right, I'd sing it for him again. I'd sing it better than I done ever sang anything, 'cause this would be the last song I'd ever sing. If I just had one more chance, that's all I'd do—sing to my baby and sing it with everything I got.

But I know he loves me, and I'm so glad that I had the chance to be his momma while my time let it happen. I know there gonna be a day when he find out that I wasn't nothin' but a hooker, but I hope that don't matter to him. I hope he still hold me close in his heart the way he do now. Somehow, he gonna have to learn to love me no matter what. He gonna be the only man who ever did.

I see this beautiful place now. You see it, right? It's sunny and peaceful with nobody around. There's some roses sproutin' from a bush in the middle of a huge garden. This place got a lake, too, and some beautiful trees. All I can smell is the fresh air blowin' through with the aroma of them flowers. I can see the petals of them roses breakin' through and bein' born in this new place. I can feel them, too. They feel like velvet. It's real windy, so the bush is rockin' back and forth—just like the branches used to do on them windy days in Oakland.

See how them tall, skinny trees is bendin' all the way over with the force of the wind? I like it when they do that. My hair would be turnin' every which way if I ain't had it slicked back like this. Yeah, it's real beautiful. I could stay here forever.

Ain't no sirens. Ain't no cryin'. Ain't no tricks. Ain't no pimps. Ain't nothin' but the roses, the lake, and the trees. And me.

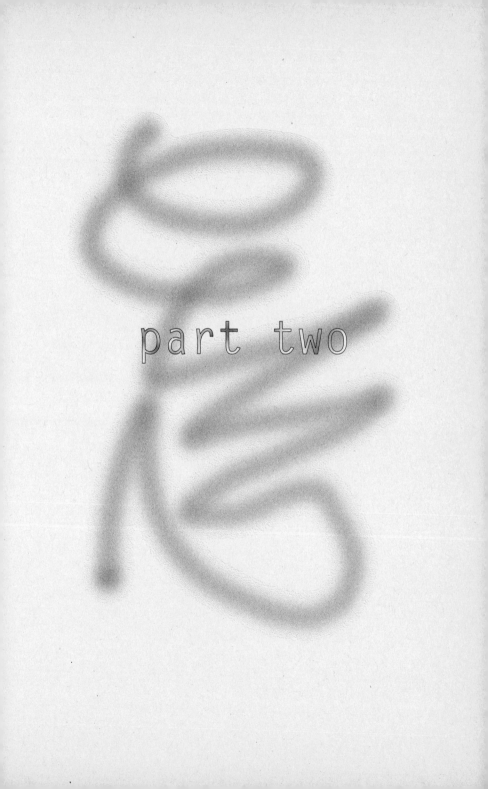

part two

Jason

Jackson would not shut up. Her mouth kept movin' and I know some crazy shit was comin' out of it, but all I could see was her lips flappin' back and forth. I was listenin' to her about as much as Charlie Brown and his potnas listened to grown folks in all of them cartoons. Nothin' she was sayin' was makin' sense anyway, especially since she really didn't have nothin' to complain about in the first place. She was just tryin' to front on me in front of our son, Dominic. Her voice was gettin' raspy, 'cause she had been screamin' on me since I walked through the door. And it wasn't even for no shit I could change. She was mad over some shit one of her girls told her about me.

"Jason, I'm sick of this shit," she said between coughs. "I know you been playin' me." She was tryin' to make tears, but her act wasn't tight, 'cause she was squintin' and frownin', but nothin' was comin' down. I mean, I could see right through the whole skit.

"What you talkin' about, girl?" I asked, turnin' my back to her so I could watch the TV set. She was gettin' on my nerves, and I was losin' patience with this whole scene. I was tired and just wanted to be home, kickin' it with Dominic. But I should have known—shit could never be that simple, not with Jackson.

"Where was you today?" she asked.

"What you mean, askin' where I was today?"

I turned away from the television set. I had to see her face to know where she was gettin' all that nerve to ask such a stupid question. Dominic was on the couch next to me, just postin' there with his daddy, holdin' a cookie between his teeth. He turned to look at her dumb ass, too.

She took a step back, 'cause she could see it in my face that she had crossed the line. I told her years ago never to ask where I was. It wasn't none of her business where I be when I'm not with her. All she had to do was take care of our son. Everything else, I could take care of. That was the deal. That's the way we always did things, at least ever since Dominic was born. And askin' silly questions wasn't part of the agreement.

"Ain't none of your business where I been," I said to her.

Damn! I had to flash on her before for askin' where I been. She was actin' like her body was weak and tryin' to catch her breath, like what I said had caused her so much grief. Yeah, Jackson was always about the big drama. She was grabbin' her stomach and frownin' up her face like she was finna be sick from all the "horrible news." And I knew she was frontin', 'cause she found enough energy to reach out for Dominic and try to pull him away from me.

"Dominic, go in the other room," she said to him, adjustin' her glasses to keep them from slidin' off her face. She was still reachin' out for him to go to her, but he wasn't goin' nowhere. He was probably scared by how she looked.

Jackson's hair been all wild and orange since last week, and it seemed to look worse last night. She put some white-girl peroxide in her hair, tryin' to look like some of them Frisco girls, but it didn't work on that nappy shit on her head. It made her hair look more nappy than it already was, and them braids she put in there to try to hide it all wasn't workin'.

"What's your problem?" I asked, holdin' Dominic back from her. She was bein' a real bitch. Like I would ever hurt my son . . . she must have been smokin' crack.

"Look, Jason, you trippin' right now," she said. "Just let him go in the other room."

"What? Why?"

"Come on, Jason, you know he shouldn't be watchin' this. I don't like it when he watches us fight like this."

She had a point, but I still didn't like her actin' like I would ever do anything to hurt my son. I love that boy, and I'm his daddy. Anyway, she's the one who be flashin' on him all the time, not me.

"I ain't trippin' at all right now, but I'm finna start if you keep actin' like this. I mean, what?! He's cool sittin' right here with me. What you tryin' to take him in the other room for?"

"'Cause we're not through . . . Shamika already told me where you was today."

"Damn, Jacki, why are you sweatin' me? I ain't knowin' what your friend told you, but I know *both* of you better stay the fuck out my business."

She stepped back.

"Look . . . See how you actin'?" Her mouth was still movin'. "I never know what you finna do, Jason. I just know how you get whenever I ask where you been . . ."

"Then why you keep askin'?"

"I just want us to be a family . . ."

"You just want me to be up under you all the time, and I been told you, I ain't that kind of nigga."

"Well, me and Dominic need you here, you know?"

For what? She was always throwin' Dominic into the picture whenever she wanted to see me. I used to get a call on my cell phone with her on the other end talkin' about "Dominic need some milk" or "Dominic been askin' about his daddy." I mean, for somebody only nine years old, Dominic was always needin' to talk to me about somethin'.

At first I bought into it and came home right away. But then I realized that whenever I'd get there, Dominic would be in the bed already, and Jackson would be sittin' around the house in some skimpy lingerie talkin' about she got somethin' else on her mind. If she was still fine, that might have been all right, but with how she look now, forget it.

"Dominic don't need shit," I said to her. "Everything he got is 'cause of me anyway, and I'm finna make sure it stay that way. Stop askin' where I been. It ain't none of your fuckin' business!"

"You ain't shit, Jason!"

Jackson picked up a toy action figure and tossed it across the room at me. I ducked and pushed Dominic's head to the seat of the couch to keep him—and me—from gettin' caught by a leg or a kung-fu grip.

She always did have a bad temper, and I ignored it when she was fine. But then her flat stomach got stretched out, and the stretch marks around her stomach started gettin' darker. They was saggin' and shit around her gut, and I couldn't ignore it anymore. The uglier she got, the worser her attitude was. She stopped wearin' makeup a few years ago, sayin' she wouldn't get her nails done with the money I gave her, 'cause it was comin' from the banks of other women. I told her that if she wanted to look tore back, that's her business. But it wasn't doin' nothin' for me, or for my son. I didn't have to put up with that shit.

So I stopped givin' her money and started gettin' toys, shoes, and clothes for Dominic myself. Then *that* started bein' a problem, too. I mean, that's what started the fight we had last night. She claimed that her silly, bigmouthed friend Shamika told her that I was in the toy store with some girl. She said her girl even told Jackson that it was the same girl who fronted me the money for my car. But I'm knowin' that Jackson was probably in the car with Shamika, spyin' on me 'cause she ain't got shit else goin' on in her life. Jackson's triflin' ass been stalkin' me for the past couple of months. She thought I didn't know, but I did.

I know that's how she found out that other girl bought my car. I didn't trip though, 'cause that issue was squashed almost as soon as it came up. The second she started sweatin' me about it, I shut her down. The car I was drivin' was my momma's favorite car, so the conversation ended right there. My momma used to go on for hours about how much she liked the 1979 Granada sedan, so even though it ain't a luxury car, it feels that way to me. But I guess she thought the action figure issue was different. I guess she thought it was all right to dig into me about that one.

Jackson asked me if the girl Shamika saw me with was somebody I was messin' with. I ain't never lied to no skeezer, even if she is my baby's momma. So I decided to tell her the truth. Hell yeah, that girl I was with from the toy store bought the damn toy I brought home for Dominic. And yeah, I had hit it before. She had a big booty, and I was all over that ass. She ain't nobody special, but she worked at Toys "R" Us and had a discount. It wasn't nothin' major. Anyway, Jackson already knew I wasn't finna be tied to one girl, so I didn't know why she was actin' like that.

But she was just bein' her usual headache, tryin' to make more out of it than there actually was. What did she care where the toy came from? It was free—and her welfare ass sure wasn't bringin' in no money, so she should have been happy. I do whatever it takes to keep my son taken care of, and if that means some other bitch is buyin' him shit, so be it. At least I was gettin' it done. I promised myself when he was born that he wouldn't ever want for nothin'. And I will always stand by that one.

I knew what it was like to be a young nigga on his own— without shit but spit—wishin' Santa Claus would come hook it up at Christmas. Or that the tooth fairy would come. Or that somebody would give me some shit for my birthday. And I wasn't finna let Dominic ever have to go through that.

When my momma died, my daddy didn't do shit for me. I guess he couldn't really, 'cause he was locked up for more than half of my life. I ain't really had no family, so Child Protective Services snatched my ass up and put me in a group home run by nuns. It was one of them "Orphan Annie" homes for real, but there was more goin' on in there than just us kids with no parents. Some kids was runaways or was pulled out of their homes for beefin' with their parents. Either way, while we was up in there, we didn't have no real family.

Them nuns started off bein' cool, too, but then I got busted for taggin' the church wall. I wasn't up to nothin'. Just tryin' to perfect my skills and make my claim that "J-Dog" was in the area—but they saw it differently. They thought a nigga was bein' "delinquent" and shit. I didn't think they would trip too hard. I mean, they had other fools up in the home who was gettin' into all kinds of shit. I was just writin' my street name on the side of the church. I thought God would want to know who was in the neighborhood, you know? Naw, but seriously, they got *hella* mad. They made me wipe off the graffiti with one of my potnas from the home who wrote his name next to mine.

Them nuns had us out there the next mornin' at, like, seven o'clock, scrubbin' down the walls of the church. And that shit was made of stone, so it wasn't easy to wipe off the spray paint. It was cold, too, so homeboy next to me started talkin' shit. He was on some old craziness, hollerin' about us bein' out there was all my fault.

"Man, I didn't make you write your name up there!" I said.

"Man, you said we wasn't finna get caught."

"How was I supposed to know what time they was comin' to church? I can't tell the future, bitch."

"Fuck you."

I stopped wipin' down the wall, holdin' the soggy rag in my hand. I was finna slap him across the face with it, but one of them nuns came over and saved him. She stood between us and told us to cut out the cursin'.

She said, "If you can't say anything that doesn't involve a curse word, then you can't talk at all. Keep scrubbing."

Well, you know niggas kept quiet for the rest of that time we had out there. I knew I couldn't say nothin' but curse words. For real, I didn't really know too much more than clever combinations of four-letter words, so she shut a nigga like me down with that one.

Anyway, after that, they started actin' funny-style, like they really believed I was a troublemaker. They started givin' the other kids extra television and radio privileges that I would never get. They would let the other kids stay after school for kickball and shit, but made me come home early. I mean, I was only ten years old, so I really wasn't too much into sports yet, but I didn't want to be locked up in the home for all them hours. It was like they was tryin' to turn me into a monk or somethin'. But we all knew that shit wasn't finna work. Not on a player like me.

After a while I got tired of lookin' at the same old church plays and wrinkled faces every day. I would sneak out and just go for walks, tryin' to soak in what was happenin' on the corner or at the school yard after school hours. That's when I started to get put on by the older fools that used to hang around the way.

There was always about four or five bloods in the school yard every afternoon, breakdancin' on some linoleum. They was cold, too. They'd be out there with the radio blastin', twistin' their bodies and spinnin' across the ground on their knees and shit. They were the first real breakdancers I had ever seen. I was hella pumped, too. It got so that I would be up in my room at night practicin' my poppin' and lockin' so that when it got time for me to strut, I would be the tightest they'd seen. Some fools was hella weak out there—especially the younger dudes my age. I ain't sayin' I could stand a challenge from the older kids back then, but I was, by far, the tightest breakdancer out there under twelve years old.

I had a little reputation goin' for myself, too. I even got put on that TV show *Home Turf* one time for this little competition I won. It was cool—that was probably the best time I had as a kid—'cause I was feelin' important and shit. Girls was jockin' me at school, and I had hella fools tryin' to be my friend. But 'cause I was livin' in a group home, I really couldn't afford to look as good as I should have when I was gettin' all that attention. I never had any money for clothes. Them nuns got money from the state to take care of buyin' me clothes, but they had my shit comin' from Kmart, and I was tryin' to wear what everybody else was wearin' on the streets. I used to be in there beggin' for them to buy me some parachute pants and some Adidas or Puma shoes, but they almost always came back to the home with somethin' else. That's when I decided to start makin' my own money.

One day, after school, I walked up to some of the fools that used to just be standin' on the corner. They was never out there breakdancin' with the rest of us. Naw, they was doin' their own thing—and gettin' *paid* for it. Man, I used to be blinded when I walked past them. For real, the fat gold chains that was hangin' around their necks was enough to pull my little ass in. A nigga like me was tryin' to get in where I fit in.

"Hey, what's up?" I asked one of them.

"'Sup, little homey. You the one who be out there breakdancin' and shit, right?"

"Yeah," I said, starin' up at him. He looked hella big to me then. I wasn't playin', so I just cut to the chase. "But I'm tryin' to make me some money."

"Oh, you is, is you?" He laughed, but he didn't dis me. Instead, him and his potnas pulled me in and started payin' me to be the lookout for the police. That was a cool gig, too. It was enough to have me lookin' fitted with the latest shoes. But you know how once you get a little taste of money, you gotta have more. So it wasn't long before I graduated to bein' able to watch the cars that belonged to the neighborhood big-timers. Some of them knew who my daddy was, so they was just bein' cool to me on the strength. But I knew some of them was impressed by how I held my own, so they taught me how to survive out there on the streets. Yeah, they was hella cool, and they never let me go home with empty pockets.

That meant the most to me for as long as it lasted. But it wasn't long before I started gettin' busted by the police for little things here and there. The first time they picked me up was 'cause them nuns called and told them to bring me in for missin' curfew. Then they just started followin' me for no reason at all, askin' me all kinds of questions about where I been and how come I wasn't at school.

I knew I should have been in school, but that just ain't never really been my speed, unless I spotted a girl to keep me interested in going for a week or two. Some days I would just go to the school lot, peek around the fences for girls, then leave that place fast before any of them teachers or security guards could spot me. I thought it was cool, too. I mean, I had all them days to myself. Shit, I saw how much money them bloods in the dope game was carryin', and I wanted some of it. I was too little to sell, but I started makin' more money by runnin' a few "errands" for them niggas. I mean, there I was, with less schoolin' than anybody else my age, makin' more than the kids at school or in the group home had ever seen. I was paid, and I just knew I was hard. None of them nuns sweated me for my gear. All they wanted me to do was pray, go to school, and stay away from them. So I prayed and stayed out of their way—shit, two out of three ain't bad. I was a hustler, man. I was makin' it happen.

But then, like with all successful underground operations, we got shut the fuck down. There was a big bust on the block and we all got hauled into the precinct—all the pimps and all of us in the dope game. Everybody got swooped up in the madness. They threw us in the holdin' cell and left us all scramblin' to be the first one to make phone calls and fill out the paperwork. I was trippin', 'cause I was goin' on eleven and now I had a record. But that's when I learned that I was on my own for real.

None of them nuns came to see me in court and wasn't nobody there to get my back when the district attorney started in on me as a "burden to society" and shit. I was tryin' not to listen. I was starin' at the walls behind where the judge was sittin', lookin' at how clean the polish was on the wood. The wall had these long, thin panels attached to it that looked like jail cells, so I started imaginin' myself stuck in the wall, holding on to the panels like they was the bars of the cell. The judge was sittin' between two flags: the American flag and one with the California bear on it. I was tryin' to figure out why everyone was always trippin' off of them flags, like they supposed to have somethin' to do with justice. They didn't mean shit to me, not then and not now.

I was tryin' to be hard, but I was scared as hell. There was nobody in my corner, so I had to do it alone. First, that shit hurt my feelings, but then I started trippin' on how them courts was always makin' niggas out there on the streets feel like we don't belong here. A few years ago a rhyme came out that started out with this man talkin' about how in most countries, jail is where they send their failures, but out here, it's America that's failed. I made up my mind that I wouldn't let the courts make me the man they wanted me to be. I'd find another way, some way, to be my own man.

I did everything I could to keep my head from believin' that "burden to society" shit when them judges moved me from the nuns' group home to the detention hall—you know, juvi—until they could find me a new place to live. I knew I made mistakes, and I knew I had to pay for my mistakes. I've never tried to make excuses for what I had to do, but there wasn't no other way for me. That's what them courts didn't want to know. I was only doin' what I could to keep myself in some decent clothes and shit. I mean, it wasn't like I had parents that bought my ass shit when I asked for it. Everything I had, I paid for myself. But instead of dealin' with that, I got sent to a juvenile hall where I was put in a cell and treated like somebody else's property.

That shit almost drove me crazy, starin' at them white walls and layin' on that cot they called a bed. I was in one of them "one-man cells," too, so there wasn't nothin' to do all day but stare at the muthafucka across the hall through the glass window. I was up in there startin' to lose it, started talkin' to myself and pullin' out my eyelashes.

That's when I first started trippin' and hearin' voices.

Don't get me wrong. I wasn't crazy or finna kill myself or nothin'. I wasn't hearin' *them* kind of voices. They was more like the voices of people I already knew. It was like I would hear somethin' somebody already said to me, over and over in my head. I heard everybody, too—my momma, Jesus, them nuns, the fools on the corner—I was hearin' them all. And they was all sayin' different shit, tryin' to confuse a nigga. At first I tried to ignore them, and then I tried to force them out. But none of that worked, so I just let them stay. They would get louder and then finally disappear on their own. It's just somethin' I learned to live with.

Them guards wasn't worth shit, neither. For real, they needed to be fired. Waking up in that hellhole every mornin' was like havin' to face another day as a dead man. The only thing that I could do in there was think. But nothing real cool came from that, only more ideas about how I could perfect my hustle. Yeah, life up in juvi wasn't no joke. They tried to schedule some activities, but most of us was too pissed off to really care about those.

We had a school up in there, but every day, the teacher would just write the assignment that she wanted us to do on the board. Then she would turn her back to us and keep readin' her magazines. To this day I ain't sure what them teachers up in there got paid to do, 'cause by what I saw, it wasn't to teach.

The other boys in there was trippin' off how them teachers wasn't teachin' us. They was complainin' to the sergeant and everything. But I was makin' use of that time. One day when the teacher told the class to write the answers down to some questions, I just pulled out a piece of paper and started writin' a letter. First I started writin' some random words on the paper, but then I started thinkin' about my momma and how she died.

After thinkin' about her layin' there on the floor with Jesus' plastic hand stuck in her face, I couldn't let go of what life was like out there in the real world. I couldn't let go of the hustles, the group homes, the stolen lives, and the punks that passed for heroes. Part of me wanted to stay in juvi so that I wouldn't have to go back to that hell in real life, but then I realized that bein' in detention was worse than havin' nothin' on the outside.

In juvi I was an animal, at least that's what everybody called me. And when you just sittin' around and not talkin' to nobody 'cause don't nobody come to visit, you start believin' that shit. So I was in that classroom daydreamin' about what my life was finna be like when I got out. I was thinkin' about the dope game, school, and them nuns. I was just reflectin' on my life, tryin' to figure out what I wanted to do with it. And then I started thinkin' about Jesus.

At first, when I was just writin' words on the page, I was mad. I was writin' all kinds of curse words and shit that made me think of death, like "blood," "guns"—you know, shit like that. But when I started thinkin' about Jesus, I started comin' up with words like "power," "girls," and "pimp"—and it didn't look that bad. I figured I could write to Jesus, get him to get some of his hos to bust me out of there. Then I could stay with some fine-ass bitch and live like a king. Yeah, I saw it all. No more cots and cold cells. No more nasty food and one-minute showers. I could have been livin' cool like the Baby Jesus I was supposed to be. But then I remembered that he was in jail for some other murder shit. And from what I heard, he wasn't gonna be out for a while.

It didn't stop his game, though. Before I got put in the Youth Authority—the state prison for kids—for doin' some more dirt, I used to see his girls workin' the corner all times of the day. I never really tripped off of them, but they would always offer to take care of me—make me into a man—as a favor to Jesus. I always got offered pussy, but never money. So I wasn't trippin' that much. I wasn't interested in all that pussy. The money was more appealin' to me, especially bein' a little kid. Anyway, any time I saw one of Jesus' hos out there in them heels, I thought about my momma and how he took her away from me. I swore I would do everything I could to catch up to him and make him pay for ruinin' my life, but then that shit changed when I thought about how much that nigga was runnin' the pimpin' scene in the West— even from jail. That muthafucka was powerful and had the most game out of everybody I knew.

I wondered how much game a man would have to have to get a woman to do *anything* he told her to do, even when he ain't around. Then I started wonderin' whether I could ever have that much game.

I figured I would write him a little letter and see if he wrote me back. I wasn't expectin' him to start callin' me "son" or nothin'—and he didn't—or to start sendin' care packages and shit. I knew that wouldn't happen, neither. But I wanted to see what he *would* do. He was the only family I had left, so I figured, what the hell? I thought he might read my letter, then throw it away. But when he wrote back, it was like he was really gonna try to be a daddy, and that blew my mind.

He was takin' the time to write to me and try to school me. And that was cool. It made me think that maybe he *had* to take my momma so that I could reach my destiny. At least, that's the way it seemed every time I read another one of his letters.

Don't get me wrong. It wasn't that I didn't care about my momma. I loved her—still do. But it was just that I had to get over that. I had to take care of myself and play this game called life with every trick I had. Wasn't nothin' for real to me. Everything and everybody was a game.

After I read his letters, I started thinkin' that no game was more important to master than the pimpin' game. Jesus was sayin' I was born to do it. And judgin' by how much play I got, and how easy it came, I believed him. I had to do somethin' to take care of myself, and the dope game was too risky. I wasn't willin' to put my life on the line so some dope fiend or policeman could bust me and stick my ass right back in jail. Naw, I wasn't feelin' that at all. But I was feelin' them words that Jesus wrote on those pages, and I was feelin' how I could get bitches to do anything I wanted and get paid in the process. Yeah, I was real interested in that.

I always had my eyes open for the letters I got back. His letters was always short, especially for a muthafucka in jail, but they was enough to make my day. Them letters was all I had, and they was real helpful in gettin' me to decide how I could use my natural skills as a hustler to make money in the Town. When I think back on it, my letters to Jesus was like cries for freedom. After a while it was like I could taste the freedom that would come with bein' a pimp like him. I already knew how some of the bloods on the corner called him "The Truth." And shit, I was finna be just like that. I wasn't about to be carin' for none of them hos. They was only good for two things—money and sex.

After watchin' Jesus as a little kid and readin' all the letters he sent to me over the years, I had learned that girls was only three things: saints, hos, and skeezers. Even when he was locked up, Jesus' game seeped into my brain and helped me keep my girls separated, and my money stacked. Yeah, he taught me all about them bitches, and how to treat each by how she deserved to be treated.

See, hos . . . well, they just give it up for anybody with money. You could spot them a mile away, 'cause they love to flaunt how much they like to fuck—and they love to show any willin' participant. The trick is just gettin' her to see that her pimp could run her pussy better than she ever could. Controllin' a ho is hard work for some folks, 'cause when a girl likes to have sex, gettin' her ass to stop fiendin' when she see a dick is half the battle. Skeezers be a little more picky— and tricky—'cause they be wantin' to tease muthafuckas. They don't always collect money for fuckin', but they want *somethin'*—a ride, some clothes, their hair or nails done—it's always somethin'. "Golddiggers" is the fancy name. Around here, we just call them hos in disguise. Once you strip that layer away—get them comfortable with their callin'—it's all good. They always crack with a little game.

Saints was girls who was, like, virgins and shit. You know, good girls. Them be the girls you see around who be all about their schoolwork. They wear them long skirts and never look like they've spent too much time around the streets. Most of them be "daddy's little girls" and spend their time talkin' on the phone with other little "daddy's little girls."

I didn't know too many saints. I had been in and out of

juvi for little things here and there—stealin' shoes or sellin' drugs. After seein' me time after time, the courts finally sent my ass up to Sacramento to the Youth Authority, where I had to serve my whole sentence. When I finally got out of Youth Authority, me and my friends from the new group home I was put in used to joke that them good girls would sooner or later end up with one of us "bad boys." They liked to flirt with us—you know, give us smiles in the hallway or on the way to school and shit.

For a while all the boys from the home used to ride to school in a van. On our way there we had to pass by this Catholic school. Every morning them Catholic school girls would be standin' next to the gate wavin' at us. Some of them was thick as hell, too. You could see it through the uniforms. It was cheap and quick entertainment, but it kept us interested in goin' to school. That was cool, too, 'cause there really wasn't nothin' to do on that ride to school but wait for them girls to turn around and give us some attention. I used to swear that one day I'd get me one of them saints and get her to start callin' me "daddy." I used to sit in class and daydream about makin' one of them girls—especially this one girl who was hella thick—cry for me the way Jesus talked about how them bitches cried for him.

One day, when we was leavin' school, I made it a point to miss the van back to the group home. I knew they did a headcount, but I didn't care. I was willin' to lose some merit points, or whatever it took, to walk past that Catholic school so I could at least get a phone number from one of them girls. I wanted to know if them good girls was for real. So I chalked the consequences up to the game and walked a few blocks down the hill to the school.

I wasn't expectin' to see the girl I had been scopin' from the bus, but there she was. She had on glasses, and her hair was pulled into this long braid at the back of her head. She was wearin' her skirt a little longer than I remembered it from the morning. She might have been one of them girls that hiked her skirt for boys, or my angle could have been off from me bein' on the bus every time I had seen her. Whatever it was, her skirt looked longer than usual.

Anyway, I think she recognized me, but she was tryin' to pretend that she didn't.

"Hey," I said to her, noddin' my head in her direction to let her know that she was the one I wanted.

"Huh? You talkin' to me?" she asked. She was smilin', but she wasn't movin' any closer to me. She was pullin' at her Starter jacket and whisperin' something to a girl next to her who had a Jheri curl.

"You!" I said, pointing at her. "Not you with the curl . . . Yeah, *you*, with the ponytail. Come here!"

"Naw, boy . . . *You* come *here*!"

I ain't never gone up to no bitch, not even in junior high school. A nigga like me looked too good to be a mark, so I told her to forget it.

But then she said, "All right, meet me over there," and pointed to a spot a few steps down.

I said yeah 'cause she was even finer up close than she looked from the bus. And I still couldn't see everything, 'cause we was separated by a wire fence. Plus Jesus had been tellin' me since birth how you had to get close to a bitch before she would let you into her dome.

"Yeah?" she asked, fixin' her glasses. "What you want to talk to me about?"

"I just want to talk to you."

"Why?"

"'Cause you a Roni, girl."

"What?"

I could have spelled it out for her—*Roni*, as in "Tender Roni"? But I guessed that Bobby Brown's 1988 game was too much for her. So far she had me believin' she was a real saint.

"'Cause you fine, that's why."

She rolled her eyes at me, but she also smiled, so I knew she liked it.

"What's your name, girl?" I asked her, stickin' my fingers through the holes of the fence.

"Jackson."

"What's your first name?"

"That *is* my first name."

At first I ain't think she looked like a "Jackson," but then after we traded numbers and talked to each other on the phone a little while, she started to look more and more like her name. She was kind of quiet, but she was always down to go out to the movies or somethin'. I called her "Action Jackson" for a minute—'cause I thought it would loosen her up in other ways—but it didn't work. So that nickname didn't stick. I had to just leave the creative shit alone and start callin' her ass "Jacki."

It turned out that her daddy's name was Jack and named her pretty much after him. I had found a daddy's girl for real. She was a *real* good girl. I mean, all we did was talk on the phone. I was steady tryin' to see how far I could get her to go, but she shut me down every time. It got so it was a challenge. I wanted her to do all kinds of shit, but she kept poppin' this virgin religion shit. I ain't never really been that type—the religious type—not since my momma died. But I played along, like I did in that group home with the nuns. I was doin' a good job, too, until I started slippin'. When her daddy left her and her momma for this white lady from Danville, Jackson's momma lost her mind and started drinkin' twenty-four hours a day. Jackson started trippin', too. She got depressed and wouldn't talk to nobody but me 'cause I was the only one she knew who had also lost his parents to some bullshit. And my dumb ass—instead of usin' that shit as a way to get what I wanted and bounce, I started really catchin' feelings for the girl. I started tellin' her how I would make her my girl and how everything would be all right. She believed me, too, 'cause then she got pregnant, and then everything changed.

She never went to high school. She stopped fixin' herself up and started lettin' her body get thicker and thicker—until it was nothin' but fat. She was only fourteen when she gave birth, so she was too young to collect from the state. Her momma was too drunk to follow up with the paperwork, so we both had to find hustles here and there to pay for diapers and milk. I had to work the streets and see if I could get some shit comin' in from other bitches so that I could afford our spot in the Acorn projects. But she wasn't thankful.

After she had Dominic, she started trippin' on me about whatever numbers she found in my pockets. To tell you the truth, before she started trippin', I wasn't even finna call most of them numbers. But after she'd make a big deal out of it, I figured why not call? It would make the fight worth it.

We started fightin' all the time. And it ain't never really stopped, except during them times when we wasn't together. But that skeezer got a problem. I mean, damn! When we not together, it seem like every few days I'm hearin' another story about how she tossin' her shit up to anybody who wants to take her out on a date. Even though we been in and out of a relationship, I hate hearin' about another mutha-fucka all up in *my* shit. So I'd get her back on my team again, and shut that shit down.

I ain't hatin' on the next man, but damn, that *is* my baby's momma. Anyway, it didn't take much to get her back. I'd call her, tell her I love her, make sure she believed me, and then I'd be back in it again. That's just how our relationship is, and as long as we stay cool with it, there ain't no problem. When we be together, don't nobody touch her just out of respect for me. Fools out there know me, so they be cool.

But anyway, even though she be gettin' on my nerves, I would never leave her to raise Dominic alone. And she ain't never leavin' me. Even when she bring me to the point where I slap her for askin' silly questions, she ain't goin' nowhere, 'cause she loves me. I'm all she got. I been tellin' her that for years, and she knows I ain't lyin'.

I think last night was the worst fight we ever had, though.

Shit got real personal when she said that I wasn't shit and threw the toy at me. She had never done that before. Her voice was ringin' in my head for hours after that, too. I mean, even though I didn't want to admit it, it hurt.

"I want more for us, Jason," she said, still tryin' to make tears. I guess she didn't realize that I could see her eyes squintin' to try to make the tears come out. "You be walkin' in here with all kinds of shit for Dominic, but you don't never have a job. What kind of example do you think you're setting for my son?"

"*Our* son."

"Whatever, Jason."

"What? Don't *whatever* me, bitch!"

It's not that she tried to dis me by sayin' "whatever" to somethin' I said—even though she was out of line for that one. It was the *way* she said "whatever" to me—like I could kiss her ass. Or like I was a bad daddy or somethin'.

The only thing that I could do was to leap over that couch and slap her in the mouth as hard as I could. I used the back of my hand, and my rings broke the skin around her mouth. I didn't mean to hit her that hard. I really didn't even mean to hit her at all, but she pushed me. It didn't look serious, but all of a sudden I felt Dominic pullin' on the leg of my pants, screamin' about how I hit his "mommy." I swear I didn't mean to hit her that hard.

All that shit was startin' to make my head spin—from Jackson cussin' me out 'cause of what I did to her mouth, to Dominic hollerin' at me any way he could. I looked down at Dominic pullin' on my leg, and he was pissed at me, pissed off that he had to watch his momma hurt. He, like me, had to watch her bleed, and he was hella mad.

To tell you the truth, I felt weird, like I had just done somethin' real serious. I mean, it wasn't like I had never hit Jackson before, but this was the first time I'd ever seen her bleed from somethin' I did. Before I could even control it, the world seemed like we had left the nineties for a repeat of my life in the eighties—when I watched my own momma bleed from the mouth.

I shook my head while Jackson's voice, and her cursin', got louder. Dominic was cryin' nonstop. His screams was gettin' all mingled with my own. My mind started spinnin', and it was all too much. I had to break out of there.

You couldn't catch the wind behind me, I was movin' so fast to get away from that apartment. I felt my beeper go off, and when I looked down at it, it looked like the number for a girl I had been messin' with from East Oakland. I really didn't feel like seein' her. I wasn't in the mood for any more complications. I didn't want to see no hos.

But it was like nothin' was makin' sense anymore. I looked down at my pager again and saw that the numbers wasn't in the right order. Then I noticed that the street signs was blurry. All I could really make out was a bunch of niggas hangin' on the corner. But even they was lookin' crazy. I mean, their faces was all the *same*, like somebody was playin' a game with my mind or somethin'.

I'm tellin' you, I was trippin', and I knew it. I finally made it across the street to my car and got inside. Once inside of the car, I laid my head back on the headrest, with my blood boilin' and Jesus on my mind. I could still see the apartment building from where I was sittin', but it was rainin', so everything outside of the car was wet and blurry. My life was fucked up and I was mad as hell at the world. But I was even madder at myself.

I tried to gather my thoughts for real, 'cause I was feelin' like my head was finna bust open. I couldn't break away from the life that had me by the balls, and it was startin' to squeeze real tight. For somebody who was so in control of all the hos around me, I felt like I had no control over myself. That shit was confusin' to me, too, 'cause that was the first time I had ever felt anything like that.

Even when I watched Jesus whip on my momma, I didn't think I was *that* confused. At least I don't remember feelin' that way. All while I was watchin', I wondered what it would be like to control somebody. It wasn't that I wanted to control my momma, but I wanted her to always be there for me. I wanted to control *somethin'* in my life. I guess I was so used to seein' it that it came natural to want a woman to control. That's how I thought life should be. I always wanted my own ho, but I had never really put my finger on *why* I wanted them. Not until last night. When I was in that car by myself, my body was drained—like all them years of hustlin' had finally caught up with me. And I was tired, dead tired.

Still sittin' in the car, I looked at the empty streets and at Jackson's body movin' behind the curtains in the apartment. I could see her body movin' back and forth, leanin' down to clean up the mess that we had made. She always picked up, and put up with, everything I dished out. She wasn't a bad mother; she just couldn't ever replace my favorite mother. No one ever could.

My eyes left Jackson behind the curtains. I reached into my pocket and pulled out the only picture I had of my momma. That picture was the only way I really had to get to know her. It was a picture she took before she was turned out to the streets. She was in high school when the picture was taken—or at least that's what I figure. I never asked her about it. Never got the chance to. But she didn't look like that by the time I knew her face. There, in that picture, her face was real young and soft-lookin'. Real pretty. She was frownin' from the sun bein' in her face, but she didn't look mad. I never remember a time when she looked mad—sad, yeah, but never mad. Not to say that she wasn't pretty later on. I mean, my momma was beautiful, but you know how the life is rough on a ho. And that's what my momma was—a ho.

I reached into my pocket and flipped open my cell phone.

I punched in the numbers to the only person I could think of who could free me from what was holdin' on to my life. I've been through so many changes over the last few weeks. But last night I was searchin' for the person I thought could bail me out.

All my life I couldn't figure out how I really felt about that nigga Jesus. Sometimes I wanted to kill him for what he did to my momma, but other times I wanted to visit him in the joint so I could see what he looked like. I wanted him to see what I looked like. I wanted to sit across from the man that gave me life and kept the lessons comin' through the mail.

I was punchin' in his phone number, but I was lookin' back at the picture of my momma. Somethin' in her eyes told me that she wasn't mad at me. I always looked at that picture when I needed somethin' to calm me down. It would always work, but it came with a price. Her voice would always pop up in my head and take over my thoughts. And last night wasn't no different. Whenever I got confused, her voice had a way of coolin' me down. It always felt like she could see what I was doin'—that she still knew what I was goin' through. I think last night she knew.

Jesus picked up the phone on the third ring, and it sounded like he was answerin' from outside somewhere. He acted like he was mad that he was bein' interrupted from whatever it was he was doin'. It was all right though, 'cause after I convinced him that I was serious about followin' in his footsteps, the nigga was cool. I had half an hour to get to him, and that was just enough time to get some gas and mob to his house—no more, no less. I had half an hour to get myself together.

"Baby, you're much too beautiful . . ."

She wasn't sittin' in the car next to me, but it felt like it. She wasn't even alive, but I could hear her like she was. Her voice wasn't distant at all; it wasn't even soft. It was rough and deep like it was when she was alive, just like it always sounded when I was hearin' her voice.

"Baby, I love you so much. Remember, you gonna be momma's prince, right? You gonna make me proud . . . mmmhmm . . . and momma love her baby."

I was smilin' before I could stop myself, but it was cool. Her voice had been comin' to me for years. All the doctors them nuns and lockdown staff had me seein' told me I needed to let her go, but it wasn't that easy. Even Jesus told me I had to get over her. But when I tried pushin' out the other voices, I never tried that hard with her. I didn't really mind hearin' her voice. She was the only person that ever really loved me, and the only person that I ever really trusted—until a little while ago, when Chinaka came on the scene.

Yeah, last night I was trippin' off a lot, but mostly I was tryin' to figure out how I could still be her prince, even if I couldn't make her a queen in real life. I was tryin' to make sure she didn't die in vain. I mean, Chinaka was right. I couldn't let her go out like that. Everything I am—and was—is 'cause of her. I couldn't let her death be for nothin'.

I started the car before the tears on my cheeks could fall off my chin. It was time to go. Jesus was waitin', and I knew he wouldn't wait for too long.

Jesus

Baby Jesus:

You need to get your shit together. You tellin'
me that you a goddamn daddy now? I'm a muthafuckin'
granddaddy? Ain't that some shit.

How you gonna be a daddy when you done just
started high school? Well, I ain't sure it's yours.
If I was you, I'd let that bitch take care of it on
her own. I mean, did you want a baby? Did you tell
her to get pregnant? If not, then that shit ain't
your problem.

I hope this don't make you start acting like a
poot-butt. Ain't nothing worse than somebody with
promise gettin' caught up behind some pussy. You
just remember that pussy come a dime a dozen, and
when one piece of pussy acts up or walks away,

there's about a hundred more waitin' for you somewhere else. Maybe right in front of you. And most
times, you ain't even gots to go that far.

If you want to care, then handle your business.
But make sure that bitch ain't tryin' to pull a fast
one. If she is, knock her the fuck out. You the one
running the scene, nigga. If you say you gots a son,
then you know what you gots to do. Don't you let
that bitch trap you. Bitches ain't shit no way.

—J

too beautiful for words

Chinaka

I met him one month ago, on the eve of my fifty-first birthday.

When I saw him standing on the corner, he was shooting craps with some of his friends, laughing and joking about something. He stepped away from the other brothers and pulled a beer out from a bag. He took an animated swig from the bottle and smiled one of the brightest smiles I have ever seen. The joy in his face could not be contained in that grin, which is why it seemed to take over his entire face. It was a blessing to have caught it, but whose blessing I was not sure. I had never seen him before, but something was drawing me closer to him. There was something strangely familiar about this young brother, but it was not the obvious. It was his energy.

Then he laughed again, this time taking himself right into the door of a car that looked just like the one I used to drive.

He threw his head back and let out a whoop like I had not heard in years. But it was a laugh that I had heard before. It was deep and throaty, loud and contagious. And I knew that I knew him.

My work had dramatically changed over the years, leading me away from the vigilance that inspired my alias as the "Molotov Queen." I was no longer a major target for the pigs, so as long as I kept a relatively low profile, no one would even offer a suspicious glance my way. My metamorphosis into an admittedly reclusive lifestyle ended my tirade of chasing squad cars and reintroduced me to the power of the written word instead. I chose to believe it was all a part of my plan—a way for me to be able to stay alive long enough to meet him. As a dead woman, I would have been of no use.

The day I met him was one of the few days I spent communicating with the people through good old-fashioned, non–tax supported street lobbying. I was passing out flyers at a bus stop about a rally to protest this government's treatment of brother Geronimo JiJaga. I wanted that brother released from prison, as well as the countless other prisoners of war still rotting away in jail from their revolutionary cries for freedom. I was out there determined to educate those who could afford to be more visible so that they could petition for him in venues that I could not. And for the most part, the brothers and sisters waiting for the bus were receptive to my message. They kept me so busy that I almost missed him, but when the bus came, he was my only focus.

He was across the street, standing on the opposite corner from where I stood. I was close enough to see his face, but I felt nowhere near him, and especially not close enough to approach him without making a special effort. Something was telling me that I had to hand this brother a flyer. I needed to get closer, and I needed a reason to talk to him.

By the time I got up to him and his friends, he was in recovery from that laugh, but the grin was still plastered across his face. I admired every inch of his handsome face, finding it difficult to imagine him as Peaches' son. He looked nothing like her. His caramel-colored skin was as smooth as lambskin leather. His brows arched slightly over two almond-shaped eyes that were almost covered completely by a set of long, thick lashes most women would die for. His nose was small and modest compared to his set of full lips. His hair looked naturally wavy and was skillfully faded into his scalp. He had a tall, athletic build—markedly different from Peaches' small frame—which could be distinguished even through his baggy jeans and long T-shirt that looked two sizes too big.

"Good afternoon, brother," I said slowly, still eyeing him for something that would confirm what my gut was telling me. I knew him. I knew I did. He started laughing without answering me. Instead, he just continued to ignore my presence in order to preserve the sanctity of his world.

But I did not move. I just used the opportunity to study his face.

"Blood, that's one of your girls?" one of his friends asked, prompting the group to break into laughter.

"You goin' kinda old, ain't you, blood?" another chimed in.

I laughed, too. The thought of us as a couple was definitely ludicrous, for me and for him.

"Naw . . . naw . . ." he said. His voice was strong and deep.

"Have you brothers lost it?" I asked.

They did not respond to me, but that did not matter at all.

I turned to him and said, "You know, usually when I greet a brother, he at least has the common courtesy to respond."

I said it soft enough so that his friends would not hear me, but loud enough for him to understand that I expected to be respected.

"What?" he asked. He was obviously not used to a sister speaking to him the way I did. Too bad, though. In those first few moments of our meeting, I could read what was going on with him. He was a classic, but one that had been badly bruised and damaged along the road. He just needed some positive attention, and a new direction.

"Look, brother. I just came over here because there is something about you that is familiar."

He looked at me seriously for one second, then dismissed me. "Naw, you must think I'm my old man or somethin'. You might have known him back in the day, but you don't know me. Folks be sayin' we look just alike."

I appreciated the comment and the candor, but there was more to it—and to him—than that.

"Who is your father?" I asked, doing my best to ignore the stares coming from his friends.

"Man . . ." He turned his back and fidgeted as if he did not want to tell me the answer to my question.

"What? You don't want to tell me?" I asked.

"Man . . . who *are* you? Why did you come over here?"

"My name is Chinaka, brother. What's yours?"

"Who do you want to know? Me or my old man?"

"Look, brother. If it is that serious for you, then forget it. I thought I knew you, but maybe not, so you have a nice day, brother. Power to the People."

I turned to walk away, and almost made it a full three

steps before I heard him say, "My father is Jesus . . . and my name is Jason."

I still cannot say what made him tell me. When I turned around, he looked as surprised as I was that he had disclosed what had appeared to be something he did not prefer to share with everyone.

But by then it was too late. I remember piecing it together: his father's name is Jesus. His name is Jason. And then I put my finger on what it was that was so familiar about that laugh. It was attached to memories of lace, fake mink boleros, feather boas, and five-inch heels.

"You said your name is Jason?"

"Yeah . . ."

"Jason, do you know a Peaches or an Angie Johnson?"

His face washed over completely, but I could not tell if it was a look of anger or just a case of simple anxiety. His brow frowned and his eyes grew intense.

"What? You . . . you knew her?" he asked. Then the ferocity receded. He moved in close like a puppy, and I realized that he was still a little boy when that pimp killed her. I never knew all of the details surrounding her death, but everyone on the street knew that "Jesus" was the one who was responsible. I heard that he beat her with his prosthetic arm, and that she died instantly, but I had heard nothing about what happened to her son. It was not that I had never thought about him, it was just that standing there watching him try to cover his pain was as unsettling as watching someone desperately try to wipe away a permanent scar. Jason's longing to know more about his mother was visible from the moment I mentioned her name.

Saying has it that the devil is in the details. Well, in her death, the devil was the main ingredient.

"Could you come over here for a minute?" I asked, moving away from the ears that had stopped listening to the impromptu game of the dozens and were making their way into our conversation.

"You knew her?" he asked again.

We moved only a few steps away, but enough to temporarily secure our privacy.

I watched as the layers of hardness peeled from his face, revealing the previous wonder I used to listen to Peaches talk about for hours. He took a deep breath, then let it out and leaned his back against the car.

"How?" he asked quietly. "How did you know her? I don't know nobody who knew her . . . how did you know her?"

I could not open my mouth. I could not see a way to explain the nature of our friendship to him in a minute, or even ten minutes, so I asked him if he wanted to come by my house. I knew that over tea and comfort, we could at least begin to scratch the surface.

He agreed to come without much persuasion, which was only a mild surprise. What was more shocking to me was how soon I had extended the invitation to him. But looking at him, I could only see one thing: urgency. Whatever our purpose was for that chance meeting, everything had to unfold quickly.

"I'm offering to take you to my place, Jason, because I trust that you have more of your mother in you than your father."

Even though his face did not completely distort at my

words, I realized that they might have been a little harsh without enough background. But I could not hold my tongue. I had spent too many years wondering what had become of Peaches' family, and her soul, in the process of being physically destroyed by this world. I had not meant to offend him, as his face had mildly suggested, but I certainly had to be careful not to disclose too much information to a brother that could potentially not be trusted.

"Look, brother," I said, "sorry about just coming out with it like that, but I have to be careful about who I bring to my place. I can't have people who could kill me and get away with it knowing where I live."

"Somebody wants to kill you for passin' out flyers?"

"I mean the police . . . and I can't take chances. I run deeper than what you see here, brother."

He laughed, then said, "Don't worry. I ain't finna go runnin' to the po-pos about where you live."

"Well, I'm going to trust that you can hold my secrets as well as your mother did," I said. "I'll explain everything later, but in the meantime, I need your word."

Everyone on the street knew the importance of giving one's word. If his word could not be trusted, then the fibers of his character were also suspect.

The problem with the whole scenario was that I couldn't know at that moment whether his word was worth anything. That was why I hoped he had more Peaches in him than his father. Peaches' word was worth its weight in gold. That pimp, on the other hand—well, the lies he told Peaches speak for themselves.

"I ain't trippin' off where you live. I just want to know what you know about my momma."

I had to take his word. There really weren't any other options.

He nodded a quick good-bye to his friends, who responded with an equal lack of enthusiasm. They were visibly confused about the quick change of heart they had seen in him. But they were not the only ones. Without question, the moments spent walking with him to my house were the most confusing of my life. I believe that everything happened for a reason, so there had to be a reason why I ran into him. That was clear. What was not so clear was what I was supposed to do with this brother once I got him to my home.

But something was whispering in my ear that this is what I needed to do to help him. Something told me that everything would be all right and that this brother needed me. Maybe it was the voice of God. Maybe it was the voice of Peaches. Maybe it was just me. All I knew was that *something* or *someone* was speaking to me that day.

I opened the door to my home with my usual haste and watched him follow me in quietly, not saying much of anything. I offered him a seat on the couch in the living room as I went straight into the kitchen to make some tea. When I came back with the cups in my hands, Jason was walking around my living room looking at the titles of the books I had neatly stacked on the floor against the wall. I had to have at least two hundred books lined up there. I never got around to getting a bookshelf. Anyway, I was starting to believe that having them along the floor like that added character to my living room.

"You read all these books?" he asked.

"Over time."

"Damn, you sure do read a lot."

"Reading is fundamental to any successful Revolution, brother."

He chuckled a bit, then went back to thumbing through the pages of a book he had picked up from the stack closest to the door. I placed the teacups on the coffee table, then walked over to where he was standing.

"What you got there?"

"Um . . ." He flipped over the book cover so that he could read the title. *"Incidents in the Life of a Slave Girl."*

"Oh, yes, Harriet Jacobs. She wrote that, you know."

"Shit, I ain't even know slaves could read, let alone write their own stories."

I laughed. There is a huge satisfaction in watching a mind begin to strip the layers of miseducation from its keeper. I could tell that Jason was struggling to appear as uninterested as possible, but he failed. He could not suppress the glow of learning in his eyes.

"Oh, yeah," I said, "and she was not the only one. Many slaves wrote about their lives. Frederick Douglass, Olaudah Equiano—there were many. You'd be surprised by the talent that is smothered by oppression, brother. And you'd be surprised how revolutionary ordinary people can be when given a chance."

Jason nodded and closed the book to look at the cover again.

"She was kinda fine, too. Maybe I should take this home and show it to my son."

I laughed—just like a young brother to notice the exterior before even thinking about giving the interior a chance. But at least he was thinking about reading to his son.

"You can borrow that—to read it—if you want to. But only if you promise to bring it back."

He shook his head and laughed, I'm sure, at the thought of learning anything from a freed female slave. But the offer still stood.

"I have tea over here for you, Jason," I said, walking away from him.

"I don't really drink no tea."

"Well, come have a seat with me anyway."

He followed me to the couch and sat down. I passed the couch and sat in an old wicker chair. It had a wide fan back that towered over me when I sat in it, and a stiff seat that was supported by a thick base extending slightly beyond its arms. It was beautifully woven together and reminded me of a time when being young, militant, and Black was celebrated and not masked. That chair used to be the official property of the Party. It was the one that held Huey in that famous picture where he is gripping a spear in one hand and a rifle in the other. That chair had witnessed so many transitions for the Party that if it could talk—oh, the stories it would tell! Interestingly enough, Huey did not even want to take that picture in the chair, and he resented it being the one image of the Party that most people remembered. He preferred an image of an intellectual army over that of a belligerent one. But to respect Eldridge's clever argument for mass appeal through the power of symbolism, Huey agreed to take the picture. A few years after that picture had reached its pinnacle of circulation, Huey mentioned to me that he wanted to get rid of the chair. I offered to take it off of the Party's hands, and he was happy to give it to me.

Sitting in that chair across from Jason, I felt like Huey. I, too, was ready to wage an intellectual and emotional battle in Oakland. I propped my feet on the base of the chair and leaned forward to give this young brother every bit of my attention.

"So, how you know my momma?" he asked, with a very confrontational stare.

"You know, in a strange way, your mother was one of my best friends."

"Then how come nobody don't know you at all?"

"None of *your* people know me, because that was the nature of our friendship."

"What?"

"None of you *could* know about me . . . I had to keep a low profile, brother. Just like I do now."

"Still, I'm her son and I remember everybody that ever came into our house."

"Well, I was never in your house. When I would see her, we'd be riding in my Granada. Going off somewhere to sit and talk."

Jason looked up at me with an interest that I had never seen before at the mention of my old car. He sat straight up and peered at me.

"*You* drove a Granada?" he asked.

I did not know why it mattered, but I answered, "Yes."

"That's why . . . she loved that car . . . she always talked about how much she loved the way the seats felt and the way it gave her room to breathe . . ."

I sat back in my chair, happy to have learned about her appreciation for my car, but saddened by the fact that she could never sit in it with me again. I sat with her son, but throughout our conversation, he fought me more than she ever did. He, like her, was content to believe that this "Jesus" was his only ticket for survival in the ghetto, and that pimping would facilitate the liberation for which his soul longed. I knew that it was too soon to attack his belief in pimping, but I could see then that he struggled with his mother's reality—vacillating between his adult perception of her as a whore and the child-based memory that knew only of her need to work at night.

He struggled for thirty minutes trying to understand my relationship with Peaches, finally letting his struggle collapse unresolved. But to me it did not matter how I came to know his mother. What was important was that I had found Jason.

"You . . . you know what your mother did for a living, right?"

"Yeah, she was a ho, I know . . ."

"Well, you probably shouldn't think about her as being just a ho. Brother, everything she did, she did for you."

"Look, don't tell me that shit . . . and don't tell me what to think, okay? You don't know me, all right?"

"But I do."

"You do what?"

"I do know you."

"Yeah, right . . ."

"Look, do you think she would have lasted—even as long as she did—if Jesus knew she kept my company for anything other than sex?"

He did not answer. He just stared at me.

"See, I met your momma when I was in the middle of one

of my personal crusades against the police. I used to be out there wild, brother. Running from the pigs *every night!"*

"So?"

"So your momma was out there with me . . . Not doing the things I was doing, but helping me out by keeping me safe. That was a major deal for her, considering how she supported herself."

He looked at me with the same degree of craziness and confusion that I would expect from someone if I had three eyes instead of two, and a parrot dancing on my head. I know he thought that I was crazy to be telling him that I knew him when we had just met, but I knew what this brother was looking for—a real way out. I also knew how he could get there. But he had to be willing to abandon everything he had internalized about where he lived, how he lived, and what his purpose was in life.

I told him about all the times I ran into Peaches out there on those streets, with her in those high heels and short, fitted skirts. We laughed only briefly at the feather boa and fur bolero she liked to wear on her "special nights." As a child, he never knew what that meant, but he remembered the boa—and he remembered her prancing in it around their apartment some nights to make him laugh.

We talked about how she walked, how she talked, and how that was all different when she was around Jesus. I told him about how she smelled like Charlie perfume, and how I would ride around in my car for days after we'd seen each other, smelling the scent of her misguided search, wishing that I could take her away from the madness of it all to save her life.

Jason's eyes lit up every time I told him something new about Peaches, and they got sad every time I mentioned anything about Angie—the true woman behind Peaches. And my heart just bled for that brother, that poor young brother whose mother had been stripped away from him, leaving him scarred by the only images he ever had of the women in his community and of women, period.

He struggled with the concept of his mother having two faces. For some reason, it seemed like he had settled on the notion that his mother was just one kind of person—a hooker whose death was her own fault for "breaking rule." No more, no less. Maybe it was the only way that he could live with her death, but in any event, it was not fair to her, or her life. And it was not fair to her family.

He claimed not to have ever really known "Angie" even if she was the one who gave birth to him. I tried to explain their differences to Jason—how Peaches was a flamboyant lover of flesh who sought out opportunities to make as much money as she could so that she could give it to her pimp. I explained how Peaches was a friend to those local pigs with open arms and accepted each insult that they hurled at her tiny, Black frame. I explained how Peaches was polite to every potential "client," even those who did not deserve it.

Then I showed him Angie. She was a sweet girl from West Oakland whose parents died early and left her with a Baptist deacon and his wife who were from Mississippi. I was never really sure about whether these "grandparents" were of her true biological lineage. I guess something in me never wanted to believe that a Black family would abandon their grandchild when she needed them most. I always thought that those people who let Angie live with them were the reason she always sought to please everyone. She wanted so desperately to be loved that she would do anything for it. I also thought they were the reason she relished the thought of rising against the system of oppression that left many of our children without parents, and without homes.

Angie was intrigued by the Revolution and was honored to walk, and work, the streets as a God-fearing Christian. Peaches just did what she had to do and asked no questions. And they both loved the hell out of a little boy named Jason.

He blinked his eyes a couple of times before clearing his throat.

"Where was you when she died? Why . . . why didn't you come find me since y'all was so close?" he struggled to get the questions out, and I struggled to answer them.

"I've asked myself those questions so many times, young brother. I loved your mother and it kills me that she's not here anymore. It's so unfair that he gets to live and she had to die. Every day I wonder why she wasn't with me that night or why I couldn't find that pimp for *ten years* after that night. Believe me, brother, I wished—I prayed—that I could find him after that."

"Well," Jason spoke slowly and quietly. "Jesus went to jail after that."

"Oh, he did?"

"Yeah, he's still in there, but he gets out soon."

"So, I guess the pigs caught up with him then . . ."

"Naw, he didn't go for that. He went for another murder." His voice was quiet and disturbed, but he did not seem to be angry with me.

"Interesting."

"He got fifteen years. That's probably why you couldn't find him."

"Hmmm."

"But you can't be mad at him like that. My momma was a ho, Chinaka. Whatever you got to say about it, she was a ho and I know that. She broke rule, and Jesus did what he had to do . . ."

That was the noise his mouth made, but I did not buy it.

"Hmmm . . . you sound like you know the rules pretty well, brother."

"Them the rules, man. I don't make them . . ."

"No, you just live by them."

He smacked his lips and turned his head away from me.

"Well, I'm not playing that game, young brother, so the rules don't apply to me," I said.

I knew he was upset, but I could not stop that. This young brother appeared to be headed in a direction that put him at serious risk—risk of losing his family, his people, his sanity, and his life. He seemed to have developed the soul of a leader and the coping mechanisms of a follower. It was something that I had seen before in our people. I'd seen it in his mother, and that troubled me deeply. I wanted him to know that he could do better, but I struggled with a way to communicate this to him without turning him completely off. It was clear from the way he talked to me that he really believed he was unscathed by Peaches' death. But I could not tell what her life as a prostitute meant to him, if it meant anything at all. He held on to that tough exterior, but I knew there had to be an opening somewhere.

"You ever heard of the People's Temple?" I asked.

"Yeah, that was that white man's church who had all them folks from the Fillmore caught up and believin' he was some kind of messenger of God."

"Right," I said, "so you know what I'm talking about?"

"Yeah, them nuns at the group home used to tell me about some people they knew who killed themselves over in Africa."

"Wow . . . and you remember that?"

"I remember just about everything."

"Well, that's good, but I've got to tell you. That tragedy had nothing to do with *Africa*."

"Don't matter no way . . . why you even ask me about that?"

"Because, brother, do you want to be the victim of a murder/suicide mission after following the likes of someone like that? The bodies of all those people are buried right here in Oakland if you want to go see them. They thought they found some rules they could follow, too, and they ended up dead from following after a crazy man."

He shook his head. "Look, I ain't talkin' about followin' no white man's religion . . . or no religion, period."

"I'm not talking about any white man's rules or religion, either. Brother, I'm talking about the system's game that you choose to play by following some pimp who's got all of you people convinced he's God."

He glared at me impatiently, but said nothing.

"All I'm saying is that you can choose how you play any game you find yourself in, Jason. It's not about religion. It's about life choices. *Life*, Jason."

I handed him a makeshift card that had my name and number on it, and walked over to the door and unlocked it.

He took the card, mumbled a "thanks," and put it in his pocket. He did not look me in eyes before leaving, but took his time walking out of my house. I watched only briefly as his slow walk took him back in the direction of the friends that I had taken him away from earlier.

I wondered if he would ever call.

Jason

Dear Jesus:

I got me some new Jordans today. Only the players got these, 'cause they cost, like, a hundred dollars or somethin'. The same girl who be buyin' me lunch every day got them for me. All I had to do was tell her that I wanted them, and she went and got them for me. I look fresh.

Matter fact, I'm not trying to sound like I'm conceited or whatever, but hella girls be tellin' me that I'm fine. I think I'm going to make a good pimp. When you get out, I want to be there to take you somewhere so that you can watch me pull hos. I be pullin' them left and right now.

I quit high school for good now. I know how to read already. I don't really see how high school is

going to help me do what I want to do. I mean, I was
hearing what you said when you wrote in that letter
that the only way for me to learn how to be a pimp
is to learn the streets. Ain't nothing in school
helping me do that, so I decided that I ain't wast-
ing my time there no more. I'm a full-time hustler
now, Jesus. I'm about to be big-time.

    Jason

Jesus

I know this muthafucka better show his face soon or I'm finna leave his ass. I only been out here for twenty minutes and I said I'd wait a half-hour, but I'm ready to go. Damn, sometimes I hate bein' a man of my word.

But shit, man, this arm is actin' up, and I ain't really diggin' it out here no more. Not with this rain comin' down like this now. The part of my prosthetic arm that touch my shoulder is startin' to be a real pain in the ass, 'cause it's gettin' too cold.

Anyway, that boy finna have to learn to be early for business meetings. Seasoned niggas like me ain't gonna wait around for every muthafucka who lookin' to be fed some game, even if we say we are. Shit, if he wasn't my son . . .

Wait . . . Is that? Yeah, it is. There go two of my new bitches.

"Hey!" I say.

I don't have to wave them over. They come 'cause they know they better when I call for them.

"Hey Jesus Daddy, we just on our way to get it done for you," the youngest one—her name is Divine—is sayin'. The other one, Candi, seem to act like she scared to open her mouth. That's all right, though, as long as she ain't scared to open her legs.

I prefer Divine of the two, 'cause she ain't shy by any means—she's feisty like a muthafucka. She's young enough to handle muthafuckas, too. I found her at the strip club the night I gots out the joint, flingin' her ass in every man's face who would give up five or ten dollars. Before I could even walk up to the front of that club, I heard them introducin' her as "Miss Divine." And when I gots closer, I caught her eyein' me. She had her ass up in some cat's face, lookin' at me and smilin'. I was up in there with Slim. Shit, he's still about the only cat in this game I'd be caught hangin' with. So when he said we should go to the club, I was ready. We was up in there celebratin' my bein' out the joint.

But, man, we always about our bread. We walked in the door and Slim went one way and I went the other. I moved over to the corner, just tryin' to scope the scene, since I had been away for a while. But I could feel the eyes on me. I wasn't worried about that, though, 'cause my eyes was on Divine.

I liked Divine right then, 'cause she wouldn't even think about poppin' her ass for a muthafucka unless he was wavin' some bread in the air. I could tell she had her head screwed on right. She's just the kind of bitch I need, one that don't require too much guidance and shit. Yeah, baby, one that don't blink unless she see green.

She rolled onto her stomach and spun around to her ass

with so much skill, she ain't really need the pole to make a muthafucka start whippin' out his bread. Not me, of course, but them other cats in the club. All I could see was money-earnin' potential for real. If the girl was that good with her clothes still on her body, I knew she could do some dyna-mite shit when they was off. She *had* to be able to do more than just dance.

And, baby, she couldn't wait to be up in my face, hollerin' about how she could spot a true player anywhere. I laughed 'cause the young girls that night was funny, with their new ideas about the game and the life. But she was pretty, real pretty. And she gots talent, so I was willin' to talk to her.

"I heard about you," she said, "and some of us been waitin' on you to get out of jail . . . You know, some of us only want to be workin' for you." She went right for it, man. I said she was a feisty one.

"Why you wanna work for me?" I asked the question, but only 'cause she was a little too eager. The way she was actin', she could have easily been a setup—an undercover cop in a thong. I've seen it before. The only way out was to test her. And to take the chance.

"I can *show* you why or I can *tell* you," she said, winkin' one of them brown eyes at me and rollin' her tongue across them thick lips. I ain't finna lie, it looked real good to a mutha-fucka like me who was fresh out the joint.

"How about you do both?" I was impressed with what I saw, but I can't have no bitches who can't spit it out on com-mand. This one wasn't gettin' no opportunity to play me. Bitches don't play me; I play bitches. Shit, I'm always ahead of the game. I could tell she was frustrated, but that was just too bad, 'cause I wasn't finna cut her no slack.

"'Cause I'm tryin' to do my thing, and word on the street say you the best."

I wasn't sayin' nothin', 'cause I really wanted to hear what she had to say about this one. A piece of me wanted to know what people had been up to while I was away, and I really did want to know what they thought about me. Part of what makes a pimp so magnificent is the legend. If the legend is gone, then a part of the game is, too. I had to hear about it.

"Some of us girls want to make more than we makin' just dancin'. Sometimes we want to do more, too, you know? That physical thing just can't be replaced, you know?"

I was noddin'—still listenin'.

"And when we be talkin' backstage, it always come up how you the best. You always look out for your girls. You know how to treat your girls, you know? And we don't have to get high off that shit if we with you, you know?"

She was movin' in closer and rubbin' her hands across my chest. She was tryin' to show me how interested she was, but everything was just everything, until she talked about not gettin' high. It ain't like I never get high—you know that ain't the case at all. But after losin' some of my best tricks to that crack shit, I didn't want no fiends on my team. I had to weed them out.

"You don't get high?" I asked.

"Naw . . . well, not no more."

"You used to get high?"

"Only before a show, you know? To loosen me up."

"Aw, baby. If you need to get high to do *this* . . ."

"No, Jesus, I said I *used* to get high. I don't no more . . . well, maybe some weed now and then, but I'm off that rock. For real, I let that go. I only did that when I was first startin' this, you know? I don't do nothin' now, but think about makin' enough money to get the things I need, you know?"

"So you want to make money?"

"Hell yeah, I wanna make money. Why you think I'm tryin' to get up under you, Daddy? I need somebody . . . I need somethin' that's finna help me do my thing."

"And you want me to make you a star? I can do that, you know. With me you don't need to get high, baby. This is Jesus you talkin' to, baby. I gots all it takes to make things happen for you."

"That's what I'm talkin' about."

I smiled and added a notch to my belt. She was on my team that night.

Now, Candi was one of them other girls from the club that Divine was talkin' about that night, but I didn't meet her until yesterday. She ain't as cute as Divine, but like I said, she ain't gots no problems spreadin' them, so I ain't gots no problem with her—not yet, anyway.

"How much money y'all gots right now?" I ask them. I *still* ain't impressed by whatever happened a few days ago. These girls still new on the stroll, and they gots to make sure they keepin' up with what this is all about in the first place.

They diggin' their hands into their boots to pull out what they both earned so far.

"Daddy, we got about eighty-five dollars so far."

"Eighty-five dollars between the two of you?" That ain't shit. These bitches must think I'm a fool.

"We just been out there for two hours. We finna . . . we finna go and make more. This is just what we got *now*."

"Bitches, I ain't playin' with you. Y'all better . . ."

"We are, Daddy. You don't even got to finish. We leavin' right now."

I know these girls gots to know what happened to Peaches. They gots to know that all that fast talkin' they doin' gots to be killed.

"Why you walkin' by my house, anyway? You gots shit to do."

"We know," Candi sayin'. She finally decidin' to open her mouth. "We just came by to drop off this CD for you."

This world is somethin' else. When I went into the joint, we had tapes and records, now we gots these little shiny records everybody callin' "CDs." Shit be changin' so fast on the streets. That rock cocaine gots these muthafuckas out here forgettin' what it's like to have order. They don't respect nothin' no more. Everything is about what they can get without thinkin' about rules and shit. It seem like there ain't no rules no more. Even though the streets always been a place where you had to fend for yourself, it ain't never been as crazy as it is now.

"It's Gladys Knight," Divine says. "I remember you sayin' you like her."

I'm lookin' at the cover, and it's Gladys Knight all right, and the Pips. One of the better records of all time if you ask me. It gots that song "Midnight Train to Georgia" on it. That song be showin' me just what a bitch would do for her man. She'll move to another city. She'll give up her Hollywood dreams for a muthafucka if he gots her lovin' him. Ain't no limits if his game is tight. Yeah, before Gladys startin' tryin' to make that bread singin' all of them new, sorry-ass songs she gots out now, she was a real act. She needs to quit bull-shittin' and come find me. I'd show her what it's really about.

"This is cool, but eighty-five dollars still ain't shit."

"We workin', Daddy. We gone . . ."

"Yeah, we finna bring home somethin' for real later on . . ."

"You better." I'm already knowin' that if they try to come home with anything near what they gots on them now, they gonna be dropped like a hot potato. "And I ain't tryin' to see less than three times what y'all carryin' now."

They're promisin' more and kissin' everything but my face, but at least they're movin' them feet in the direction they need to go to make it happen. If I'm finna be on top like I was before I went into the joint, these bitches gonna have to work. I ain't that far from the top now, 'cause my hos was workin' while I was away. My Top Ho, this ho named Angel, been keepin' my money in one of them safe deposit boxes at a bank. It's all cash up in there, and she was sendin' me notes in the joint about how much each ho was bringin' in. So far she ain't done nothin' tricky, but I be checkin' up on her ass just in case she try to get frisky.

Yeah, I ain't where I was before I went in the joint, but I'm finna be there again soon. Slim's runnin' the scene now, but he ain't gonna be there for long. That's my muthafucka, but this is business. I gots a plan. I'm finna stack all my bread, weed through the bitches that ain't bringin' in what they should be, and build myself a whole new empire. You see, like I said, the streets done changed, and since there ain't no rules no more, I'm finna start pimpin' niggas *and* bitches. There be some freaky muthafuckas who want to fuck niggas who dress like bitches. Well, I gots it in my head that I'm finna give them what they lookin' for. Ain't nobody doin' that right now. Them transvestite hos be renegades, but they bringin' in *bread*. The way I see it, all money is green. Even faggot money.

Damn! Jason better come on, 'cause I'm startin' to get a little itchy—like I want to go out on the stroll just to make sure my new girls understand the procedure. I gots some of my other girls showin' them the ropes; shit, it ain't that hard. But you never know what evil is lurkin' around the corner, tryin' to make your girls reconsider everything you done spent your time teachin' them. There's always somebody tryin' to undo your shit.

To tell you the truth, I think muthafuckas out there still trippin' off my bein' in jail all them years. I think they still tryin' to figure out how a muthafucka could keep on pimpin' from the joint—and then come back to the streets like he was never gone in the first place. See, that's another difference between me and these other cats, man. I don't stop just 'cause some shit done gone wrong. That's when I kick it up. I just come back stronger.

That judge slammed his gavel on that bench and hollered out "fifteen years" at a muthafucka. But I ain't even flinch. I just winked at him. I knew my game would be strong enough to stand fifteen years with me off the streets. That's the thing about my gospel, baby. It don't get tired. And anyway, fifteen years was better than spendin' the rest of my life in jail, or bein' on death row. Lucky Slim had a lawyer who was a client of his who came through for me. Yeah, he came through for me on that one. He owed it to me, though, since the reason I was facin' a murder charge in the first place was

too beautiful for words

'cause I was defendin' my girls, and a bitch who happened to work for him. Gettin' me that lawyer was Slim's way of sayin' thanks.

I ain't no fool, though. I know Slim probably had some dirt on that lawyer cat, and he defended me to get away from havin' to face his wife when Slim's ass showed up at the front door demandin' money for the job one of his bitches had done the night before. Yeah, with them options, that lawyer was probably happy to defend my ass.

Anyway, the murder wasn't somethin' that could have been avoided. I told you I'm a jealous, wrathful pimp. It wasn't like somebody had a gun to my head to make me stab that fake-ass pimp who was tryin' to make a home in my backyard, but what was I supposed to do? Let that mutha-fucka graze? Shit, not on my grass.

It was right after that shit went down with Peaches that word hit the streets about how some poot-butt was on the scene in some fancy threads that he probably picked up from the last muthafucka who fell for his shit. He rolled up on the stroll hollerin' from a blue sedan about how he was finna take over me and Slim's shit—and take all our hos. It was obvious he wasn't from around here, but he was actin' like he knew all the players in the game.

One of my hos came back to the crib talkin' about how she ran into some pimp who was tryin' to make her choose him. First, I couldn't understand how somebody could call himself a pimp and then stoop to tryin' to *make* a bitch choose him. Then I was mad. I was ready to whip on that poot-butt until he gots it through that skull that I—and the West—was not to be toyed with. It seemed like the more she told me about what he was sayin', the more I wanted to break him like I break my hos. That perpetrator had to be stopped. A point had to be made.

I was mad as hell when I went lookin' for him. My ho had already described him to me, sayin' he had one of them long Jheri curls and a black and white suit that matched his wingtip shoes. They said he was wearin' a cape—like the muthafucka could fly. Well, shit, I know now he wishin' he could have flew! I grabbed my knife, loosed up my arm in case I had to use that muthafucka, and set foot out on the stroll. My arm was still broke from a few nights before. Yeah, it was fucked up bad 'cause of that Peaches shit. It didn't have no hand, and the arm was bent. But I didn't need no hand to make that muthafucka work if I needed it to.

I remember everything about that night, too, especially how loud it was. It ain't usually that loud on the streets at three-thirty in the morning—but that time it was like Mardi Gras out there. I was eyein' anybody who even looked at me sideways—and still lookin' for that infiltrator with a long-ass Jheri curl and a cape. And you know, I was stoppin' muthafuckas left and right, man. I was in a damn maze with that shit. It was the eighties, and every other muthafucka I saw had a Jheri curl!

Then I came up on this little, pretty muthafucka who was tryin' to make a play for one of Slim's hos standin' between two buildings. He had his back to me, but I could tell he fit the description—all the way down to the cape and wing-tips.

The girl he was talkin' to saw me come up from behind and started tellin' that fool he should leave. But do you think that muthafucka would listen to her? Naw, he was still too busy tryin' *make* her choose him.

"Go on, now . . . You really better leave," I heard her say.

She was wavin' in the opposite direction than where I was comin' from, so I guess she was tryin' to tell him where it would be safe for him to go.

"Aw, baby, don't leave now . . . I ain't through talkin' to you," he said.

He didn't even know I was right behind him.

"That's how you get your hos, muthafucka?" I asked, steppin' up behind him a little closer. "You beg for their shit?"

I had reached him already, so nowhere around there was safe. The girl knew it, too. That ho got out of there fast, leavin' him all alone with me.

He turned around real fast, almost gettin' some of that Jheri curl juice in my eye. But he missed me, 'cause I moved my head back just enough and just in time. I didn't waste no time grabbin' for my weapon, neither. He couldn't do nothin' but look at me and try to be as hard as he was talkin' about bein'. But I could see it in his eyes that he was drownin'—kickin' and spittin'—while he was standin' there lookin' at me. I'm tellin' you how these young niggas be gettin' in over their heads with this pimpin' game.

"Who you is, man?" he asked.

"You don't know, trick muthafucka?"

"Trick?"

"Yeah, bitch . . ."

"What's all this, nigga? You breakin' up my game. Why you all up in my mix?"

"'Cause you up in mine, phony muthafucka. I'm here now, 'cause you causin' wrinkles in *my* shit."

"Ain't my fault your game ain't ready for mine. If your girls wanna leave you for me, that's their business—and mine. Not yours."

He was pissin' me off more and more by the second. It was gettin' so that I wasn't even finna let him finish his last sentence, but I wanted him to remember that night. I wanted him to remember me. He was finna die knowin' not to play with anything that belongs to Jesus.

"*All* business that goes down in my world is *my* business, muthafucka, especially when it makes my girls uncomfortable," I said. "When they ain't comfortable, they ain't happy workin'—then you messin' with my bread, and then I ain't happy."

"Well, I wasn't meanin' to upset none of your hos."

"This ain't about upsettin' no hos, man. This is about upsettin' me."

"Who *are* you?"

"Jesus, muthafucka!"

I was boilin' by then, and he knew it. I could tell he didn't think I would actually come lookin' for him. He started fidgetin' and shit, and his eyes gots big like he was seein' a ghost.

"Shit, man. I didn't know . . . No disrespect, man . . ."

"Shut up, muthafucka. It's too late. You been all through these streets, disrespectin' my name *and* the game out here. You already know what's comin'."

"Man, I ain't disrespectin' the game. Don't you know? Hos on the streets is fair game when there ain't no pimp around to protect them. It's your fault your bitches is lookin' at me and not you."

I had to laugh, 'cause he was sure his knowledge of the game was untouchable. He had everything memorized like he was studyin' from a rule book. He was so weak. I could have left him right there and he never would have showed his face around the West again. But the way this cat was workin', he probably would have been in another town smearin' my name 'cause he thought he could get away with it. I couldn't let that happen.

By this time, at least a dozen muthafuckas was standin' on the opposite corner, watchin' me and him. I had been quiet the whole time—ain't really been my style to get loud over no shit like this. I was used to just handlin' my business. So that's what I did.

I looked at him and said, "Jesus don't play by nobody else's rules, nigga!"

Before he could say any more shit to get on my nerves, I pulled the knife out of my coat pocket and stabbed him. I was just stickin' and pullin' and twistin' and jabbin' that knife all through his guts. I wasn't even concerned that somebody had called the police and that sirens was comin' down the street faster than my mind could pull me back to reality. I remember just wantin' to watch him die.

See, when I beat Peaches, I didn't stick around 'cause I really didn't want to watch her die. I didn't want to see that shit happen, so I split. And I was tryin' to stay low, until I came across this muthafucka. Then I just lost it—and the police caught me, 'cause I was slippin'. I admit it. I know I gots bad reflexes—some call it a "temper"—but you know, that's just me.

When the police pulled up, they caught me red-handed, man. I was leanin' over that muthafucka just to make sure he was dead. And I made sure I saw it in his eyes before I got up for the police.

They jumped out the squad car yellin' for me to freeze. They was ready, too, even had their guns pointed at a nigga.

They watched me pull the knife out of that cat and put it back in my pocket. They watched me stand up and raise my real hand over my head. And they watched me turn to face the wall—all before they ran over and shackled my ass. I was lucky they didn't shoot me. But shit, I was payin' for most of the jewelry their wives had around their necks, so I ain't get roughed up too bad. Anyway, that lawyer Slim sent to me was cool. He had me plead self-defense in court. I was baptized in the holy water of true players, baby. And my words was made manifest when I was put to the test—when they sent me to jail.

Naw, I didn't flinch when that judge gave me fifteen years. Fifteen years wasn't so bad considerin' what I could have gotten.

Jail turned out to be just like the hustle on the streets, man. Remember, this is Jesus, and I ain't no ordinary player. I was gettin' hauled away by the cops, and my bitches was still joggin' alongside the squad car claimin' they would wait for me. They was all over it, too, talkin' about how they was finna stick with me no matter what, hollerin' about how they knew my bein' sent away was a trial for them to test their loyalty.

Hey, baby, they started it—and I just finished it.

I told them that just as Jesus was resurrected from the dead in the Bible, I was finna come back stronger and better. And I wasn't lyin'.

I took that promise seriously. For every one of them fifteen years I spent behind them dingy bars in that tiny cell, gettin' shook down by guards who wanted to test my manhood and gettin' threatened by those who couldn't get down with my way of thinkin', I was only concentratin' on how things was finna be when I gots out. I was finna take over everything. Of course, before that could happen, I had to make sure that my girls had loyalty.

I was sure all doubts was cleared by the time they actually shipped me over to that jail. And my roster was sittin' tight once word gots out that I had successfully took my business to a place where the demand for new pussy—and whatever could look like one—couldn't possibly be beat.

Now, before you get ideas about how them jail bitches gots on the temporary roster, remember I already said that pimpin' came to me naturally—and it ain't gots to do with nothin' but bread. It's a gift, man. I'm a survivor.

In jail, I took the game to another level, 'cause I ain't never been about none of that faggot shit—but some muthafuckas be into it all. I mean, I came in there as the new cat, so there was some who thought I was finna be up for beddin' with the one-eyed Willie. But I ain't never been a trick. Shit, I would sooner die. And I let that be known right away. I walked up in there, popped my collar, and let them muthafuckas know—I was not the nigga to fuck with. Before they knew it, I had them jail bitches on my block payin' me to make sure nobody took their shit without my permission. And it ain't never been all about muscle, 'cause there was some muthafuckas up in that joint who could have whipped my ass in a one-on-one, especially since they took my arm away. But I had the gift of gab, baby, and they believed that if some shit ever did have to go down, my wrath was gonna be spiritual.

My game in jail also spread when my hos came to visit. I remember one of them real good. Her name was Marie. She was a Filipino girl who had just come to Oakland from

Frisco, runnin' away from her parents. She used to talk about how her family gots pissed that she had decided to go with some black cats, so they disowned her—cut her out of a will she said was thicker than anything we could imagine. She was real cute, too—exotic-lookin' with a whole heap of attitude. Just right to be my Pacific Islander grinder. Cats in jail started askin' about her, and before she knew it, we was passin' her off as the old lady to half my cell block. We was real slick about it, too. It took a lot to change her look every week when she showed up as somebody new, but the niggas and Mexicans—and some of them white boys, too—was payin' out the pocket for a piece of little Marie.

I remember the first time she walked in there to visit me.

"Hey, Daddy. Some of the girls chipped in and bought you these cigarettes." She winked at me. "We thought you could use them in here." She ain't never had no accent, just the look: dark skin, straight black hair, chinky eyes, full lips, and some righteous ass.

"How y'all doin' out there? Anybody messin' with you with me up in here?" I knew the answer, but I had to ask the question.

"Hells no! Everybody out there is still talkin' about how you took out that fake pimp right in front of the cops. For reals, I think they're too scary to even try to talk to any of us."

"Hmmm . . ."

Not many of them pimps would wait too much longer to move in on my bread.

"And anyways, we know you comin' back to take care of us, Jesus. We all know it. If a girl starts havin' doubts, it don't take long before she gets checked by one of the other girls."

I knew what she was sayin' before was too good to be true.

"Doubts? Who's havin' doubts?" I asked.

"Uh . . . well, I was just givin' an example."

"Well then, finish the example, ho."

I was starin' at her hard at that point, so I knew she was gettin' nervous. I reached over and started strokin' her hair, then I grabbed that shit tight. I was pullin' at her head like I was tryin' to scalp her. Nobody around us saw me do it, but I guess one of them guards saw it. I know she was doin' her best not to let it show how much pain she was in. But she couldn't hide the fact that her head was bein' yanked with every second that passed and she wasn't tellin' me which one of them bitches was havin' doubts. She finally caved in, though.

"It was Gina . . . But she ain't trippin' no more. For reals, she ain't trippin' . . ."

The guards rushed in the room and pulled her away from me. I let go when they came around so that they wouldn't put me in the hole. I had been in there when I first gots to the joint for some shit I had to do to defend my manhood. And I wasn't tryin' to go back in that muthafucka. I'm tellin' you, that stank, rat-infested bitch ain't no place for a pretty muthafucka like me to be. So, yeah, I let Marie go without trouble.

She knew the conversation wasn't over, though. She signaled that she would wait for my call. I was sure she just wanted to buy time so I could calm down, but I had already made up my mind that Gina had to be dealt with. I had to strike the fear of God—or Jesus—in that ho. The next time Marie came to visit, I told her to bring Gina.

I hooked Gina up with one muthafucka named Tiny who was the craziest cat in the joint. I used to watch him stare at shit the same way my momma used to stare at shit, so I knew how to deal with him. One day I asked him if he wanted to "marry" Gina. It ain't no surprise how fast he jumped at the chance, and just like I figured, he nearly ripped her little body to shreds. Marie came cryin' to me about how Gina was bleedin' and shit and how I had to handle Tiny for doin' that to her. Well, when I said I wouldn't do shit for a bitch that was havin' doubts, she changed her tune and started bringin' in more money than she was before. I still wasn't sure if I wanted that bitch to scream my name, but at least that ho learned her lesson.

I calmed down after a while, but mostly 'cause of Marie. She was a little dope hustler on the side. I gave her my permission to do a steady date with one of the older cats on the block who kept my supply of heroin comin' in on the regular.

Just like I thought, when I gots back to my cell, wrapped up real neat in them cigarettes was a decent supply of my soother, enough for me to have on my own and even share if I was feelin' like it. I can't really remember how long it took me to get through that box, but I tell you this, it was enough to keep my mind from goin' crazy up in that place.

Damn, that shit was rough, but it gots better when one of those black guerrilla cats on my cell block walked up to me in the rec yard. He was tryin' to be real discreet by creepin' up on the side, but he still looked like he wanted somethin'.

"J-J-Jesus . . . Uh, look here, brother. I saw y-your-your old lady come in the other day."

"What?!" I almost choked on my cigarette. "What you talkin' about, you seen my old lady?"

"Yeah, your . . . uh . . . ." He stuck out his tongue and made an hourglass shape with his hands.

"That was just one of my bitches, man. She one of my *hos* . . . she ain't nothin' close to bein' my old lady."

If she was my old lady, this nigga would have been pickin' up his teeth off the ground—especially after makin' that hourglass shape and shit.

"Aw . . . mm-mmm-man, that's good to know. I . . . uh . . . n-noticed y'all was havin' some p-p-problems."

"Nigga, why you over here stutterin' up in my face? What, you like her or somethin'?"

"Well, I n-n-noticed she was f-f- she looked good, man."

"So, what? You want to try to see if we can arrange a little rendezvous between the two of y'all?"

"Aw, m-man, th-that-that would be righteous."

Them black guerrilla cats was always tryin' to lecture the rest of us about how we wasn't up in there for no reason but the wrong reason—like killin' a white man is better than killin' a black man. Shit, man . . . This pimp don't see no color but green. Anyway, with this cat comin' up to me like he did, I knew one thing: them guerrillas was just like the rest of us. My philosophy was still secure. All men, at least all the straight ones, will do whatever, whenever, for even the smell of some pussy.

"She ain't free, man. What you gots?"

"I was th-thinkin' I could arrange to get you s-somethin' from the outside, man . . . How . . . How much she cost?"

I didn't answer right away, 'cause there was too many variables. We was in jail, and conjugal visits was only for the inmates' old ladies—or those that was soon to be. I had to come up with a plan, and of course, with each thing that made it harder to pull off, like spreadin' my game beyond just my cell block, I had to tack on more bread. Before long, cats was payin' up to two hundred dollars for a half-hour with little Marie and some other hos I brought in there.

I guess after five muthafuckin' body exams a day and bein' faced with tricks dyin' to suck another man's dick in their cells, these muthafuckas was ready to get some real pussy. It was funny to me, too, 'cause cats always want to talk about how they broke, but when a good piece of ass walks by, they be findin' some bread, baby. Hell yeah, they can find the bread when they want to.

Anyway, I don't look back on them days with any kind of special feelings. Marie started turnin' to crack, and that ended her reign on my roster. Shit, everything I did up in there was just to cope with my situation anyway. The only highlight was when I would get them letters from Jason.

The way he wrote them, it looked like he took his time, like he had thought about shit real hard. He wrote just enough to get me goin' without boring a nigga to death. Every letter was short and sweet, and by the end of it, I knew I was right by sayin' I'd help him be a pimp.

For one, I know I can't run this game forever. This game requires some youth with the skill. You need to be young enough to keep these bitches on alert, man. I ain't never gonna be broke, so I always knew there was finna be a time when I would have to get creative and shit. A muthafucka like me gets old like the rest of them, so I was glad I had a Baby Jesus to sip on my secrets, and get drunk from the taste of my game, baby. I always *wanted* to see Jason hold the honor of bein' "Mack of the Century," so hell yeah, I was finna help that boy.

See, when I was readin' Jason's letters, I was hearin' myself—seein' myself—in him. That muthafucka been tryin' to live up to everything he promised in his letters. That's why, when he called me tonight, I made time for him. I'll be his guidance counselor, his—what they call it on TV?—his "mentor" and shit. Shit, the way I see it, as long as he willin' to make bread and keep our legacy goin', ain't nothin' to worry about. Call it my retirement plan if you want to.

The boy was spit from *my* seed, baby, so he gots some natural sense of what this is all about. All he need from me is to fill in the gaps, give him some pointers. By the time I finish with the player, his game will cut through anything and anyone. Shit, he finna be a legend in his own right.

Listen to me—soundin' like a bona fide daddy. I can't help it, though, 'cause I love this life. I have to. I can't sit around like them other cats in jail used to, waitin' to get their next taste of whiskey. Like I said, a nigga can't be broke. And I ain't never finna be homeless again, so I do my thing to make my money.

Ain't no bitch—male or female—finna hold me down. As far as I'm concerned, all the bitches in the world can lean over and kiss my ass.

I can see headlights comin' down the street now. They comin' kind of fast, but slow enough for me to catch the make of the car. I would know that brown and tan Ford anywhere—from the way that boy wrote about it in his letter. He wrote about that car like it was his pride and joy. I guess in a way it was, since one of his bitches got it for him. And that music blastin' makes it even easier to know who this is rollin' down my block.

The car is pullin' up to the curb now, so I guess I'll get on up from these steps and get in. Soon, me and Jason ain't finna be sittin' in no old-ass Granada. When I get his shit straight, he finna be pickin' up his old man in nothin' but Bentleys, Cadillacs, Mercedes-Benzes, and Lexuses. Shit, we finna be rollin' down the West with all these bitches screamin' for us to take them on and keep them locked in.

But it's cool for now, I'm sittin' next to my son. I'm holdin' a Gladys Knight CD. I gots my soother, and I gots my bread.

"What up, Jesus?" Jason says.

"Yeah, nigga . . . let's go."

And we gone. More bitches to be tamed, more bread to be made. It's all in the game, baby. It's all in the game.

Jason

Dear Jesus:

   I ran into this guy at the gas station the other
day who said he used to be a pimp. We didn't start
out talkin' about pimpin'. But he saw me slap this
one bitch and he came over talkin' about how I
needed to find the Lord and how if his whole game
could change, my game could change, too. It's a
trip, though, 'cause the more I laughed at him, the
more serious he got. But I'm not tippin' off him.

   Pimpin' is the best life a nigga could hope for,
man, 'cause don't nothin' in this world come for
free. And when you a pimp, at least you controllin'
how much them other folks, like them white folks
that run downtown and them oil companies or whatever, control you. Some people say that people love

workin' for big businesses, 'cause it's easier than
makin' somethin' up yourself. I think people love
to coast—do just enough to get what they need.

People be doin' all kinds of shit for love. But
that ain't for me. I hate love. And it don't matter
anyway. Love don't mean shit when there is somebody
bigger that can take it away. I mean, ain't we all
gettin' pimped anyway?

Jason

Chinaka

With the skyline of downtown Oakland as a backdrop, the Festival at Lake Merritt had officially commenced. The water glistened, licked by sun rays that created an air of serenity and peace, and the festival that always welcomed its heartland to the body of water was under way. Every summer hundreds of brothers and sisters in search of free entertainment and good food gathered around the city's lake. The music would be blasting as loud as we could raise the volume as brothers and sisters stood around, laughing and talking with one another until each fraction of the day's sunlight had dropped beneath the horizon. For years, there was nothing like it.

The water smelled horrible, as usual. It was always in desperate need of cleansing, but that did not matter. Covering every corner of the concrete and grass surrounding the lake—and for at least a seven-block radius beyond that—

young and old, happy and anxious faces were looking for a good time. There would be many people of all colors, even Whites, there as well, celebrating with the sea of Black faces the beginning of summer.

From jazz music to the loud bass of hip-hop, the sound of voices rose and drifted somewhere among the trees that lined the city. The enticing smell of all preparations of chicken and fish warmed the hearts of those willing to stand in line for hours just to get a taste. With greasy fingers and huge containers of juice, the festival would be alive and kicking. We all came together to have the biggest cookout the city could handle.

Then the pigs shut it down like they habitually do to every freedom that Black people enjoy. Last year was the last year the city could enjoy the festival in the summer, as the tradition had dictated. Brothers and sisters were not aware of the fact that city officials had determined the summer attraction to be a haven for criminals and drugs. Instead of just letting us be happy, they insulted us—then tried to steal our celebration away by moving it to the fall. College students who went to school in other cities could no longer participate, and since many did not see the festival during its usual time in the summer, I guess they naturally assumed it to be gone forever.

Only a few of us caught word that there would still be a festival. And about three weeks ago, only those few actually walked the lake in an attempt to rekindle what we knew would eventually die altogether.

The music was not quite as loud, but the food still tasted incredible and the laughter still rose above it all. Conversation loomed of a countdown until there would be nothing at the lake to celebrate, but for a few hours, we just hung around and soaked in the smell of the earth.

I was there with my friend Laurie, a Haitian sister who had moved to California from New York about two years ago. We met at an underground meeting and have been good friends ever since. I have not fully recovered from all of the friendships that I have lost, but I could not deny her sense of humor and, of course, her willingness to participate in the struggle.

Laurie and I decided to go to the festival out of curiosity. We wondered the night before about whether the festival in the fall would be able to maintain its original feel, and whether the place would be swarming with pigs. If it were covered in midnight blue, we would have turned around in a heartbeat. But when we arrived, there were not enough pigs there for us to classify them as having "swarmed" the lake.

I decided before leaving the house that I would use this occasion to look good. For years I believed it superficial to pay attention to the way I looked, concentrating instead on building my temple of knowledge. Laurie thought that what was visible from the outside was a reflection of the inside, so I needed work. After looking in the mirror, I decided she had a point. I still looked like it was the seventies—maybe it was time for a change. Laurie convinced me to share her eye shadow, lipstick, and some brown powder that she said would even my skin tone. I was never a fan of makeup, but it did clean up my blemishes and make me look several years younger than I actually was. With the baseball cap on my head, I looked—and felt—like a different person. It was not as altering as a disguise, but it changed my look enough to make someone take a second look. And I have to admit, it was fun.

After swiftly walking past a few pigs who were standing at the entrance of the park adjacent to the lake, Laurie and I followed our ears and let the music guide us. It led us to the crowd of about sixty young brothers and sisters who had discovered their own way to rebel against the "new" festival.

"What is that?" Laurie asked.

"It looks like they're dancing," I answered.

"Yeah, but look at them, girl!"

"I see it."

"Wow, I haven't seen anything like this in years!"

A contrived path as deep and endless as a *Soul Train* line met my eyes. The bodies forming the dance showcase were barely touched by the goddess of age and wisdom, and they were the perfect vehicles of pure athletic dance. The sun kissed their bodies, and they thanked it by clapping to the rhythm of the music.

I watched them with great joy, remembering when my body could move into positions such as theirs without hours of subsequent aching. I was thrilled by their energy.

"Come on, girl, let's get in closer," I said, pulling Laurie's shirt so that she would be at my heels as we made our way toward the front row of the line.

Bodies rocked back and forth, which made our journey easier. The movement of the line naturally brought us closer, much in the way of a tidal wave. As we were swept in, the crowd jumped and started to shriek with pleasure. We could tell that someone was dancing his or her heart out in the center, but the tall brother in front of me was my obstacle to sharing in the delight of the crowd.

"Yeah, take it to back in the day! That's old school!" the brother yelled, while laughing hysterically and waving his fist in the air. This time his excitement cleared a path for me to stick my head in and take in the talent that was being coached on.

I caught sight of his body as he was landing from some acrobatic maneuver that brought his legs down from the air in a slow motion after what looked like a handstand. From that move, the brother grabbed ahold of his baseball cap and twisted it to the side, gliding his feet across the ground with more skill than Michael Jackson and with as much ease as a cartoon image. But this brother did not need any special computer graphics to make his moves impressive.

I moved in a little closer, to join the rhythmic clapping that molded the music to the wonderful contortions of his body, and came face to face with his sexuality. The dance move that he had chosen at that moment brought him inches from my face. It was a playful sensuality, and everyone close by laughed and cheered when he did it. That is, everyone but me.

"What's wrong, girl?" Laurie asked. "I know he's young enough to be your son, but he's fine, so don't let that scare you."

I could not move. There he was, right in front of my face, not knowing that it was me. I felt my smile fade, but no one else's did.

"Grab her, blood!" said the brother standing next to me. He moved away so that the brother dancing could easily grab my arms and pull me into the center of the path. I was in the dancing zone, but I was not interested in dancing.

I was more interested in the fact that the face staring back at me was Jason's. But apparently he had not taken a moment to recognize me. My new look must have thrown him off.

"Come on, lady . . . You scared of me or somethin'?" he asked, playfully twirling me around to the cheers of our audience.

"No," I said, and started to dance as best I could, trying to keep up with a dance that I had seen before, but not in recent years. We danced, but it was anything but playful. His gestures were filled with flirtation, like he really believed he held the secrets to a powerful, irresistible form of seduction. I was immune to him, though, at least to the part of him that lured women. I was not amused by the sexual overtones of his dance, but I was overcome by a strong remembrance of Peaches.

She used to dance at the drop of a nickel if a good song caught her attention. Never mind where she was or who was watching, Peaches was always ready to shake her butt. There were times when we were driving back to her corner that she would turn on my radio and start dancing in the car. Now, I'd seen people dance while sitting down, but none was as creative with the obvious constraints as Peaches. She did not care if she was sitting down, her leg would make it up in the air by the end of the song—even if she had to push the seat all the way back to create extra legroom.

I thought of Peaches as I danced with Jason, and part of me started to dance for her. I tried to imitate some of the moves that she used to do, but I could not replicate them with as much skill as she performed them. I caught a couple of stares and claps with some of those moves, but I knew the real inspiration. I wished that others had the opportunity I did to watch these dance moves at their inception.

"Okay, then," I said. "We can dance if you want to get down."

He did not recognize my voice at first, but as our time in the spotlight continued, I noticed him recognize my face as something familiar. But as we danced, our secular movements became spiritual, and we were possessed. Our possession was not of a person's spirit, but of a people's spirit. Our gestures were guided, and when I looked over at him, he was moving in slow motion—as was I. I tried to speak, but there was nothing that I could say. There were no words at that moment, just dance. Our dance. The magic between us was as if our ancestors had come to teach us a lesson, and we were being forced to comply.

I looked at his face and his was as confused as mine, but we verbally acknowledged nothing. We just kept our feet moving and searched for the spirits of the diviners and African deities who danced with us. We could not see them, but we could feel them. I knew I could feel them coursing through my veins and expressing themselves through my body. And I could tell by the look in his eyes that he felt them, too.

Somewhere in the middle of our act, between a peaked movement with the divinities of the other world and a quick meeting of our eyes, he let me know that he knew who I was. I raised my finger to my lips and incorporated a silent "shush" into my contribution to the dance. He nodded, choosing to honor my want to keep quiet at that moment.

Once our bodies were returned to us, he discreetly let me twirl my way back into the line, leaving room for another, much younger, woman to dance with him.

Laurie followed me through the crowd as I rushed through, wiping my brow of the sweat that had accumulated there and tucking in the stray hairs that had fallen out of the cap.

"Girl, you can't hang anymore, huh?" she asked.

"No, I guess not." I was not sure whether she would understand what had just happened. I knew that any explanation I gave to her would have to be thorough in order to satisfy her thirst for information. Like me, she was very inquisitive. But unlike me, she did not have so many skeletons to hide from the rest of the world, nor was she given the "gift" that Jason and I had apparently been given.

I looked back over to the crowd, which had dispersed with Jason's final dance move. I guessed that no one wanted to go after him in the *Soul Train* center. I could not blame them. No one could follow such a performance.

A crowd of young women swarmed to Jason like he was a superstar, complete with requests for autographs and phone numbers. He seemed to love all the attention and was happy to oblige. Still standing over to the side and only partially listening to Laurie's observations of the whole scene, I watched as one enamored girl after another caressed his arms, stroked his cheeks, and flirted with him.

"Why do you keep staring at him, girl?" Laurie asked.

Her question brought me out of my trance. I was staring at him, and it was difficult for me to stop. I was drawn to him, consumed by the desire to celebrate him, and to warn him of his looming danger if certain life choices did not change. Since he had walked out of my house, we had not spoken, but I knew he wanted to, because I was not the only one concerned by our second chance meeting.

The power of my name was at work, and I knew that God had led me to this brother again. I watched him collect at least ten phone numbers, but his eyes kept glancing my way. The energy between us was very thick, and we were still in the afterglow of our mystical brush with the Fantastic. Others walked through and continued to enjoy what remained of the festival, but Jason and I could not move. We were connected, but we were unsure of what to do about it.

Laurie tapped my shoulder to get my attention. She told me that she had to find a restroom and asked if I needed to go with her.

"No, I'm fine," I said, "but I'll be right here waiting for you."

"Yeah, I bet you will . . . Still staring at your little boyfriend."

I did not even cut her a glance to let her know how ridiculous I found her statement. Instead I kept my attention focused squarely on Jason.

After he had collected his last phone number from the crowd of adoring fans, he spoke into his friend's ear and moved slowly in my direction. I turned so that I could face him squarely as he approached me. My soul was calm, but as he moved in, the energy between us got stronger and stronger until he finally said:

"Why you keep followin' me?"

"What are you talking about, brother?"

He started to laugh, acknowledging a joke that I did not get.

"I'm just playin'," he said. "Anyway, you kind of a good dancer."

"Oh, *kind* of!"

"I ain't tryin' to slight you, but you know, I be doin' my *thang*."

"Yeah, I saw. You really have a lot of talent, brother. You know Peaches used to do her *thang*, too. You reminded me so much of her out there."

He looked to the ground and shifted his weight from side to side. He looked like he wanted to say something to me, but I wondered if he knew what it was. He had come to me, so I knew that the animosity that he had left my house with must have been fading.

"I didn't recognize you at first with that hat on," he said. "You got makeup on, too?"

"Yes, I do. What's the big deal? Can't a revolutionary wear lipstick?"

"Yeah, Chinaka . . ." he said, chuckling, "but you be all about the drama sometimes."

"Well, until I'm free, there will be drama."

"That's what I mean. Look at you! You're free!"

"Am I, Jason?"

I was always one to believe that functional paranoia preserved my life for all of those years. It was healthy.

"Hell yeah, you're free. You not in jail or nothin'. Nobody's after you . . ."

"Yes, but just because I'm not in a cage does not make me free. Anyway, I'm glad I ran into you. Have you given any thought to our conversation the other day?"

"No," he said quickly, looking straight into my eyes. He

stood there looking at me with all the defiance he could muster, but I knew he would not be standing in front of me if he had not been giving some of what I said any thought.

"You're lying," I said.

He turned to look at the crowd, but turned back to me quickly and asked how I figured that he was lying.

"Because I know you want me to think that you don't care about anything—not about your momma, not about your daddy, not even about yourself."

"No, I don't care about *hos*. That's what you need to think."

"Why do you want me to think that, brother? Sisters might be impressed by your dancing and your looks, sure. But that doesn't make them hos and it doesn't mean that you don't have to care about them. I've seen people stop caring. It's not pretty what that does to you as a human being."

"Chinaka, why are you trippin'? See, this is what happened the last time. You start off cool, then you start on this *shit*. That's why I left your house . . ."

"Speaking of which, when are you planning to call me or come back so that we can finish our conversation?"

He shrugged his shoulders. "I don't know if I am comin' back."

He seemed to revert to a little boy when I mentioned the visit to my house. I could see the ladies' man transform into someone who desperately wanted to be loved, and maybe I was the one tapped to give it to him. I never believed that he was looking for a sexual love. He was the proud recipient of such affection all the time. Instead I felt that he was in search of something deeper—the kind of love that would free him from the captivity that held him with more security than anything I had ever witnessed. His personal jail held him tighter than any government or law enforcement restrictions on my freedom, because it gripped on to his heart and would not let go. The jail he lived in did not restrict his body; it restricted his mind. And that was the worst.

"Well, I hope you do come back over, Jason. There is still a lot for us to discuss."

"Yeah, all right."

"I'm serious. I know you want me to forget that I found you, but I can't. I can't let you go now. And I know that you are determined to make me believe that you don't care about any of this, but I also know that if you've got any of Peaches in you at all, you care. You might try to fake it, but you really care about what happens to you."

"Look, I ain't never said that I don't care. You need to stop tryin' to tell me what to think."

"Fine, so I'll stop telling you what to think."

I folded my arms and smiled at him, which seemed to make him angry. He stepped back and looked at my entire stance before I finally conceded to his stare. I felt that it was more important to keep his ear than to run him away with my own stubbornness.

I knew that I came on strong, but again, ours was a relationship of urgency, and there was no word that could leave my mouth fast enough.

Something inside of me said that he was going to listen, too. It was almost as though he struggled to hear me, but—like his mother—wanted to hear about what built my world, and what could build his.

"You know, I do care about shit, Chinaka. And I'll tell you another thing." He paused to take a look around and twist his cap so that the bill was facing backward and I could see every feature of his face. "I love my momma with everything I got. I'm just . . . I'm from the ghetto and this is what I know."

"Hmmm."

"Anyway, forget about that."

"Okay, I'll try . . . for now."

"I came over here to see if you felt that crazy shit that happened out there."

"Of course I did."

He leaned in to whisper, "What was that?" then stepped back. He looked frightened by the experience and even more reluctant for anyone else to hear about it.

"Honestly, I think that was a sign for us, Jason. It was a sign that we're not done. You and I . . . we've got work to do."

"Damn, everything is serious with you, man."

"Well, what did you expect me to say?"

"I don't know . . . let's just forget it."

"If you think you can . . ."

"Anyway, I was surprised you could dance at all. I didn't know Black people like you ever danced or had fun, even though I see y'all got to wear hella makeup to do it."

"Hey, I do what I have to do. There's a time to laugh and a time to get serious. There are many serious things going on right now out here, brother. You've just got to start looking at them. Start noticing your enemies. Spot them and let it register. Then continue with your mission."

"I do what I got to do. But let me guess . . . you want to tell me about the *enemy*, right?"

"I thought you didn't want me telling you what to think anymore."

He smacked his lips, rolled his eyes, and walked away from me, mumbling something about how I ruined "it" and that he was not "messin' with" me anymore.

"Bye, Jason. Hope you stop by soon!" I yelled behind him.

He did not turn to acknowledge my parting words, but I knew that they had reached him. I did end up seeing him again after that meeting at the festival, and I knew I would. All I had were my instincts, and I trusted them. And again, when I looked at Jason, they chanted the war song of urgency in my heart.

His struggle was not easy, but something told me that he had enough strength to fight through whatever was really bothering him in order to reach his interest in redeeming his mother. Maybe he would accidentally redeem himself in the process.

I chuckled to myself because I saw humor in his frustration. I've always thought of frustration as a good thing. It does not do much for initiating change or creating balance in one's soul while it is there, but at least it demonstrated that the individual was wrestling with an issue. Jason was frustrated, but I felt that it was because of something much more important than my not being able to fill his appetite for learning about my relationship with his mother. And I did not think it had anything to do with my not flattering him the way every other woman that came into his life did.

What was intriguing about him was his spirit. I was drawn to him because of my love for his mother, but he was quickly carving a niche into my heart for himself.

His quiet but undeniable talent and magnetism were probably what attracted all the younger girls to him, but not me. I was attracted to the traces of the warrior left in his stare. And, of course, to the budding flame that kept him frustrated about being the person he had built for others to praise. I knew I could guide him.

I knew there had to be a way to strip away from him the layers of anger that had accumulated over the years. I knew I could get through to him if I could just get him to *believe* that he was more than what the ghetto told him he was. I wanted to beat at his door until something in his subconscious woke to the rhythm of my drum. I knew he wanted to hear my music, or he never would have come to me after our dance that day at the lake. I knew he was trying to quench his thirst for more.

Peaches was so entrenched in the lifestyle that she had chosen—and that had chosen her—that she could not let go of it in order to embrace a new way of life. She had decided that it would be too much energy to jeopardize her relationship with that pimp to leave him for what I had to offer her. But in Jason I saw an opportunity to fix her broken record.

He was badly scratched, but he emitted airs of promise. Maybe it was in the bounce that remained in his step, or the confrontational way in which he demanded answers to his questions. Whatever it was, it was calling me. He was calling me—to help him rediscover the revolutionary that he was born to be.

"Okay, I'm back," Laurie said, tying her sweater around her waist. "What did I miss?"

Still thinking about Jason, I took a deep breath and looked at the sky. We used to pray to God for liberation from slavery, and there I was trying to get a pimp-in-training to cleanse himself of the spirituals he sang for money. But I believed it could be done. We did not have a choice.

"Nothing. You didn't miss a thing. Let's get going before some pig decides to harass us for standing in the same spot too long."

"Oh, come on," she said, "where do you think we are, New York?"

"No . . . I think we're in Oakland."

Jesus

Baby Jesus:

You sound like you been doin' a lot of thinkin' lately. The way you lay out the pimpin' game is one way to look at it. We gots the same frame of mind as them big-timers downtown. We know what the Man be thinkin' so yeah, we one step ahead of the game.

Like I been tellin' you since birth, pimpin' ain't a way to pass the time. It's a callin', man, and if you feel it, then you ain't gonna be able to fight it. This game is a road to havin' some shit that really mean somethin', man. You can get whatever you want if you play it right. If your game is tight, hos will give you their lives, their souls. You won't ever have to spend another night wonderin' about how you gonna take care of yourself or

how you gonna pay for all the shit that makes you a
man. It's about makin' bread off of them muthafuckas out there who ain't gots no game. The streets
is a simple case of the strong crushin' the weak.
That's the only way to live, man. Watch your back.
Know who you gots on your team, but be ready to
defend what's yours.

Never forget. If you stay ready, you ain't gots
to get ready.

    ¬J

too beautiful for words

Jason

I pulled up to that curb holdin' the weight of the world on my chest. It was a weight so heavy that only little pockets of air could get through. My body was trippin' and I couldn't figure out what was happenin' to me. I'd had bad days before, so the fact that I was trippin' wasn't new. It was the *way* I was trippin' that had me sideways. Man, I was gettin' dizzy for, like, seconds at a time. Then it would disappear. Shit was crazy, but I was handlin' it.

I could see Jesus gettin' up real slow from his steps, but it was only a matter of seconds before he was sittin' next to me in the car, diggin' in his pocket for some shit that could get him high.

The seconds it took him to reach me was real seconds, too. But they felt like an eternity—enough time for the sight of his old, street-wise body to make the thoughts of my momma more intense. All I could picture was him walkin' around my momma's apartment when I was a kid, runnin' the place and makin' my momma turn into his personal servant. I mean, she turned into a different person *for real* whenever he was around. Back then, I couldn't stand his ass, but when he became all I had to lean on, I had to suck up those other feelings. It's always been like that. I always had to suck up my feelings, like they never mattered.

I always had to be the one sacrificin' everything just so everybody else could have the kind of life they wanted. I thought that was cool for me, but lately I been thinkin' about what I want, you know? It's bullshit that everybody else gets to have me the way they want me, and I don't get nothin' for myself. I got some shit going on, too.

Every second that passed by as he walked over to the car was like watchin' the world demand even more from me. I mean, between not bein' able to shake the feelin' that the world was breathin' down my neck about my momma and *not* bein' able to shake Jesus, I was dealin' with some issues. This was the first time I was seein' him since I was a little kid—since the night he killed my momma. It was tough.

Then I saw her. I know I did. I tried to close my eyes and make the shit disappear, but it didn't go nowhere. I could hear the keys go clink on the table and the shouts and screams for a Jesus to help her. I saw her body laid out on the floor. I could hear the sirens and the mobile bed. I could see the badges and squad cars. Shit, I could smell the blood. But I had trouble gettin' used to the image.

Maybe that's 'cause it wasn't supposed to be that way. In movies and TV shows, it's always the other way around. It's always the momma who be watchin' the police wheel the body of her dead son away. She's always the one who got to cry into the sleeve of a neighbor or somethin' 'cause she got to deal with the fact that her son is dead.

You know the scene. The son was probably in some dirt, usually a hustler or doin' somethin' in the dope game. The father usually ain't nowhere to be seen—or if he is around, he'd be drunk as fuck. After the momma fights her way through the crowd of cops, she starts cryin' and pullin' at the people around her—you know, neighbors and strangers—to get out of her way so she can get closer to her son. Everything she do is to get closer to the body of her dead son. Yeah, that's how it usually go.

You don't never see it the other way around—not on TV anyway. People don't want to see a young boy watch his momma get rolled away by the same cops who got paid off by the man who killed her. They don't want to know what it feels like to watch the emergency team search for a way to cover a boy's dead momma from him, just to stand there helpless 'cause there ain't no way to hide a plastic hand in her face. Ain't no way to hide blood on the floor or the broken tooth I found in the corner that night before the police officers took me away from the apartment. Ain't no way to hide that shit, and there really ain't no cool way to live with it.

For the last fifteen years I been tryin' to get over how I never got a chance to pay my final respects. I mean, they never even gave her a funeral. Yeah, it took me a minute to be able to handle that one. She may not have been much to other people and shit, but she was my momma. She meant the fuckin' world to me. I spent all these years bein' hard and tryin' to convince myself that shit ain't matter. I said I wanted to be a pimp so I could be the one controllin' muthafuckas. That way I couldn't ever be the one gettin' played.

And shit made sense—a whole lot of sense to a nigga like me. I mean, what else did I have?

For real, I thought I was doin' cool since my bills was gettin' paid, with enough left over for a haircut and line every three days. I mean, bein' a hustler is what made it possible for me to see my twenty-first birthday. Other muthafuckas I know ain't been that lucky.

My looks and my game are my lucky charms. That's my payoff for havin' to star in this fucked-up game of life. And it ain't like niggas in the ghetto was the only ones usin' what they was born with to make life a little more manageable. I mean, a nigga did have a TV in them group homes. I watched the Fonz sport a leather jacket and snap his fingers for ten fine-ass, big-tittie skeezers to be at his hip. Shit, they used to *run* to be next to that fool. Game is everywhere, and the only ones who was makin' it where I came from was those who could spit it the best. I used to feel sorry for myself, but I had to shake that feelin'.

After my momma died, I spent most of my time alone, except for the few hours here and there that I spent half-ass listenin' to them church people—and them Muslims—who would come around me preachin' all kinds of pimpisms in the form of some religion. I ain't really see no difference between what they was hollerin' and what Jesus was doin' to my momma, so that shit got boring after a while. I had heard it all before.

Don't get me wrong. I believe there's a God, but you know, I have to wonder what blood be thinkin' sometimes. I mean, my momma got a cross hangin' around her neck in that picture I have, and I remember her with it when she was alive. She had pictures of Jesus all over the house and even fell for a pimp with the same name. I remember havin' to say my prayers before she let me hit the sack, but after she died, I just couldn't bring myself to pray no more.

The way I saw it, why pray to a God that never answered when I had a Jesus who wrote me every month? I mean, I only saw one Jesus tryin' to help me stay alive in the ghetto. Sometimes I would just sit alone and wonder if people was wrong about God and what He was really supposed to be about.

"See, young brother, you got to stop lettin' the white man control your life." That's what them Muslims used to say when they came to the block. They was a trip, with them bow ties and tight-ass suits. But they was kind of cool. At least they seemed to want to get us out of there. They would come walkin' up to us on the corner talkin' loud and hookin' us up with bean pies and newspapers.

"Say, brothers," they used to say, "standing on the corner doing nothing with your life is the plan of the white man. It's part of the white man's plan to keep the black man idle while the rest of the world continues to progress."

We would always just look at them and say somethin' to make them think we was feelin' where they was comin' from, but for real, we was just sayin' whatever they needed to hear to get them out of there. It was cool for them to spend *their* lives livin' by the teachin' of a man they never knew, but what they was spittin' didn't always make sense to the fools on my block. Their political and hustler "isms" we understood, but we could have done without that religion shit.

That's why I never really understood why my momma was so hung up with the church. I mean, I never got a chance to really ask her what was goin' on in her mind when she was talkin' to them pictures on the wall. I used to spend hours sittin' around, squeezin' my eyes and racin' my brain tryin' to remember what she used to say when she was talkin' to them. I remember watchin' her from the bedroom, 'cause most of the time she only talked to them when she thought she was alone. But I watched her. I never thought she was crazy, though. I just wanted to know what she was sayin' to them.

Don't ask me what she even saw in them pictures anyway. One was of some white man who was supposed to be the son of God, you know? I used to look at that picture and trip off how he had half the world prayin' to Him to make their lives better. I used to trip off how the same thing was goin' on with the Jesus that was my daddy. That nigga had *all* the hos on the street—including my momma—prayin' to him. And when I was tryin' my damndest to hate that muthafucka for what he did to my momma—and to me—I couldn't. Believe me, I *tried*. But I couldn't.

See, him and his game was all I knew my whole life. He had to be right about somethin' to have half the West prayin' to *him*, or at least the money he was bringin' in—even from jail. I couldn't hate the only nigga who bothered to write me letters. I couldn't hate the muthafucka who was teachin' me how to survive in my hell.

Jesus always be sayin' that things ain't always cut and dry. And he's right. Life don't always make sense like you want it to, and even when you try to stay in control of it, you ain't always gonna win every time. The ghetto got all kinds of loopholes and ditches. If a muthafucka ain't careful, he could get stuck.

I was thinkin' about all that shit last night, in the two seconds it took Jesus to get up from his steps and get in my car.

Like I said, the seconds was creepin' by, and my head was spinnin'.

Part of me wanted to mash my foot on the gas and get out of there, but not 'cause I was scared. I ain't never been no scary nigga. My mind was just trippin' and I needed a minute to get it all together. But I knew there wasn't no time for all that, so I just had to adjust. I had to let the night just run its course. All Jesus had to do was to hurry up and get in the damn car.

I leaned over and unlocked the door. Jesus took his time openin' it, fumblin' a little with the door. It was almost like he was lookin' for me to get out and open that muthafucka for him. I ain't the doorman, though, so he had to do that shit hisself.

"What up, Jesus," I said.

"Yeah, nigga . . . let's go," he said when he finally got into the car. He reached out to pull in the door. He let it slam shut.

"Yeah . . . Okay."

He didn't even seem fazed with this bein' the first time he was seein' me in fifteen years. I didn't want to be the only one trippin' off that, so I didn't say shit to him about it. I did look at him, though. I could see why people said we looked alike. I got his eyes, his nose, and his lips. Shit, I got his face! But his was old-lookin'. He was missin' a tooth, and he looked out of shape—surprisin' for a nigga comin' out the joint. He didn't look at all like what I thought he would look like. He looked tired and old.

I had the beats goin' in the car, bumpin' a mixed tape that I made a few years ago from that "Born to Mack" Too Short record and some of that NWA from back in the day. I remember when I made the tape. I used to listen to this tape whenever I was tryin' to just chill—you know, and vibe off of how these niggas must have been followin' me to get my story, then go back to the studio and put it on wax. They wasn't talkin' about nothin' but my life. I mean, all them skeezers them rappers used to brag about, I was gettin', too. That tape I had in there was like my theme music.

Jesus used to write me and tell me how he didn't like rap, even though if he had actually listened to the words, he would have tried to take my tape for his own collection in a heartbeat. He was bobbin' his head though, so I knew he didn't mind the music.

"So, where you want to go, nigga?" He said it slow and looked in the rearview mirror.

Before I could even answer his question about where we could mob, he reached into his pocket and pulled out a little package of foil. Inside the foil, I could see the weed and hop he was about to smoke. I wasn't trippin' when he pulled it out. I mean, I didn't smoke that shit, but who was I to tell another grown-ass man what to do with his body? I did look in the rearview mirror, though. I had to make sure we wasn't bein' followed. There will always be one thing that eats away at my skin, man—and that's the police.

There ain't a black man in the ghetto who like the police. It ain't like it's 'cause we a bunch of criminals and shit. It's more like, them muthafuckas are probably the worst gang that ever existed. All you see around my 'hood is crooked cops who don't do nothin' but drive around and find another nigga to lock up. I be doin' what I can to stay out of their line of fire. A nigga might not wake up from that blaze. That's why I checked the mirror and rolled down the window. If there was heat, at least my shit wouldn't smell like what Jesus was smokin'.

He stopped askin' questions about where we was goin' but I had my foot on the gas and took off toward the freeway.

"Yeah, baby. Let's ride," he said.

I didn't say nothin' back to him. Instead I just looked at him. Part of me wanted to laugh at him for callin' me "baby," but Jesus was from the old school. He always talked in that seventies slang and shit. I guess I couldn't blame him. He was up in jail for most of the eighties and nineties, and I knew all he really had was his memories.

Jesus was grinnin' from ear to ear. He seemed so happy to get to what was cased in that foil. His fingers was movin' fast—faster than I thought fingers could move—to roll up that dope. But he rolled it, all with that one hand, too. I guess he was used to doin' it that way. He looked like he had been waitin' to smoke that shit all night.

"Hey, baby. Hope you ain't insulted by these vapors," he said, and lit it up.

"Naw," I said, and I pressed down harder on the gas. I wasn't finna mash too fast, 'cause the registration tags on my car wasn't right. But I wanted to get the hell off of his block.

Jesus' head was noddin' and his eyes was rollin' around. Part of me was happy to watch him destroy hisself, but there's somethin' cold-blooded in watchin' a dope fiend find his heaven. I mean, it ain't exactly a bedtime story. They smile like they happy, but if you look close that ain't happiness you lookin' at, it's somebody who come so close to death they forget about everything else. But like I said, it ain't easy to watch a nigga die—even if he think he is foolin' his mind into thinkin' somethin' else is going on.

Anyway, I had to keep my eyes on the road, so that kept me from havin' to watch too much of it. The rain was fallin' pretty heavy by then, so my old windshield wipers was makin' a squeaky sound. The drizzle that was happenin' early on was gettin' angry. It was startin' to pour.

Jesus didn't notice a thing, though. He was laid back in the passenger seat with his prosthetic arm propped on the armrest and his other one limp in his lap. His leather coat was hangin' off his shoulders and his head was slowly movin' up and down.

"Cool, man . . . cool," he said to hisself.

Right. Cool. I watched him from the corner of my eye, just tryin' to peep how he would come down—or up—off of that trip. He lifted his head up and gave me a strange grin. This was the man I thought could rescue me from that nightmare I lived in as a kid.

"Nigga, I'm your daddy, right?" he asked.

"Yeah," I said. Then after glancin' at the blankness in his eyes, I said, "You been schoolin' me since birth."

"And you *still* earnin' that pimpstick!"

True, I was still in school to be a hard-core pimp like him, but I had been graduated from the kind of school I really needed to survive in this world. I had already figured mostly everything out. All he was doin' was fillin' in the blanks. But I don't think he would ever admit it.

I kept drivin', promisin' him that the place where we was going was finna be filled with bitches. He seemed happy that I would show him my pimpin' skills. But my head was burnin' with the words of everybody who had somethin' to say about pimpin'. My girl said she wasn't gonna raise Dominic around me if I took pimpin' to the level we all knew that I could. She threatened to take him away from me if I ever got caught up in the life for real.

Then I had Chinaka on my mind. She was a drama queen—funny how I seemed to pull them—but she was cool. It's a trip how a lady I just met a month ago seems to know me better than all the people I done known my whole life. She got so much to say about this world, and most of it I don't get. But I listen to her anyway, 'cause my momma did. My momma used to know her.

"Let's go to Frisco," I said to Jesus, who was still feelin' hisself for knowin' the secrets of the pimpin' game. I kept it friendly to keep him out of my grill, but my head was still spinnin'.

He nodded and kept lookin' out the window at the rain. I kicked up the speed of the car and headed toward the tollbooth. All night I had been listenin' to what everybody else had to say about my life—and about me. I had to get out of Oakland so I could hear my own voice for a minute. I just had to hear *myself* think.

I tried to let my mind wander to a time when shit wasn't so crazy, but I couldn't think of no time that was like that. I ain't sayin' that I've never had a minute to just chill, but it seemed like even then, I was always into *somethin'*. Most of all—maybe it's 'cause we was on our way to Frisco—I kept thinkin' about what happened last week when I was out in the Fillmore with this one ho, Tina.

We was standin' on a corner on McAllister in front of a liquor store just chillin'. There was a couple of fools out there, but they wasn't trippin' off me. They was too busy sellin' rocks to be trippin' off me. I mean, we was cool. You know, we traded a few words, but for the most part, they was doin' they thing, and I was doin' mine.

Tina had been hoin' for a while, but she hadn't chose nobody yet. I wasn't trippin' off her that bad. She would come over to the apartment when Jackson was at her momma's house and I would have her walkin' around in a thong and pumps cleanin' up the place. Sometimes she would give me some money just 'cause she said she liked me and thought I was hella cool. She ain't done nothin' for me, but I was keepin' her around to see if she had potential. But shit, if she was finna choose somebody and get serious, then I wanted to be the one to take her money.

At first, I couldn't figure out why she was so quiet. Tina could talk your ear off, but that night, she was quiet—just standin' around lookin' hella suspect. I figured out why when this pimp from around that way started trippin'. He came up on us like a snake, suckin' his teeth when he talked and eyein' me like I owed him money or somethin'. I wasn't finna go out like no sucka, so I stopped talkin' to that ho and looked back at him. I didn't recognize him, but that didn't matter. There wasn't too many fools I did recognize from Frisco.

"What you lookin' at, nigga?" I said.

"Yo' shirt . . . that shit say 'Player, ' right?"

I didn't have to look at my shirt to know what it said, and I sure didn't need nobody to read it for me.

"What about it, nigga?"

He laughed, so I was startin' to get mad. I wasn't botherin' him. I was talkin' to that bitch Tina—who moved close to the wall of the store like she was tryin' to hide—and he came over to *me*. He was all in *my* mix.

"Tina, what's up, baby?" he said. I ain't know what to say at that. He wasn't talkin' to me no more, but to that bitch. Then I tripped off how he just ignored my question like *I* was the bitch.

"Aw . . . hell naw, nigga!" I turned my back to Tina so I could see his whole face. I know he could tell that I was gettin' fired up.

To tell you the truth, I was hella scared. Even though I was probably only, like, ten minutes away from the West, I was in Frisco with none of my potnas, about to have funk with *this* muthafucka. I ain't know him for shit, and I didn't know where his potnas was, or how many of them could come around the corner and jump me. But I kept my poker face, and just stared at him. I wasn't finna go out like no sucka. I'm from the city where they pop they collars. She was about to choose me. Fuck that nigga. He was a hater.

He stared back, then looked at my shirt again. Then, real slow-like, he said, "Player . . . that kinda sounds like a word in Spanish that mean 'beach.' Kinda sounds like 'bitch,' don't you think?"

"What?!" I said. I stepped back and raised my hands. "You want somethin', nigga?"

"Naw . . . I don't want shit from no *bitch*."

I didn't say shit else. I jumped at the chance to kick his ass, 'cause I wasn't finna be no more "bitches." I swung at him, and he swung back. I landed some, and he landed some. Nobody jumped in to stop that shit, and so it got wild. Matter of fact, everybody had crossed the street and was watchin' from over there. I landed a hard one to his nose, and I know that shit stung bad, 'cause he closed his eyes and backpedaled until he stumbled to the ground. I had already spotted a bottle, so I jumped at the chance to grab it so I could break it over his head.

I turned around to get the bottle, but when I turned around, he was lookin' at me. He was wobblin', but he had his hand in his pocket like he was finna pull somethin' out of there. I wasn't sure what it was, but I was hopin' it wasn't no gun. I could fight a knife, especially since I had the bottle in my hand. But a gun? My piece was tucked in my car. All I had right then was what was in my hand.

"Hey, man . . . what you trippin' on?" I asked. I didn't even know what I was fightin' him for really. I mean, I figured it had somethin' to do with Tina, but shit, he took it too far when he called me a "bitch."

"Hey, man . . . that's my girl you Mackin'," he said.

"Aw shit, you fightin' me over *that* bitch?"

I laughed and lowered my hands. I ain't know that Tina had a muthafucka who was willin' to fight me over her ass. That was crazy. But what was crazier was me fightin' back. I didn't want to fight over no bitch—especially one that gave it up for free to muthafuckas on both sides of the bay.

"I ain't fightin' over her, man. She already mine," he said. "I'm just trippin' off how much of a bitch you is to be over here Mackin' her on my set!"

"Aw man . . . I ain't too proud to leave. You just came at me wrong, blood. That's all you had to say in the first place . . ."

He didn't say nothin' back, but I was sure it wasn't over. I backed away, but I still had a tight grip around the neck of that bottle. I stopped talkin', 'cause what I was sayin' wasn't doin' no good no how. I spit on the street and looked at him again.

"Hey," he said. "Ain't that muthafucka Jesus yo' daddy?"

I spit again and asked why he was askin'.

"'Cause I'm just wonderin' if he know how much of a bitch his son turned out to be."

"Muthafucka, call me a bitch again, and I'ma kill you."

I wasn't knowin' how I was gonna do it, but I was mad enough to find a way. This nigga was trippin'. He didn't know me.

"Man, Slim my uncle. And you over here tryin' to Mack *my* ho."

"Your *ho!*" Tina jumped in it. "I ain't *nobody's* ho, mutha-fucka . . ."

"Shut up, bitch!" he yelled.

"Yeah, Tina . . . shut up." I had to think for a minute, 'cause if he was really Slim's nephew like he was sayin', he had a way to get his faulty information to Jesus before I could reach him. The only way I had to get in touch with Jesus was letters. Everybody knew that Jesus and Slim was potnas from back in the day, and the last thing I needed was for me to be the cause of bad blood between them. Especially not over no ho like Tina.

"Look, I said I ain't know!" I said. At this point, I just wanted to get in my car, get my gun in hand, and get on the fuckin' bridge. But it was too late. Fools was startin' to gather around like we was the sideshow or somethin'. We was lookin' crazy out there tryin' to work things out over that bitch, so I decided to make a move and think about it later. I threw the bottle at him and it broke at his foot. I ain't expect to hit him. I was just tryin' to make a distraction so I could get to my car.

I made it to the car, but then I heard a few pops and it felt like somebody had lit a match under my skin. My shoulder and my chest was burnin', but I knew I had to get the hell out of there. I didn't see no blood, but it was gettin' hot under my collar.

"Jason! Jason!" Tina was yellin' at me. She came runnin' over to the car, but I knew I ain't had no time to be playin' around with her. "Oh, my God," she said, "Is you okay? I ain't mean for you to get shot . . ."

"Bitch . . . get away from me. Just get away . . ."

I jumped in the car and started the engine. I wasn't sure where I was finna go, but I was sure I wanted to live. I was just hopin' there wasn't no traffic on the bridge.

Jesus

"I ain't trippin' off that shit, man," Jason sayin' to me as we rollin' up to the line at the tollbooth. "Bitches ain't shit."

"I hear you talkin', man."

"Jesus . . . Blood . . . this is more than just talk. I know what went down between you and my momma wasn't personal."

"Nothin' in this world I do be personal, man. You get that?"

"I always knew that bitches had to be kept in their place, blood."

"That's cause I'm your daddy, nigga!"

I believe him when he say he not finna start actin' up about what happened between me and his momma. I really don't like talkin' about that shit, but at least he know that what went down between me and Peaches was business. I'm sorry she had to die, 'cause I never meant to hurt Jason. I mean, damn! He *is* my son. Pimpin' is cold-blooded, but I ain't a robot, you know. Everything I do be about business, but not everything be cut and dry.

"Jason, our business be takin' muthafuckas to some crazy places." I'm finna tell him the real deal with this pimpin' game.

He ain't comin' into this game all half-assed, representin' me. And he ain't finna get knocked out by somebody whose game is tighter than his. Nobody should have tighter game than this bloodline. Nobody.

"What happened between me and Peaches, man, I didn't want that to happen. But the secret to bein' a pimp ain't really no secret at all. It's more like a test."

"How you mean?"

"I mean, you finna always be tested on how far you willin' to go to protect what's yours. To protect your bread. Bitches gots to be kept in their place, man. That's number one. Ain't nothin' more crucial than makin' sure your ho don't get out of line."

"Hell naw . . . nothin' is more important than that."

That's some good shit. This boy already understands the fundamentals. Really, everything else is about how much he was born with. He finna be cold. I know he gots what it takes. This boy here next to me is a winner. I can feel it. He's in a class that people ain't ready for. Shit, I might be able to retire sooner than I thought with this pretty muthafucka.

Jason looks just like me. I read all them letters where he would tell me about how girls was tellin' him the same shit they used to tell me. But damn! I never thought lookin' at him would be like lookin' in a mirror twenty-five years ago. The only thing different about my face and his face is the hair. He keeps his close to his head, and I let mine hang. But shit, if he keep his money as close as his haircut, then he'll be all right.

"Number two, don't let nobody else in your shit," I say.

"For *sho'*."

Yeah, this muthafucka finna be right. Once he gots the full swing of the Mack Commandments and gets sworn into the life of a true Mack, he'll be able to recite the words of the true player prophets. I already know my boy ain't no snitch, and that he understands the basic tenets of this here life. Yeah, he'll get the language later on.

Damn, Jason gots the music poundin' up in here. This beat feels good, though, especially after years of havin' nothin' in the joint. Ain't nothin' like the rhythm of a song, man. And this boy knows how to handle his car, too. It ain't like the car is pimped out and flashy like some of the rides I done had. But it's doin' enough to stay afloat. Part of the natural charm this boy gots is the way he don't even try and he *still* gets farther than some who been at this game awhile. Oh, yeah, he finna be all right.

"Here, put this in there," I'm handin' him the Gladys Knight CD I just gots from them young hos. He's lookin' at it like I'm handin' him a dead rat or some other nasty shit.

"What's that?"

"It's Gladys, nigga," I can't believe he don't recognize this cover. "See, that's what's wrong with y'all these days."

"Aw . . . blood, I know who Gladys Knight is."

"You think you do, but I bet all you know is one muthafuckin' song. Y'all don't know nothin' about sweet young Gladys with the lips of a goddess and curves like them streets windin' around the mansions in them hills."

He's laughin', but I'm serious. He's puttin' the CD in now, but I can tell he ain't really sold.

"See, you gots to listen to the beauty in her voice, baby. Can't nobody sing like Gladys. Now, your momma . . . she came close."

I don't even know why I'm talkin' about Peaches. I ain't talked about her in a long time. Maybe it's 'cause lookin' at Jason all grown up gots me thinkin' about her. Ain't that a bitch!

Fuck it, though. She did what she was put on this Earth to do, and that was to give me a Baby Jesus. Fuck her.

We at the front of the toll line now, and we ridin' up to the attendant booth. I can see this fat girl in there, lookin' out at the short line of cars leadin' up to us. Jason ain't even seen her yet, but we about to have some fun.

"Look there," I say. "See that girl up there in the booth?"

"Yeah, what about her?"

"Put your money away."

"Why? You finna Mack your way through the toll?"

"Naw, nigga. You is."

He's laughin', but I'm serious.

"Look at her eyes, man." If I keep talkin', this nigga finna be spoonfed.

"Yeah, I see them."

"Man, look at that bitch. She ain't never had nobody who looks half as good as you come up to her fat ass. See how she don't even look up from that register, man? She gots problems lookin' in people's eyes already, nigga. She's a perfect candidate."

"Blood, she's fat."

"So? I ain't sayin' fuck her. I'm sayin' get us to Frisco."

He's noddin' now, like he understand. He claims he gets it. He's even sayin' it now, talkin' about the way them bitches be fiendin' for some attention.

"Do what you gotta do then, nigga," I say.

We pullin' up to the booth now, and Jason's startin' to put it to this girl.

"Say, baby . . ." He startin' it off like all the players do. I ain't finna listen to everything he gots goin' on right now. A Mack needs some room, baby—and I ain't finna be the one to crowd the young cat.

Well, we're pullin' away now, headin' over to the bridge. He's all smiles and shit, like he just did somethin'. His game was all right, but there ain't no need to get all excited.

"Not bad, there, young player."

"I knew I could get through."

"I knew you could, too, but don't get too happy. What you did was cool, but remember, a *real* pimp gets paid for his game. That was just one step up from parking-lot pimpin', baby."

"Aw, fuck that, nigga. I did get paid . . . sort of."

"Aw, nigga . . . I ain't talkin' about no *two dollars'* worth of game."

I'm talkin' about the real shit. I'm talkin' about the kind of game that gets your Cadillac turned out and your suit tailored to perfection—all with cold, hard cash, baby. Two-dollar bitches ain't nothin' but trouble. For one, they usually talk back and give their pimp a hell of a time, and that shit don't ride in this camp. Them cheap hos don't really believe they worth nothin', so they act like it. I need a bitch who feel like her pussy is gold. That way she'll be happy to demand gold before she serves it up.

"I was jokin'," he sayin' now. But a pimp that's big-time don't even joke about havin' no two-dollar hos. We gots our minds on the big prize—the major leagues. Bread don't wait around for no sucka, and it's our job to weed all of them out to create more for us. This some big pimpin' we after, baby.

"I ain't finna quit pimpin'," I say. I'm tellin' him about this thing here. "'Cause this is where the world is headin', man."

"Is that right?"

"Hell yeah, man. The pimpin' we do is only part of the big game that the world sees. Folks been lovin' me 'cause of my name for years. And that's cool. I can live with that. But all that says to me is that there's more than prayin' goin' on in them churches. Think about it, man. How powerful would my game be if the church wasn't already Mackin' the minds of these hos?"

He's noddin' like he gets what I'm talkin' about.

Some of them fools in jail would try to tell me about how the churches be out there bad, workin' folks for their bread and their souls. Yeah, them Muslims used to come onto my cell block hollerin' shit about the white man's God and the black man's God. Wasn't none of them about my God—the green God. Shit, that's what all this shit is really about—them little green men starin' back at me from that paper, man. Don't nothin' else make a goddamn difference.

Like *I* said, real pimps get paid. Now, you show me the man who flashin' his bread around this world, and I'll show you the pimp inside of him. Jason was right when he wrote in that letter about them big-time oil companies, them big-time companies on Wall Street—all that shit—bein' the pimps of the *world*. Us? We just do what we can to hold our place down in this game. But I can see how shit goes down in this world. I know what's goin' on.

"See, nigga . . . I ain't had to change my name for this pimpin' game. Them hos know what this is all about. They be comin' to me with tithes and offerings. You ain't gots to keep hos on dope if they think what they do is holy."

"You a fool, blood."

"A muthafuckin' breaded fool, nigga. See, when you gots it all together, you don't need no dope, and you don't need no liquor to get them hos devoted to you. That's my philosophy, baby. That's what keeps my game pristine."

We crossin' the Bay Bridge now, and the rain is violent out here. This shit is beautiful. I can't really see the water splashin' around from this weather, but I can hear it. And I love it, too.

Damn, the view from this bridge is the thing about Frisco. Muthafuckas always hollerin' about the Golden Gate Bridge. Shit, that muthafucka don't gots squat on the Bay Bridge. Man, comin' from Oakland, you get the best view of them lights in Frisco. Ain't none of them stiff suits workin' this time of night, but you can always count on the lights from them buildings to brighten up the sky—even in all this rain.

"So you sayin', then, that you ain't never considered leavin' the life?" he askin'.

I ain't finna lie to the boy. When I was first gettin' started, I thought I should have been doin' other things, but only 'cause of the threat of goin' to jail. My attitude about that changed when I went to Chicago and realized that them police officers be down for you as long as they get their cut.

And the only other time I ever reconsidered bein' in the life was when I first gots to the joint. Spendin' them first few nights up in that place can make the hardest, coldest mutha-fucka wonder what the hell he was thinkin' about to get his-self up in there.

"But I wouldn't change nothin', man," I say. I said it with some authority, too, 'cause I want this boy to know. "For *nothin'*, man."

"You ain't never thought about, like, folks risin' up against all this? I mean, what would you do if people stopped buyin' into the pimpin' game?"

"Nigga, is you crazy?! People ain't finna never stop wor-shippin' prostitution, man."

"I'm sayin though, what if there *was* a revolution and bitches . . . women . . . started, you know, flashin' and didn't want to be hos no more? What would happen then?"

"First of all, bitches ain't never finna stop hoin'. It's the world's oldest profession. People will always want to fuck, baby. That's the way of the Maker. And anyway, there's always finna be them straight-edge muthafuckas who don't have no game on their own, but gots bread and willin' to pay for the ass. You'll see for yourself. When you gots bread on one side and the need for game on the other, baby, you gots pimpin'."

"But . . ."

"Nigga, what's with these 'buts', man? I thought you had it all together, but now I'm startin' to think you ain't really understandin' what this is all about."

"I get it, blood. I'm just tryin' to ask some questions . . ."

Where is all this shit comin' from, anyway? He goin' on about how he don't think there will ever be a "revolution" as long as pimpin' is on the minds of the people who don't gots shit. And I'm hearin' what he sayin'. I done heard it all before.

But comin' from him, this shit concerns me.

"Player, who you been talkin' to?"

"I been talkin' to everybody. I'm a friendly guy."

He's laughin', but I'm serious.

Shit, I see now that's finna be his problem. He obviously been talkin' to the wrong people.

"I'm just messin' with you. But seriously, did you ever know about this lady named Chinaka? She was my momma's friend . . ."

What the hell is this? Forget what that boy's sayin' now, I ain't never heard of nobody named "Chinaka" . . . or whatever. And I knew *all* of Peaches' friends. Her friends was my friends. She didn't have no friends of her own.

"Naw . . . wait. Who is this bitch you talkin' about?"

"Chinaka. She's hella cool, actually. But thing is, she used to be one of them Black Panthers . . ."

"Aw, hell naw!"

I *know* he must be testin' me. Like I said, I knew *all* of Peaches' friends, and I made sure my girls stayed away from them Black Panther bitches. They wasn't nothin' but trouble to my bitches, and even worse to the pimpin' game, 'cause them bitches believed muthafuckas didn't need no money. And some of them thought they was men—tryin' to control shit! Them *bitches* was fightin' and carryin' pieces like they ain't need *no* men. I would never have no parts of somethin' like that, and it don't sit too good with me that Jason is.

Naw, I ain't never heard of this Chinaka bitch, but she must be scopin' my shit and lyin' on Peaches. She probably just tryin' to get into the pimpin' game like some other bitches out there who think they gots enough game to handle another bitch. Some of them other pimps dig that shit. They think it's cute, but I don't. I don't like to see no bitch controllin' shit, especially a gun.

From what I can see, this Black Panther bitch already been workin' on gettin' Jason in her corner. And she probably did her job, and did some research on our family. Shit, she must be tryin' to get to me. That's the only thing that make any sense. I just can't see Peaches sneakin' behind my back with some strange bitch I never knew. I'm finna have to let him know.

"... and she been hollerin' about how one day there will be a revolution ..."

"Nigga, hold on." I gots to sit up in this seat for this one. My music is startin' to skip, but I can't be bothered with that right now. Ain't nothin' more annoyin' than a wishy-washy muthafucka—especially one that's tryin' to waste my time. This boy gots to get his priorities straight.

If he finna put his heart into the pimpin' game, then I can respect that he gots some questions and shit, but all this bitch quotin' he doin' gots no place in the life.

"You second-guessin' the life, baby?"

"Naw, I'm just conversatin'."

"Well, this game been livin' this long without you ... and I sure hope you not tellin' me I been wastin' my time all these years ..."

"Naw, blood. Calm down. I was just conversatin'."

"Well, you doin' the wrong kinda conversatin', boy. You might as well drop this shit, 'cause there won't never be no 'revolution.'"

And I mean that—there won't. Muthafuckas don't gots enough energy for that shit, man. We been there. Done that. Niggas tried to fight that war. They lost.

"Even for women?"

"Bitches ain't never finna put their lives on the line just so another man can keep them broke while the bitches look bad, man. They be choosin' this life 'cause they get treated good. They get sex. They love sex. Bitches don't love dyin' for a nigga. They love fuckin' him."

"Is that right?"

"Hell, yeah, that's right! Pimpin' is *it* for the world, man. Other muthafuckas disguise the shit. They get up, put on a stiff-ass suit, come downtown and walk into buildings that gots other muthafuckas' names on the outside, and feel like they doin' somethin' special. Shit, all they doin' is gettin' pimped."

"I know . . ."

"And it makes them feel good. They can brag about how they work for 'such and such, ' while the big boss man sittin' back in his chair with two or three bitches suckin' his dick while he countin' the money his 'director' and 'adviser' of whatever done just made for him."

"I know . . ."

"We ain't doin' nothin' that the rest of the world ain't doin', Jason. You gots to hear me on this one, 'cause the one thing you gots to know is that we just doin' enough to get our piece of this American pie, nigga. We not hurtin' them bitches. Fuck a bitch. We run our own society to get bread from our community's natural assets, man."

"Yeah, I know. This is what she . . . um . . . this is capitalism for real."

"Look, nigga. Call it what you want to, man. It's called makin' money to stay breaded."

"Makin' money on those people with lesser game."

Now he startin' to sound like the muthafucka who been writin' me for almost fifteen years talkin' about how he serious about pimpin'.

"That's the way it works, man, 'cause there will always be muthafuckas with no game, baby."

"And there will always be somethin' out there for them, right?"

Always. There's somethin' out there for everybody. We just gots to find out where it is.

"There's only two ways to live in the ghetto, Jason."

"Oh, I know, blood. Sink or swim."

"And with me as your daddy, you gots the best strokes to stay alive, baby."

He's laughin', but I'm serious. Things ain't finna change no time soon, and they ain't finna change no time in my lifetime.

"I ain't really trippin' as long as I got what I need . . ." he's sayin'.

". . . to keep the bankroll thick, baby."

I'm tryin' to tell this boy—it's all about the bread. It's all about the paper, what them boys out there callin' "dead presidents" or "ends." That's the way this shit has been set up. Who are we to think we can change this shit? I already know not a muthafuckin' thing is finna change.

"Yeah, I get that it's about the scrill, man. But I don't know, sometimes . . ." Jason gots his fist balled up in his lap, and he leanin' over to the side, rubbin' his forehead like he gots somethin' on his mind.

"Spit it out, baby."

"I was just thinkin'," he sayin'. "I was just thinkin' about if I could be a . . . you know, be African."

Be *African*?

What the hell is this nigga talkin' about?

Jason

Dear Jesus,

   I read your letter, and I hear what you sayin'.
You sayin' that the gift of a pimp is bein' able to
know the game tighter than anybody else so he don't
get played. I guess you mean that he can't get
played more than he let hisself get played. I been
thinkin' about that. There's people out there who
gonna always have more money than us. They be the
ones who own houses and businesses and got fools
workin' for them all the time. Even when they sittin' back in a bathtub with four—maybe five—bitches!
They like pimps, too, right? So, if niggas be going
to work every day for they companies, ain't they
gettin' pimped? Does it make a difference if they
know they gettin' pimped? Are they hos?

I don't mean to be askin' all these questions, it's just that I been thinkin' about this a lot, and I think I got the answers. I been seriously thinkin' about how I can make some money. Shit is gettin' crazy out here and I be wonderin' if I'm still gonna be livin' when you get out. Fools is gettin' smoked left and right 'cause of the dope game, and niggas tryin' to cover they turf. I mean, it ain't like LA— we don't got no crips and bloods. Niggas in the Town be too ready to be down for themselves to be worried about some click. But shit been gettin' crazier and crazier. I'm gonna try to make it, though.

Jason

Chinaka

Boom! Boom! Bap. Bap. Boom! I could hear the sound of the drums beating and echoing through the land. Boom! Bap. Boom! I could feel the rhythm reverberating through the air, and I just adored the sight of glistening, dark skin and muscles contracting as each drummer landed another hand on the instrument of dance—it was so beautiful. They were so beautiful.

I could feel it in my body even though the sounds were created in my mind. I could smell the heat in the air. I even coughed up the dust that was flying around from my feet as they hit the dirt with the other African strangers in my circle. Oh, I was feeling every intense beat and every one of those drums' booms that worked their way into my reality. Boom! Bap. Bap. Boom! Bang!

The sounds were so beautiful, then they became erratic and violent. The echoes were no longer peaceful. They were coming in faster and harder. And stronger and more pronounced. Then they were chaotic and pounding, until they finally accomplished what they intended to do from the moment the drumming began—wake me from my sleep.

I stumbled through the darkness of my living room, passing each piece of furniture with care, still listening to the sporadic pattern and the groans on the other side of the door that were getting increasingly louder. I listened to the inconsistent pounding that I then recognized to be far too irregular to be the music of dance. I wondered how it ever could have passed as such in my mind, but dreams are funny that way.

It was music, just not the music of dance. No, the sound on the other side of that door made music of a different kind, the kind I knew all too well, having been in the struggle this long. It was the music of curse words and pain, of wounds and of debts. And I knew exactly whose song it was.

I unlocked the door as fast as I could, making every sleep-inspired lethargic effort to move my body with the speed for which duty called. I dragged my feet across the floor, hoping for the best, but already knowing the worst. I was always efficient in these situations, but I never looked forward to them—never.

When I opened the front door, Jason's body poured into my house, using every precious breath to ask me if he could hide out with me for a while. His lips were moving and his vocal cords were trying to work, but sound could not pass through the blood that was spewing from his mouth and chest.

"Just be quiet, brother," I whispered to him, as I slid his body away from the entrance. His face was angry and terrified. His eyes were filled with the greatest amount of fear that I had ever seen in all my years of hoarding wounded bodies. They were just so determined—determined to be afraid, determined to live, yet longing to die. They were the eyes of a soldier, and they sparked something in me.

I was definitely awake by then, and as prepared as I ever could have been for the wakening of a soul. That night was the night.

I closed the door behind us with a kick, allowing the door to slam shut. Then I picked him up and led his pain-stricken body to the back of my house—farther away from the entrance, farther from the watchful eyes of suspicious cowards, and closer to the help that awaited.

The couch and all other furniture back there were covered in plastic. They've been that way for years—and believe me, they have been used.

I covered them in plastic once I had acquired my fifth replacement couch to rid my place of the smell and traces of bloodstains that brothers and sisters had left behind from stab wounds, bullet wounds, and billy-club wounds. My house was virtually transformed into an operating ward on many important occasions, but that was all right with me.

I had the windows boarded up in the seventies—shortly after my suspicion grew about the people who could see into my private ward. My suspicions are still very much alive, but they have been calmed by the fact that my place—and I— had never been shut down by the pigs. For some reason, I guess by way of some divine intervention, the police never found my haven of refuge. My place was one of the only remaining points of asylum for my many comrades in the Revolution. And it always will be as long as it stands.

But Jason's body occupied the couch that night, and he bled just as much as any revolutionary. The brother was not fighting any war of liberation—at least not so far as I could see—but I could still see the making of a soldier in our army.

He did not know what I knew, nor was he concerned. He was still gripping his shoulder and his chest, sharing his hands, and their application of pressure, between the places where bullets had obviously torn through his skin.

"Just sit back . . . Lift your legs . . . Apply pressure here . . ." I made the demands like a professional physician's assistant, but behind all of it, I saw only his soul. I had to look beyond the bravado and false pretenses to find it, but once spotted, it would not go away. Once spotted, it could be seen with the naked eye, even through the oppression he faced every day.

Then I thought about the Party, and about "seizing the time." I became energized. Jason was my soldier to claim. I was going to seize him.

"Chi-Chinaka . . . help me . . . I'm dyin' . . . please . . ." Jason finally said, coughing and hacking the blood that was clogging his breath passages.

I nodded so the brother would know that I was still there with him.

"This fuckin' . . . pimp. He shot me . . ." I could not believe Jason was actually trying to explain what happened. I was caught between a feeling of terrible awe at hearing his pleas for help and a feeling of sadness for the state of perpetual dysfunction that brothers and sisters seemed to embrace.

"Please," I said to him. "Don't talk, brother. Of course I'm going to help you through this. We both know you are *not* going to the hospital."

He nodded, succumbing to the involuntary convulsions of his body.

We both knew the hospital was out of the picture. Unquestionably, that's why in his moment of torment and fury, he found his way back to my place. There was no way that I would turn that brother away, not with the pigs likely to be looking for him. As soon as he rolled into that hospital with bullet shot wounds those nurses would be on alert. And, certainly, as soon as his name came up on the registration form, those pigs would be at the hospital with their clubs and handcuffs, ready to shackle the brother for any crime they could pin on him. But try as they might, they could never pin on him the crime for which he was truly guilty—just the ones symptomatic of everything else that was wrong with the ghetto.

I was just glad that he remembered where I lived. After our chance meeting at the lake, I wasn't sure if he really wanted anything more to do with me. But clearly, he did. And I am glad he made the right move. Who knows what could have awaited him with any alternative decision? Of course I would help him.

I picked up the phone and dialed Kephra's pager number. Years ago, Kephra resigned as a physician at this hospital in Alabama and moved to the Bay Area searching for a racism-free existence. He wound up working with the rest of us in search of that existence by lending his healing skills to the Movement.

That brother would come over on many a bloody night with his "toolbox" in hand, ready to help keep another wounded brother or sister alive. This time was only different in that the circumstances bringing us together were initiated by acts of hate—instead of through the constructive struggle of love.

I punched in a special sequence of the numbers "7" and "6" as a signal for him to come to my address. It was something that we developed about twenty-five years ago to mean that his skills were needed at my place immediately to kill the work of the Beast with the perfection and accuracy of an African's healing hands.

We used to say the sequence verbally and pass it on through Party members as if we were in an extremely sophisticated game of telephone. Then our system improved when technology made it possible for pagers to communicate our messages.

I hung up the phone and glanced at the clock. It was two-thirty in the morning.

Jason was still gripping his wounds with intensity, trying to hold together his life. I walked over to help him cope with the pain of having bullets wedged inside his body. His eyes went blank—empty from something missing in his life. They looked at me with a longing for help, but I could only stare back at them and wonder how anyone in their right mind could have ever let this precious life deteriorate into something that could be considered less worthy.

His brow wrinkled with pain every time he attempted to open his mouth, but he felt like he needed to speak.

"Chi . . ."

"Stop trying to talk, brother," I said. "I'm here, and help is on the way. A doctor will be here in any minute."

He nodded and closed his eyes.

"Hey!" I said. "But you have to stay awake, Jason. Come

on, brother. You've made it this far. Just hold on. He'll be here any second now."

My mind chased Kephra through the streets, hoping to make his legs carry him faster to my place. I was confident he would come to us—nothing had ever kept him away before. No confirmation calls had ever been needed, but as I was holding Jason's head up—rocking back and forth—I was praying that he would make it in time. He was an older man, nearing his seventies, but he was committed to making his best effort to save every Black life that he could. I was hoping his best effort was fast enough this time.

"Hey, brother," I said, trying to keep Jason focused on something other than death. "Any minute now, brother. You can do this. You're hard-core, remember?"

He opened his eyes.

"That's right," I said. "Aren't you the hardest brother out there? That's what you tried to show me before, isn't it?"

He looked away, but his eyes were still open. I was going to challenge him again, but then there was a knock at the door.

I carefully lifted Jason's head and propped it up with two pillows. After comforting a few coughing fits, I ran to open the door for Kephra. He marched in without the need for direction and began the cleaning procedures that had saved many lives.

He opened the "toolbox," and inside were several pieces of cloth, cleaning materials, and other objects that might not shock those accustomed to Western medicine. But also in that box were elements of an African ritual that cleaned the body of impurities and left it open to the ancestral spirits lingering around him. If I had not witnessed his magic many times, I probably would not have believed how easy it was for him to call upon spirits to help guide his hands, and how consistently those spirits came to heal their sons and daughters.

It was always amazing to watch a healer at work, especially one with as much skill and love as Kephra. He was truly a doctor for those in the Party and others without more conventional American options. And he was the best.

I responded to every order that was given to me—for water, towels, whatever. Everything else was in their hands. All I could do was watch him and hope we would be able to keep that young brother alive. All I had to do was pray for Jason to hang on. And I did.

I lit some incense to cover the scent of blood and began what would be a long process of cleaning the blood that had spurted from Jason's body during his journey from the front door to the back of my house.

After four hours, my *house* had successfully recovered from Jason's emergency, but *I* was still working on it. Inside of me, everything was stirring to the rhythm of a rebellious nation. I could not let the brother go back untouched by this experience. I could not let him return to the streets with revenge on his brain, especially not in the way that he was probably used to. This experience had to be for something. Maybe he would accept it; maybe he would reject it. But I had to say something.

I walked to the back of the house and into Jason's temporary room with a lifetime of knowledge and a torch of wisdom, hoping that he would accept my pass. Kephra was gone, leaving me with careful instructions for how to care for Jason, and I had every intention of following those directions. But more than just his body needed healing.

I turned on the light switch, but turned down the light until just a dim haze filled the room. Jason looked up at me and smiled. He looked happy to be alive, although I don't think he realized it. Then his smile faded to a smirk, and he turned his head to face the wall closest to him—and away from me.

"How long am I finna have to stay like this?" he asked, referring to his position of lying on the couch, wrapped in bandages to cover the wounds.

"As long as it takes, brother," I answered, lighting a candle next to him.

He turned his head back to me, then glanced at the candle. His eyes wandered to his chest. He tried to move his shoulder a little, but all extraneous movement was shut down when a grimace crossed his face.

"It's going to hurt for a while," I said. "So you probably shouldn't move so fast."

"Oh, I ain't trippin', I can handle the pain. I can take a hit . . ."

"That's not what I'm talking about," I said.

He stopped talking and looked at me curiously.

"You know, you're a lucky brother."

"Oh, man . . . here comes the lecture . . ."

"I'm not a lecturer, brother. But you will listen to this one. You owe me that much, don't you think?"

He looked away, but nodded. He did not want to hear what he already knew, and he certainly did not want to hear it from a woman—that I could tell. But he stopped talking. If he really did not want to hear it, he would have gotten up anyway and crawled out if he had to. Nothing was really holding that brother to my couch, and to my "lecture," but his own will.

"It's going to hurt you to walk away from that pimp life you got going on, brother, but you know you have to leave it."

"Man . . . Chinaka . . . It's not that easy. Ain't nothin' out there for me *but* that. I'm from the West, man. I'm Jesus' son. It's my destiny to be a pimp."

"You were raised in a system that wants you to pimp your own as a way of keeping our nation apart."

"What *nation*? Damn, Chinaka, what imaginary world do you live in?"

"I'm talking about the nation that is being destroyed by the savvy of brothers and sisters scared into conformity by this oppressive, capitalist system."

"What are you talkin' about . . . a 'capitalist' system? What the hell is that?"

"Money, brother. Money made on the principle that other people—mostly poor, dark-skinned people—will be exploited. Money, and I'm talking *wealth*, made by the few on the lives and deaths of millions who dwell in poverty."

"Man, what does that have to do with me?"

"When you're pimping, what is your purpose?"

"To get paid, man!" He was getting frustrated and started to raise his voice. I could not have cared less, though. I knew this would be the last time he would listen to me if I did not get it right. I had to get it right—for him and for Peaches. I missed my opportunity to save Peaches, and there was no way I could continue to live if I missed this opportunity as well. I had to seize the time!

"To get paid," I repeated. "And you do that by having a woman with low self-esteem sell her body for you, right?"

"Hey . . . them girls don't do nothin' they don't want to do."

"And what alternatives do they have?"

"I don't care."

"Seriously . . . you get paid from their labor. They give you the earnings from their labor, and then you walk around flashing wads of money, right?"

"They ho 'cause they like to do it, Chinaka. I ain't never asked nobody to do no shit they wasn't willin' to do from the jump."

"Do you really believe that?"

"What?"

"That they *like* to 'ho'?"

"Hell yeah. Maybe not you . . . but some of them bitches out there love to ho."

"Just like slaves loved working for the 'massa, ' right? Just like Peaches loved to ho?"

"That's not the same."

"Actually it is. It's all a part of the same system, Jason. And when you sit here and justify everything that you do to these women, you're no better than those people who exploited your ancestors on those cotton and tobacco fields. You're helping to destroy your own people."

"Then I guess I am, then."

"For *what*, brother?"

"'Cause I want to be fitted, that's what for. I want to have the same shit as them big players. I want nice things and nice cars. I want to be ballin', 'cause I ain't never had shit my whole life, Chinaka. I just want to be paid."

"For what? What will money do for you?"

Confused, he looked at me again and asked, "What do you keep asking me that for? I already told you."

"That's really it, then? All this killing and pimping and hustling has been so that you can just hold on to some money?"

Jason rolled his eyes. I often wondered what happened to the Movement, but my conversation with him was helping me to understand that the most painful episode in someone's life is recognizing for the first time—through the eyes of someone else—that his or her entire existence has been a lie. The Movement died when brothers and sisters like Jason learned to believe the lie. They internalized the lies in those schoolbooks, in those movies, and in the news. They became slaves to their own misery, and by having done so, have even expedited the concretion of those lies into their own lives.

"Look at these pictures," I said, jumping up from my seat to point to some of the inspirational remnants of the Movement that I had framed around the room. I walked over to one showing hundreds of brothers and sisters storming the California State government for freedom, standing defiantly in tilted black berets, strapped with guns and armed with the spirit of our past. They were beautiful in their pride of being able to boldly display everything black, from their clothing to their consciousness. Then I walked over to another picture, this one showing children lined up diligently in front of the Party schools—raised to be soldiers and to wear the uniform of the Revolution.

"We tried to prepare your generation for what we knew would take several lifetimes to complete, but this country took that away, Jason. I'm trying to give it back to you, but as fast as the oppression grows, that's how fast you all ignore everything we did to make *you* count. This Revolution is about counting beautiful, precious Black lives, Jason—not about counting money."

"What Revolution? I don't see no kind of Revolution happenin', and especially not if money ain't involved."

I looked again at the pictures on the wall, this time focusing on the pictures of the Panther members leading community education rallies and testing for sickle cell anemia. More important to me than the faces of the Panther members in those pictures were the faces of the people being freed from the prison of their own ignorance about the medical condition. Their energy leaped off the black and white photo, leaving the gloss behind to spark the feeling that we had done the right thing. We were doing right by the community, and we had to find a way to bring it all back.

"Say there is no Movement if you want to, Jason, but it is happening now. It comes in many forms: art, music, dance, literature, political demonstrations, marches, conversations, whatever. But there are many who are a part of it. And I bet there is something in your heart telling you that you'd rather be a part of the Revolution than a part of pimping."

"Oh, here you go again, tryin' to play Jedi mind tricks with all this tellin' me what I want to do."

"That's not it at all. Look, why did you come to *me* tonight, Jason? Why didn't you go to your friends or to one of your girlfriends?"

He was caught off guard by my question, but did his best to recover.

"I. . . I was . . . thought you could help me. I don't have nobody else."

"You thought I could help you, or you *knew* that I would not let you die?"

"I guess I knew you wouldn't let me die."

"How did you know that?"

"Man, I don't know . . . I just knew."

"You knew I couldn't let you die. And you knew this because you know that I love my people *that* much. You knew that I would bring you into my home, and you knew that I would do whatever I could to keep you alive. I'm here for you, Jason, because I loved your mother. I love you, too. Where do you think that love comes from? Because, you know, your 'game' or whatever does not work on me."

He shrugged one shoulder. Maybe he really did not know why he came to me, but at least I had his attention. He could not walk out on me this time.

"It comes from knowing that there is more to us than what is demonstrated or presented to us every day," I said. "That's where my love comes from."

"What? Oh, now you poppin' this shit about there bein' more than what's 'presented' every day? Man, what's 'presented' to me is them cards that was stacked against me since birth. And I don't know why you claim to care so much, like it makes a difference. It ain't helpin' nobody around here do nothin' different. Shit ain't finna change just 'cause you *care*. The dope game and the pimpin' game is gonna last forever. And I ain't finna be the muthafucka to change none of that."

"Only because you think you're too weak."

"Aw . . . I don't have to listen to this shit."

I glared at him. He glared back.

"Jason, I just want you to understand one thing."

"What?"

"None of this is because I'm trying to get on your nerves or come off as some holier-than-thou kind of savior. Yes, the pimping game is as much a part of this country's social fabric as meat and potatoes, but that does not mean that you have to be a part of it. When you are, you are not only jeopardizing your life and the life of your family, your son. When you pimp, you *help* continue the cycle of poverty that your people must endure. You aren't creating wealth. You aren't taking away that deck of cards that were stacked against you, brother. You are creating more deep-seated poverty, and now you and all the people don't only have to worry about being exploited by the system at large. Now you all have to be worried about being exploited by you. That's not living, Jason. That's *barely* survival."

He did not say a word.

"All I have to say is that you have to save your son from all of this, brother. That baby deserves more, and I can tell you that Peaches did not want this for you. She wanted you to find your own way, but pimping is not what she had in mind, brother. Not at all."

Then I turned around and looked at the pictures and into the eyes of countless revolutionaries—some who had died and some whose lives had been swallowed by the Beast and spit out Revolution-less as peddlers of oppressive marketing schemes for the enemy. But some of us managed to hang on. I had not let myself deteriorate into that, and I was not about to let him think there was anything acceptable about those who had.

"Do you think any of us were born into a neighborhood that was *designed* to foster our healthy development? We *made* those communities happen for ourselves. We fought for our voice. I lost over thirty friends to the struggle, and they died fighting to make Oakland, Chicago, New York, New Jersey,

Mississippi—wherever there were substantial concentrations of Black people—a decent place for us to live. They died trying to give young brothers like you other options. It's not about what you were born into, Jason. It's about what you're willing to do to make your life, and the lives of your people, better.

"Look, are you prepared to take another bullet to the chest for the continued *oppression* of your people?" I continued, lowering my voice from the riled spirit he was conjuring up by his pathetic excuses for apathy and conformity.

He laid his head back on the pillow and stared at the ceiling.

"What do you want me to do, Chinaka? Why do you keep pushin' me?"

"What do I want from you?" I smiled. Finally he asked a question I wanted to answer. "Brother, I want you to accept the challenge. I want you to respond when there are expectations that are set for you. I want you surpass everyone else's standards for you and set your own. The only limitations that you have are the ones that you put on yourself. This is *your* world, Jason. Don't just get by on a hustle that means nothing. Breathe! Use it!"

He sighed.

"What about your son?" I asked.

He moved his eyes in my direction without turning his head.

"Are you prepared to lose your son to the same lifestyle that we lost Peaches to? To the same lifestyle that is claiming her only son?"

He turned his head and raised it from the pillow, looking at me with anger in his eyes.

"You can be mad if you want to," I said, "but be mad at the person allowing this to happen to you, and that's yourself."

He grunted and laid his head back on the pillow, saying nothing and staring at the ceiling.

"Are you prepared to make a change in your life and accept the call to join us in fighting for a Revolution?"

He did not say anything, and I know it was because he was confused. I saw that in him from the start of my "lecture." I knew he wouldn't answer anything right away, and that was okay. It showed me that at least he was trying to process everything.

I mentioned to him that Peaches found her own way to contribute to the Revolution, and that while I did not expect him to turn into Nat Turner that instant, I did expect him to not let her struggle have been in vain. I did not want *my* struggle to be in vain. My failure to convince Peaches that she could leave the life resulted in her death. I could not allow that same fate to meet Jason.

"Everything she did was for you," I said, walking over with a towel to wipe his brow of the sweat that had accumulated there over the few minutes that he had been challenged to accept something new as a way of life. "Some 'hos' are able to escape the thralls of oppression, you know."

I put the towel on the table next to him and walked over to the light. I was ready to cut it completely off and let him think about his life for a while. Then I started to wonder who was the one that really got away: Peaches or her pimp? I wondered how I found Jason and I wondered how he would hold on to the rebel stirring inside that would help him make his contribution to the Revolution.

"You know," I said, with my finger on the light switch,

"you can stay and rest awhile, but remember this: America is the only place that has ever had a 'Negro' or a 'nigga.' Africans were brought here to this land, but it was the Negro who was freed from slavery—with all of his King James devotion and brainwashed tendencies. Our job is to find the African in us again, and let that African breathe freely in us *all* the time, not just when the going gets tough. Brother, we have to work on ourselves, you understand, to liberate the souls of our murdered ancestors and to liberate our children.

"That couch you're on now is for revolutionaries," I continued. "Think about that, and I'll talk to you later. Get some rest."

I clicked the light off, and the room went dark but for the flicker of the candle next to his head.

I closed the door behind me and walked away, leaving Jason alone with the pictures on the walls and his own thoughts about Revolution . . . Peaches . . . and the choice I hoped he would make.

What happened to the Movement? Well, one thing was for sure—a piece of it was brewing in that room. Only time would tell how it would explode.

Jesus

Baby Jesus,

I'm gonna keep this short. A true pimp can't get played, man. That's what I been tryin' to teach you all these years. How to be a man. How to be a real pimp.

But the time is comin' up for me to teach you what's going on for real. I got word today that I'm finally gettin' out of this muthafucka. It seemed like I was never gettin' out of here, so I had stopped countin' the days. But I am. I should be home next month.

So here it is, nigga. The moment of Truth. If you serious about doin' what you was born to do, I'll see you when I get out. You gots my number, and you know where I live at.

      —J

Jason

So, last night, when we rolled into Frisco, I was thinkin'
about everything I had learned about life and how I was supposed to live it. All the way from the Town, Jesus had been
spittin' his philosophy on why pimpin' was the way for me,
but I still hadn't shook that vision of my momma's body with
his hand stuck in her head. I tried hard to shake the thought
by picturin' my momma with Chinaka—dressin' like her,
talkin' like her—but that image didn't stick.

Chinaka let her hair fly around natural, not in a real Afro,
but somethin' like it. Every time I saw her, except for that
time at the lake, she was dressed like she was ready for war.
Her face didn't have that many wrinkles for a lady her age,
but her hair was all white, so I knew she must have been
through some shit. She was, like, the total opposite of my
momma—in every single way. Maybe that's why they was
friends, I ain't knowin'.

In my mind, I wanted to make my momma look like them other women—like Chinaka—who wasn't about hoin' or trickin'. I knew it wasn't the truth, and maybe that's why it didn't stick. It didn't matter, though, 'cause my momma was true in her own way. I just wish she would have spotted the enemy.

Yeah, I know them Black Panther chicks had to have their own set of problems, but at least it didn't come with pimpsticks and plastic limbs. At least they could spot the enemy. Or so Chinaka be claimin'.

The night I got shot, I was hella lucky. I ain't never heard of no muthafucka bein' able to drive across the bridge—shot—and not crash into the side of the freeway or somethin'. That shit was a miracle, and I had to pay attention to it. I asked Chinaka that night about what she be talkin' about when she say "Revolution." The way she explained it to me, the Revolution was about makin' change, you know? She said that it wasn't somethin' that was finna just *happen*. She said it had to be a process. It had to come in bits and pieces.

"When you're ready to make the appropriate sacrifices in your life, Jason, you'll be contributing to the freedom of your people," she said.

"But y'all was already fightin' for that, Chinaka. You always blastin' on prostitution, but damn! I mean, not all bitches . . . I mean, women . . . want to fight and shit. Some just want to be hos," I had said.

She looked at me from where she was standin', then came over and sat on a little plastic-covered wicker stool next to the couch I was layin' on.

"Look, brother," she said. It was a trip, 'cause she had been talkin' pretty loud, but that time, she was damn near whisperin'. "There were many chances in the Party for sisters to sleep their way around. I mean, if a sister really wanted some upward mobility in the Party, for the most part she had to be willing to sleep with a man already in power."

"Then why you sweatin' me?"

"Because there is always an option in any situation that looks closed, brother. Yes, there were sisters who slept with the leaders of the Party, but there were also hundreds of other sisters who laid their lives on the line every day without so much as blinking an eye at a brother who made a sexual advance her way."

"Well, that's them . . ."

"That's a lot more sisters than you think. You know, many sisters know how to spot the enemy, even if he is dressed as a brother or a comrade in the struggle."

She talked about spottin' the enemy like they was lookin' for the Man or somethin'. I mean, I could feel not really wantin' to trust everybody that looked like they're your potna. Fools be good at makin' you think they're down when they're not, so I knew what she was talkin' about. It was just a trip when she said that she believed I could spot the enemy, too—if I wanted to. Well, I guess I must have wanted to.

I had been tellin' Jesus that I was serious about bein' a pimp for a while. And I was—until last night. I really can't say what happened to me in that parking lot, but my visions was takin' over. The mental stress was buildin' and all I could see was my momma dead, my girl a single mom, my son a hustler, and me bein' shot.

Before Chinaka, I had never even thought about my life as anything but a pimp—I mean, I declared pimpin' when I was barely a teenager! I thought I was finna live my whole life and die right there in the West. All I *knew* was the West. And I just never saw myself nowhere else, or doin' nothin' else but followin' in the ways of the land. When Chinaka said that I was scared to live and have expectations, she was kind of right. I mean, all my life, I was fightin' lies. I would watch NBA players and NFL players and think that I could do that—but I knew it would never work out. Everybody knew I couldn't do that shit. Every time another one of them counselors told me that I could do whatever I set my mind to, it felt like a lie. They knew I couldn't do nothin' without a high school diploma. And I had a baby! The cards was stacked against me so high, it was scary to try to knock them down. I mean, what if I was a failure? I wasn't ready to take the chance.

Chinaka called me "weak" when I got shot, but she was wrong. I ain't weak. I couldn't really tell her that then, 'cause I thought I was finna die for real. I thought her face was finna be the last face I would ever see. I was hopin' she'd be able to keep me alive, 'cause I knew there was nobody else who would really do it. I mean, I kind of surprised myself when I showed up at her door, but it was like I was possessed by somethin' that just wanted me to live. I just knew she was the only one I could go to.

Before that night, there were many times that I had wished to die. I thought it might be easier that way. But when it was really finna happen, I started trippin' on all the things that I hadn't done with my life. I thought about all the things I had thought about doin' and never got a chance to do—like start a dance class for little niggas to keep them off the street. I just couldn't go out behind no bitch. I mean, I know I'm gonna die. But not like *that*.

Chinaka asked me if I was ready to die behind how I live my life, and leave Dominic and Jackson alone to face this world, but I couldn't really answer her. I wanted to tell her that the answer was no, but there was too much to think about with that question. I mean, it would be messed up if I purposely left them alone. But there wasn't no guarantee that I was finna die just 'cause I was tryin' to be a pimp. I knew I was gonna die someday. I mean, we all are. I couldn't say for sure that my leavin' the life would be any safer for me than bein' in it. It's not that I was so hung up on bein' a pimp, 'cause really, I was just gettin' started when you compare what I was doin' with the legendary players on the scene.

But for some reason, I couldn't answer her until I was with him. I didn't really know the answer to her question until I looked into Jesus' eyes and saw what I needed to know. I had to see him—the man, not the words on paper, not the legend. Sure, I knew in many ways it was all the same, but I also knew that where the pimp ended, there was me. When I watched him sit next to me, schoolin' me on the ways of the pimpin' game, I saw somebody who looked like me, but who wasn't like me at all. At least not like the me I wanted to be.

When Chinaka was askin' me them questions, I was startin' to hate her, man. I was startin' to think she might be worser than Jesus—like she was tryin' just as hard to recruit me to her team. Then, when she left me alone, I really started trippin' off of what she was talkin' about. Even though she don't know it, I actually took some time to look at them pictures she had on the wall in that room. And I saw what she was talkin' about.

I saw all of them marchin' and doin' some work in the community, and somethin' just touched me. I was like, damn, if they could do that back then, how come we couldn't do it now? Man, lookin' at them faces and really trippin' off of how hard they had to fight to get food to the community, and to try to keep the police from killin' us all made me think about how I ain't really have a *right* to destroy it.

I mean, I know I ain't have nothin' to do with the way the 'hood looks now, but damn, you know? If I could try to fix it a little—just to say "thank you"—what was keepin' me from doin' it? You know, I was like, there are so many other fools in the West who should just peep what Chinaka got goin' on up in that house. They would come out changed.

If the question was whether I was willin' to lose Dominic to the one-sided game that Jesus dug into my mentals, then hell yeah, I had the answer. I finally told Jesus my answer, and I hope that sooner or later, everybody will get the point. If Chinaka was there with me last night, I would have told her the answer, too. Then I would have thanked her for askin'.

When me and Jesus got up near the pier, I told him that I wanted to pull over and show him somethin', so he wasn't trippin' when we pulled into the parking lot. Jesus wasn't trippin' off anything I did last night, for real.

He was too busy livin' in that world he had created for hisself—and was trying to create for me—where he controls everything that crosses his path and the rest of us just sit around all day thinkin' about how we can make his life better. I wasn't buyin' it no more, though. None of it looked good to me.

I was feelin' strange, like I was gettin' lighter the more I decided not to follow the man sittin' next to me. I wanted to run, but I didn't. I just let the energy rush through me, and went along with it.

The rain had stopped comin' down, so I rolled the window down some more and let the fresh air into the car. The taste of salt water was all around, but I wasn't trippin'. I was just tryin' to keep Jesus from noticin' how jumpy I was gettin'. The last thing I needed was for him to flash, 'cause I was still healin' from my bullet wounds. But, shit, I was strong enough to fight his ass if I had to. It would take more than that arm to get me.

I had come all the way to Frisco to get away from what everybody else had to say about my life, and all the way there I had to listen to Jesus' ass. But when we got up close to that pier, I could finally hear my own thoughts—even while Jesus was talkin' about somethin' else.

I had finally blocked that muthafucka out to hear what was goin' on in my own mind.

Chinaka said that she would give me time to think about how I wasn't finna let my momma's death be in vain, and how I was finna make life better for my son. Well, I finally had the answer.

"Nigga, what you gots to show me?" Jesus asked, still sittin' next to me in the car.

"Well, there's some real serious shit goin' on in my life, and I had to talk to you about it. You know, before I could be sure."

"Aw, nigga, be sure about what? Don't start actin' like you ain't sure now. I heard about you gettin' shot over this shit, but I ain't trippin'. You startin' to make a little money . . . and now you thinkin' about throwin' it all away?"

"No, I ain't *thinkin'* about throwin' it all away," I said, imaginin' Slim's nephew on the phone flappin' his gums like a sucka.

"Then, what *are* you doin'? Man, you my son—my spawn—and we was made to pimp. How many times I gots to remind you of that? We keepin' the legacy goin' in this game. I'm talkin' about at least three generations of big pimpin' goin' on, baby, startin' right here."

"Three generations?"

"Yeah, baby. Me, you, and Dominic. Ain't no man finna die in this family without havin' mastered our purpose here."

Jesus had never said nothin' before about bein' a grandfather. I used to think it was 'cause he didn't see no purpose in havin' another mouth to feed when I was stugglin' myself. Then I thought it was 'cause he didn't have no family, no *real* family anyway, besides me, so he didn't know how to be a granddaddy. I didn't think he wanted to be one. All he wanted was a "family" that could keep him paid, and that's what he had. His hos was his family.

"Our purpose . . . meanin' pimpin'?"

It was gettin' harder and harder for me to pretend that I was really all about this pimpin' game. I was sayin' the words, but in my heart I wasn't believin' none of it. Then somethin' snapped and I didn't feel like I had to pretend no more.

"What else are we talkin' about, man?" he asked.

We wasn't talkin' about nothin' but the pimpin' game, but *I* was thinkin' about other conversations. I didn't want to die knowin' I could have changed my life, but didn't. I didn't want to get older and flash on my girl, leavin' her dead on the floor with Dominic considerin' his role in life as a hustler. I had already been lookin' at my life, and I knew it was time for me to play a different hand with the cards I had.

The cloud in my head was clearin', and everything was startin' to make sense to me. I wasn't finna join no Black Panther group or start livin' my life in Chinaka's back room and shit. But I knew I could do somethin' for the "Revolution." I knew I could start by making sure the pimpin' game in *this* family didn't go no further.

I reached under my seat and felt the cold metal of my gun press against my sweaty hand. Hell, a nigga was nervous as hell to grab that shit after what had happened to me when I got shot. But shit had to be resolved. Somebody had to take the bullshit away. I was a grown-ass man and was able to handle my shit, but the conclusion I had decided on was makin' me nervous as hell.

I pulled out the gun and held on to it with a tight grip. I can't tell you if Jesus saw me when I first put my hand on it, or if he even knew what I was reachin' for, but he didn't stop me if he did. I knew he was lookin' at me when I had the gun in full view, though. It was cocked and pointed at my head. I asked myself, what if loyalty and hate was the same thing, and the only way out of them both was death?

My mind was spinnin', 'cause there was too much goin' on in there. Too many "what ifs" and too many "how comes." I just knew I had to end this shit before it was too late and I changed my mind.

One of the things I always liked about myself was that I was loyal. Loyal to myself, loyal to my potnas, loyal to the game that I had been taught as a kid, and loyal to my son. But I also realized that I hated my potnas. I was jealous of the fact that they all had mommas to go home to when the day was over, and that their mommas was always givin' them hell for bullshittin' the days away. I hated the game that I had been taught as a kid. I hated the way I used it against my son. I hated the way I used it against Jackson. I hated the way it had me pissed off at all women, how it made me want to control them and shit, and how it almost made me miss out on what I learned from Chinaka. But most of all, I hated Jesus.

I hated him for all the obvious reasons, but even more than that, I just hated his ass for bein' alive. Chinaka was right. It wasn't fair that he could be so cold-blooded and live. It wasn't fair that he could walk the streets like he was the most righteous pimp on Earth but be nothin' inside but a fuckin' hopped-out ex-con. I wasn't hatin' him for cheatin' the game—he beat the system—and, all right, that was part of his legend. But I hated him for bein' my daddy. And I hated myself for lettin' all that get to me.

Jesus wasn't even fazed by lookin' at me with the gun to my head. He just looked at me with no expression—a cold, poker face that I knew was hidin' a plot to do whatever he needed to do to save his own ass.

"Aw, man . . . Boy, you done flipped out."

I wasn't mad when he said that. Matter of fact, it just got me more fired up. He was right. I was trippin' for havin' the gun pointed to my head. I mean, part of me wanted *some* kind of instinct to make him try to save my life. After all, he was my daddy, even if he was a daddy who wasn't shit. Even if he was a daddy who let everybody but me claim him as "daddy."

Without me even thinkin' about it, the gun changed directions. It felt like it switched by itself from bein' focused at my head to pointin' straight at Jesus. I knew his poker face would change if it wasn't *me* who was finna die, but him.

"What you pointin' that gat at me for?" Jesus looked surprised, but his body didn't move at all.

"'Cause this trip is over, *Hay-soos*."

He still looked surprised, but I knew I couldn't give him no time to think of a way out of this one. He was laughin', but I knew he wasn't happy. And I wasn't tellin' no joke. His real hand was still on his lap, with the plastic one still by his side. He wasn't movin' it—I think 'cause he didn't believe I would really pull the trigger. I guess they all thought I was too weak.

"This trip is over, blood. We ain't finna ride on . . ."

"Boy, what the hell you doin'? You too scary to do somethin' like this, muthafucka."

"This is for my mentals, nigga, and for my momma . . ."

"Nigga, pleeease . . ."

"Ain't finna be no more pimpin' in this family. It ends tonight."

Jesus was beginnin' to see how serious I was. He moved his head and started to open and close his fist. His face got bright red, but he kept on laughin'. Then he stopped and started mumblin' some shit again about me not havin' the guts to take him out. I had to show him I wasn't the scary little boy he thought I was. I had to show myself.

So I pulled the trigger. I *had* to pull the trigger.

"Like I said, man. I ain't *thinkin'* about throwin' it all away . . . I *am* throwin' it all away."

I pulled the trigger again.

"And I been thinkin' about bein' African again . . . if I can find it in me."

I pulled the trigger one last time, then wiped the gun off and tossed it carefully on the backseat.

You ever watched a man die? I mean, have you ever sat through the last seconds of somebody's life—seein' in their eyes everything they ever did or wanted to do? I tell you this, if you ever want to see fear strike in a man's eyes, just watch him die. I ain't gotta tell you how ill it was to watch him struggle for life. He gripped his coat, as if holdin' on to it would somehow make him stay alive. I couldn't watch the twitchin', the blood spittin', and the eye rollin' for too much longer. That shit ain't clean and glamorous like they show in the movies.

Watchin' a man die will let you see everything you thought you knew about him go right out the window. I saw all that in Jesus' eyes—that and more. I saw a scared, sad man. I saw a dope fiend searchin' for his paradise. I saw an angry nigga. I saw a version of me I hope I never see again.

In life, we all take chances, hopin' for things to work out the way we need them to. But last night the circumstances brought just me and him. Yeah, just me and him, guts and glory, a whole lot of game and a little Revolution. You see, I *had* to pull the trigger, 'cause nobody else could do it.

But I knew I was on my way to finally gettin' some peace of mind—or should I say, some piece of my mind back.

When Jesus gave up his fight, I ain't said a word. I just started up the car again, put it in neutral, and let it roll toward the dock. I jumped out in time for me not to roll into the bay with the pimp lessons and man everybody called "Jesus." He was on his own for that next ride.

I left the car, and Jesus, dead on my road to recovery. And it was my turn to be born again. I know I'll be on that road for a while, but at least I'm on my way. I just wished my momma could have seen me. I hope she'd be proud of me. Shit, I'm proud of me.

I turned my back to that whole scene and never looked at the car sinkin' into the bay. Instead I just kept my feet movin' toward the bus station, so I could get home to my son and come anew.

I mean, I get it now. This whole shit—life in the ghetto—it's all temporary. That's what my momma was singing to me all them nights. That's what Chinaka been tryin' to say. Life is too temporary to waste. I've got to put in work—real work. I'll make a difference—my way.

Angie

Ain't nobody ever said that when you die, you through knowin' what's goin' on with the people you done loved. It sure ain't been like that for me. I mean, I be knowin' everything that happens with my baby and with Chinaka. I can even feel them—late at night when they sleepin' and thinkin' it's just them. It be me and them in they dreams. In they shadows. I ain't tryin' to scare them, I just be watchin' over them, makin' sure they safe. And they gotta know that I'm there with them, especially when they together. It's what I prayed for before I came here. It's what I always believed would happen.

I know Jason done did what he thought was best, and I ain't placin' no judgment on his precious soul. I can feel the weight liftin' from his heavy heart—the same weight that was lifted from mine. I just hope he can hang on, 'cause I got a feelin' things gonna get better from here on out.

I be wantin' to tell him what I couldn't tell him the last night he seen me. I be wantin' to tell him how good I feel now, and hold him real tight like I used to. I be wantin' to tell Chinaka how I know what she done did for him and hold her again, too. And for real, I want to let them both know that it's okay to not be mad at him. They can't hold a grudge against that man forever—not when I'm the happiest I done ever been, you hear me?

They all right, though. They gonna stay all right, too. And that baby, Dominic—he gonna know what everybody did for him, and why they did it. Most of all, he gonna be able to feel love, you hear me? That's right. My grandbaby gonna see the beauty in knowin' about love. Lord, what people be doin' for love . . .

I know now that man ain't never really love me. I mean, what kinda fool was I to think he did? I don't be worryin' about them kinds of things, though, not no more. I let all that go when I got here. Look at me now . . . my spirit's free! I got so much greatness in my soul now; I don't even bother myself with all that craziness no more. I just had to stick around long enough to know my baby would make the right choices. And I'm so proud.

Yeah, baby. Momma's proud, and I don't care who hear me! Your life is much too beautiful for words. I done always said that. You are, to me, the best thing that Earth done ever seen. I still believe it—yes I do. Even from here—you're much too beautiful for words. Much too beautiful for words.

And we all can be.

Amen.

Reading Group Guide

We hope that you have enjoyed *Too Beautiful for Words* by Monique W. Morris. The following questions are intended to facilitate your group's discussion of this insightful and provocative book.

1. On a number of levels, this book is about liberation: Jason's and Peaches's liberation from Jesus' "game," sexual liberation, and the liberation of African Americans vis-à-vis social revolution. At the end of the book, has Jason liberated himself by killing Jesus? Why or why not?

2. From jail, Jesus sends Jason letters that contain fatherly advice. Which lessons does Jesus share with his son? Which lessons does Jason ultimately accept?

Based on his relationship with Jesus, what types of lessons will Jason impart to Dominic?

3. What is the role of free will in the novel? Was Peaches a good girl gone bad who just got randomly caught up in prostitution? Or is she to blame for making the choice to follow Jesus? To what extent is Peaches responsible for the roles she played and to what extent is she a victim of fate?

4. How does Jason's getting shot change him? Why does it take an event like that to finally get him to listen to Chinaka? How does his life change after the shooting?

5. The title of the book, *Too Beautiful for Words*, is not only a song that Peaches sings to Jason, but it also sets the tone for the recurring theme of beauty throughout the book. What are the different perceptions of beauty that Morris examines through the eyes of Jesus, Peaches, and Chinaka?

6. There are competing views of the roles of women in this novel. How does Jesus' view conflict with Chinaka's? What statement does Morris make by creating a female heroine for this novel?

7. Jason believes that pimping is about "controllin' how much them other folks, like them white folks that run downtown and them oil companies or whatever, control you." This statement leads to one of the guiding

questions in the book, "I mean, ain't we all gettin' pimped anyway?" Do you agree with Jason's statement? Within this framework, who is really getting pimped in this novel? Who are the pimps and who are the prostitutes?

8. While Jesus is beating Peaches to death, she recites the Lord's Prayer, thereby conjuring up early images from the novel when she was in church. What does religion mean to Peaches? How does it play a role in her life? What message is Monique Morris trying to relay by naming the pimp Jesus?

9. Part 1 of the book ends with Jason watching his mother die. Part 2 ends with Angie watching Jason kill Jesus. Why did Jason feel that he had to kill his father? What does this say about the legacy of violence that Jesus has passed down? Will Jason ever be able to free himself from Jesus' influence?

10. Throughout the course of the novel, many people contributed to Chinaka's revolution. What was Peaches's contribution? What was Jason's? How did these contributions change the fabric of the novel?

11. At the end of the book, Morris shows Peaches watching over Jason as he kills Jesus. However, this final chapter is not told from Peaches's point of view, but rather from Angie's. What does this mean? How are Peaches and Angie different? Why is this the only time that Morris refers to her by her birth name?